What People Are Saying About *The Birdhouse*...

Laura Hilton's *The Birdhouse* is one of those wonderful books that starts good and gets better and better. Readers will have a hard time laying the book aside. "Just one more page" turns into "just one more chapter." Laura has crafted another riveting story in The Amish of Jamesport series. Readers will reconnect with characters of the previous two books (though it is not necessary to have read those books first) and will meet new characters, as well. The plot is fast-moving, and the characters are well developed and believable. Themes of trust and forgiveness are woven in throughout the story. Anyone who enjoys a romance with a message will want to read *The Birdhouse*.

—*Susan Simpson*
Author

Amazing. Beautiful. Heart-touching. All wonderful words to describe Laura Hilton's latest book, *The Birdhouse*. It was heart stirring to read the "miry clay" experience from Josh's point of view. I wept as I read his side of the experience. Having read all of Laura's books, I have to say this one touched my heart the most. It is truly an evangelistic story. I foresee hearts and lives being changed by this book.

—*Cindy Loven*
Co-author, *Dianna's Wings, The Parables of Trevor Turtle* and *Swept Away* (Quilts of Love series)

Laura V. Hilton has exceeded my expectations once again! *The Birdhouse* is a compelling story articulated with intensity and sensitivity! Lost faith and hope, as well as lies and misunderstandings, take this beautifully crafted story to a profound level, while a deepening, passionate love is reignited with both palpability, discernment, and discretion. A story of renewed faith, hope, and love, this story will leave you thirsting for more!

—*Nancee Marchinowski*
Reviewer, www.PerspectivesbyNancee.blogspot.com

Author Laura V. Hilton has become one of my favorite Amish fiction authors. Her stories never disappoint. I am always drawn into each one, savoring each page and waiting on pins and needles to see what happens next. Her characters are real, so real that I often forget the stories are fiction.

—*Judy Burgi*
Reviewer, ChristianFictionBookReviews.org

No girl *rumschpringes* like Greta, the jellies seller, thanks to the sweet and tart storytelling of Laura V. Hilton in *The Birdhouse*. How complex can a return-to-Amish-life get? *Gut* and complicated, *chust* like Josh, the birdhouse guy. A bundling of plots and twists.

—*Alan Daugherty*
Columnist, Angelkeep Journals, *Bluffton (IN) News-Banner*

THE *Bird* HOUSE

LAURA V. HILTON

WHITAKER
HOUSE

Publisher's Note:
This novel is a work of fiction. References to real events, organizations, or places are used in a fictional context. Any resemblances to actual persons, living or dead, are entirely coincidental.

All Scripture quotations are taken from the King James Version of the Holy Bible.

The Birdhouse
The Amish of Jamesport ~ Book 3

Laura V. Hilton
http://lighthouse-academy.blogspot.com

ISBN: 978-1-62911-566-5
eBook ISBN: 978-1-62911-588-7
Printed in the United States of America

Whitaker House
1030 Hunt Valley Circle
New Kensington, PA 15068
www.whitakerhouse.com

Library of Congress Cataloging-in-Publication Data

Hilton, Laura V., 1963–
The birdhouse / by Laura V. Hilton.
pages ; cm. — (The Amish of Jamesport ; book 3)
ISBN 978-1-62911-566-5 (softcover : acid-free paper) — ISBN 978-1-62911-588-7 (ebook)
1. Amish—Fiction. 2. Man-woman relationships—Fiction. I. Title.
PS3608.I4665B57 2015
813'.6—dc23
2015029543

1 2 3 4 5 6 7 8 9 10 11 22 21 20 19 18 17 16 15

Dedication

To the God that healeth, the One that saved me.

Acknowledgments

I'd like to offer my heartfelt thanks to the following:

The residents of Jamesport and the surrounding areas, for answering my questions and pointing me in the right directions.

My husband and children, for going with me on vacation and helping me observe; also, for beating the starter to get the minivan running again when it decided enough was enough and had a meltdown just outside Kansas City.

The amazing team at Whitaker House—Christine, Courtney, and Cathy. You are wonderful.

Tamela, my agent, for believing in me all these years.

My critique group—you know who you are. You are amazing and knew the right questions to ask when more detail was needed. Thanks also for the encouragement. Candee, thanks for reading large amounts of material in short spans of time and offering wise suggestions.

Also, thank you for my street team members, who work tirelessly to support my books.

My husband, Steve, for being a tireless proofreader and cheering section.

My daughter Jenna, for reading over my shoulder and editing as I wrote; also, for naming the horses.

My children Michael and Kristin, for taking over kitchen duties when I was deep in the story.

My daughters, Kristin, Jenna, and Kaeli, for help with the household chores.

And in memory of my parents, Allan and Janice, and my uncle Loundy, and my grandmother Mertie, who talked about their Pennsylvania Amish heritage.

To God be the glory.

Glossary of Amish Terms and Phrases

ach: oh
aent/aenti: aunt/auntie
"ain't so?": a phrase commonly used at the end of a sentence to invite agreement
Ausbund: Amish hymnal used in the worship services, containing lyrics only
banns: public announcement in church of a proposed marriage
boppli: baby/babies
bu: boy
buwe: boys
daed: dad
"Danki": "Thank you"
dawdi-haus: a home constructed for the grandparents to live in once they retire
der Herr: the Lord
Gott: God
großeltern: grandparents
dochter: daughter
ehemann: husband
Englisch: non-Amish
Englischer: a non-Amish person
frau: wife

grossdaedi: grandfather
grossmammi: grandmother
gut: good
haus: house
"Ich liebe dich": "I love you"
jah: yes
kapp: prayer covering or cap
kinner: children
koffee: coffee
kum: come
liebling: a term of endearment meaning "darling" or "little love"
maidal: young woman
mamm: mom
maud: maid/spinster
morgen: morning
nacht: night
nein: no
onkel: uncle
Ordnung: the rules by with an Amish community lives
rumschpringe: "running around time"; a period of freedom and experimentation during the late adolescence of Amish youth
ser gut: very good
schatz: sweetheart
schnuckelchen: beautiful girl
snitz: dried apples, usually for pies
sohn: son
süße: sweetie/sweetness
to-nacht: tonight
verboden: forbidden
"Was ist letz?": "What's the matter?"
welkum: welcome

Chapter 1

Greta's diary, 2012

Who I am, and all I believe, is marred with just one glance into angry steel-blue eyes. He seems to control my air, my ability to breathe. He makes me crave everything I know is sin. Pure becomes tainted, and lines are blurred. It's my fault; I'm the one who isn't strong enough. I've been damaged, broken. Josh's words haunt me: "There's a consequence for every choice you make."

2015

The hairs rose on the back of Greta Miller's neck, and her skin prickled the way it did whenever someone stared at her. She should be used to the attention. Used to feeling like a caged circus animal, with all the tourists who came into the Amish Country Store. But this seemed different somehow. She turned away from the boxes of cereal she'd been unpacking, and her eyes met Joshua Yoder's penetrating gaze.

He stood stock-still, not ten feet away, his hand holding his hat slightly above his head, as if he'd stopped mid-lift. His blue eyes narrowed.

Her mouth went dry. Her chest hammered.

"Greta...." He lowered his hat to his side and approached, a smile slowly forming on his lips.

Nein. She couldn't deal with him and those emotions today. Or any day. She fled down the aisle and ducked inside the door marked "Employees Only." She would find some work to do in back until her shift ended.

As she dashed past the employee break room, she glanced at the clock. Fifteen minutes till she got off. He should be long gone by then. She wiped away a renegade tear.

After Greta clocked out, she made a few purchases—a bottle of olive oil, a jar of yeast, a fresh pineapple, and several avocados—and surveyed the store. Nein sign of Josh. She sagged with relief.

"Bye, Greta." Her cousin Rachel waved from the cereal aisle, where she'd taken over the task of unloading boxes.

Greta waved back on her way out the door. "See you tomorrow."

Greta stepped outside and into strong masculine arms that swept her up against a solid chest and swung her around and around. She screamed, trying to pull away. The man stopped swinging and released her waist. *Josh.* His hands immediately cupped her face, and he pressed his lips against hers. Hard.

They softened as they moved, igniting an unexpected fire. She couldn't keep from responding. Something inside her flared to life. She had a brief taste of peppermint before reality set in. Nobody had the right to kiss her. Not anymore.

She shoved her hands against his firm chest. "Joshua Yoder!"

He let go with a wink, then bent and retrieved his hat, which had fallen off sometime during the assault, and plopped it on his head before jogging over to his buggy and jumping in.

Leaving her reeling. In more ways than one.

She grabbed the nearest support beam on the porch and watched him flick the reins and drive off with a grin and a wave.

The door swished open behind her, and the store manager, Joel, stepped onto the porch, adjusting his hat against the glare of the sun. "Greta Miller. Must I remind you that we don't approve of such public displays of affection?"

She couldn't tear her gaze away from the buggy as Josh proceeded through the four-way stop. Leaving her behind.

As he'd done so many times before.

She should be used to the sting of rejection. The pain of abandonment.

Then again, she never expected him to kum from out of nowhere, swing her around, and kiss her.

Not after....

Her lips still tingled.

Such strange behavior, even from Josh.

"Greta." Joel's voice was sharp.

She dragged her attention away from the departing buggy to the bearded man standing next to her.

He held out a full white plastic bag. "Must I remind you...." He started to repeat the question, but Greta tuned him out. She glanced at the bag—her groceries?—then lowered her gaze to the ground.

It's not my fault! she wanted to say. *He kissed me when I wasn't even looking!* But that would require an explanation, and she didn't have one to give. So, she got the blame for being assaulted in broad daylight.

"I'm sorry," she assured her boss. "It won't happen again."

It shouldn't have happened in the first place.

Especially not after....

Joel gave the plastic bag a shake, causing the two glass containers inside to rattle against each other.

Her face heated as she reached for her purchases. Hopefully, the avocados weren't bruised.

Joel frowned. "What's gotten into you? You've been so skittish this past year. It's affecting your work. Probably a gut thing Gizelle is going to start soon."

Greta cringed. "I'm…I'm sorry. It's just…my daed…." *And Josh's return.* "Wait—what? My sister…working here?"

Joel's eyes softened. "I thought your daed would have told you. He arranged for Gizelle to take over your job, since you're going to have other obligations. We're all praying for him, you know. If your sister needs some time before she starts—"

"She won't." Not when their family needed every penny to cover their everyday expenses, plus the extra medical bills from Daed's accident ten months ago. They needed far more than Greta earned, so she'd spent every free hour making jams, jellies, and baked goods to sell at the tiny roadside stand in front of their haus. She'd thought she would continue doing this just on her days off, but apparently it was about to become a full-time venture. Mamm had mentioned sending her to farmers' markets, festivals, and other events. Tears burned Greta's eyes. Couldn't her parents have at least discussed it with her? Instead, she'd found out secondhand from her boss.

"Have a gut afternoon." Joel turned to go back inside, nodding at a couple Englisch customers who were just arriving.

Not even a "We'll miss you"? But he wouldn't say that. It wasn't their way. Besides, he would still see her at church gatherings.

She put her bag of groceries on the front seat of the buggy, tied the strings of her black bonnet, and unfastened her horse, Whippoorwill, from the hitching post. Then she started home, the sting of betrayal still burning.

A buggy was parked along the side of the road. As she started past it, a man stepped out in front of her. *Josh.* His straw hat was askew. Sunglasses concealed his eyes. She'd never dreamed he'd look so gut in them. So dark. Mysterious. Handsome. He wiped his hands down the sides of his pants. She caught her breath and flicked the reins.

He reached for the horse, stopping her. "Greta, wait. We need to talk."

A car inched around them. "The middle of the road is not a gut place."

Another vehicle approached and passed.

"If I kum over to-nacht, will you walk with me?"

He'd given up that right long ago. They weren't courting. She shook her head.

Josh released Whippoorwill and stepped back, his shoulders slumping. He nodded, accepting her refusal.

Something the old Josh never would've done.

He lowered his head. "I won't bother you again."

Inside her, something shifted, and the words tumbled out almost without conscious thought: "Jah, you can kum. After dinner."

He glanced up with his heart-stopping grin. "Danki. We really do need to talk." Then he turned back toward his buggy.

Her stomach fluttered. She'd probably regret changing her mind. She and Josh had nothing to say to each other.

Not one single word.

But better talking than kissing, for her sanity's sake.

~

Josh couldn't believe she'd said that he could kum over. He wouldn't be calling on her, exactly, but at least he'd been granted permission to go to her haus. Under duress. His stomach rumbled, reminding him it was past suppertime, and he hadn't yet been home to eat. Instead, he'd taken care of business in town for Daed and Grossdaedi. And himself. He smiled.

He left the horse and buggy at the end of her driveway, by the mailbox—an old habit from when they were courting, and his visits would last late into the evening. To-nacht, however, he wasn't coming for dinner. He'd probably be allowed to stay just long enough to say what he needed to say, then told, in no uncertain terms, to go away. Permanently.

Josh winced, though he knew he deserved nothing more.

The thing was, he didn't know what he would say. Just that he had to talk to Greta.

Maybe he should apologize for his impulsive behavior at the store that afternoon. But he'd wanted to get her attention. Instead, he'd stirred up a host of familiar feelings and a history of memories he'd need to live down.

He needed to stop and pray for guidance and wisdom before he went any farther, so he stepped to the side of the driveway and bowed his head. *Lord Gott, I hurt her so badly. I don't know how to begin making restitution. Give me the words. Give me the strength. Soften her heart.*

He raised his head as he started walking again, bypassing the front door and going around to the back. The rear of the haus came into view, and he stopped and stared for a moment. One side of the porch roof listed heavily, and the steps appeared to have rotted. Didn't Greta's brother know how to use a hammer? Or was he too swamped with other chores to take care of a haus and an overgrown yard?

The back door opened, and Greta appeared, wiping her hands on her apron. She held the door open. "Hallo. Want to kum in?"

Josh eyed the steps again. "Nein, I want to talk to you. But if it's not a gut time, I can kum in for a few minutes." And maybe find out how bad her daed was injured. The whispered comments he'd heard varied from "hurt his back, needs surgery" to "just lazy, spending all his days in bed."

Greta glanced behind her. "I'm doing dishes. You're welkum to join Daed at the table while he finishes his tea."

Josh nodded, then carefully navigated the steps and walked past her into the kitchen. He inhaled. "Something smells wunderbaar."

Greta's daed looked up with a smile. "Joshua Yoder. I haven't seen you around in forever."

Andy Miller appeared frail, his face drawn and ashen with the look of a man in constant pain. He held a fork in his hand, a half-eaten slice of coconut cream pie in front of him, a steaming mug of tea to the side.

"How are you doing? I heard you were in an accident."

Andy scowled. "Jah. An accident." He shifted. "Have a seat. Talk awhile. Gut to see you again. We've missed you."

So, the accident was taboo as a topic of conversation? Josh glanced away. "I've missed your family, too." He avoided looking at Greta. After all, it was his fault. All the blame fell on him for causing so much hurt. Pain. Ruined relationships. He pulled out a chair and sat.

"Greta, get your young man a slice of pie and some tea."

She wiped her hands on her apron and did what her daed asked, but the look she gave Josh clearly communicated, "Not my young man. And don't you forget it."

Not that he could forget it if he tried. Pain knifed him again. He looked up. Her long lashes framed her beautiful green eyes. Strawberry blonde curls escaped her kapp. His fingers flexed with an inexplicable desire to touch her hair. Dangerous thoughts. He glanced at the pie. "Danki, Greta. Looks great." Did she hear the huskiness in his voice?

"Have you had dinner?" Andy forked off another bite of his dessert. "She grilled bratwurst and served it with some fancy salsa she made from pineapple and avocados. Actually, pretty tasty."

"Sounds gut. But I'll eat when I get home." He didn't want their food. Not when he knew their budget was tight.

"Nonsense. We've hardly any left over. It'll be a snack for you. Greta, get the bu a brat and some of your salsa."

He should've kum a little later. To give her daed time to eat and Greta time to clean. Instead, he was causing more work. "Really, I'm fine."

A plate holding a brat in a bun, covered in fruit salsa with onions and a few other unidentified things, landed on the table in front of him. Delivered with a frown.

He couldn't blame her.

"Did Greta tell you that Gizelle starts work at the store tomorrow?"

Josh saw Greta's back go rigid. "Uh, nein. Is Greta going somewhere?" He hoped not. In an effort to appear as if he didn't care, he picked up the sandwich and took a bite. It was ser gut.

"Nein, but we're going to put her to work selling baked goods and jams and such to the tourists. And at farmers' markets."

Josh straightened, set the sandwich back on the plate, and swallowed. He'd get to see her almost every day, then. He tried to control his grin. *Danki, Lord.* "Really? I'm selling birdhouses and feeders that I made, and fishing flies and baskets made by David Lapp. I'll be glad to send my driver over to pick up Greta and her food items. Be easier than hauling them all by buggy. And we're going by here, anyway, so she won't need to contribute toward gas."

"That would be wunderbaar," Andy said. "We'd appreciate that, Joshua. Gott surely smiled on us when He brought you back home again."

An iron skillet slammed down on the counter.

"This tastes wunderbaar, Greta." Josh took another bite of his meal and glanced at her daed. "I'd be happy to help William with the repair work and chores too, if he needs it." Which he clearly did.

"I can't pay, but one of the benefits of having a man courting my dochter is, I can put him to work." Andy chuckled.

If only. Josh rolled his shoulders and took another bite. He wasn't sure why her daed didn't know they were no longer courting.

But Andy would figure it out soon enough.

~

Greta finished the dishes, including Daed's and Josh's, her tongue firmly pinned between her teeth so she wouldn't blurt out anything disrespectful. Or spiteful. But really, she had only herself to blame for inviting Josh in.

And they desperately needed his help.

Josh pushed to his feet. "Nice talking with you, Andy. I'll stop by tomorrow after the sale and see what I can do to help. Now, I'm going to take Greta on a walk, if it's okay."

Her daed nodded. "See you tomorrow." A smile lit his eyes.

Greta didn't want to dash his hopes. Not when so little brought him joy these days.

Josh held the door open for her, then followed her down the rickety steps. She felt embarrassed that he'd seen them in the current condition, a not-so-subtle signal of the family's state of need.

She turned and looked at him with barely contained anger. "We aren't courting."

"I'm aware of that." He bent his head and fell silent, walking by her side down the lane.

"You wanted to talk?" Controlled annoyance edged her voice. She winced at the realization.

Josh looked up. "Nobody mentioned you wouldn't be working at the Amish Country Store anymore. Why didn't you tell me? Why didn't Rachel?"

Why did he think he deserved advance notice, especially when even she hadn't gotten as much?

She shrugged. Tears threatened. "Nobody bothered to tell me, either. I found out today. At work. After you left." She wiped her eyes, embarrassed at her roller-coaster emotions. "I thought I was going to sell jams and baked goods on my days off. But apparently, that wouldn't bring in enough money, so Gizelle is taking my job, and I...."

His hand grazed the top of hers. The one up by her face. "You get to have the adventure."

Greta blinked and jerked away. Her skin tingled from his touch. "You've been around Onkel Samuel too much."

Josh smiled. "Gut man. Lot of wisdom to share."

They turned at the road and strolled past his horse, Sea Grass, calmly grazing.

"It hurts to admit when you make a mistake—but if it's big enough, it hurts only for a minute," Josh said quietly.

She glanced at him, failing to understand his statement. But she wouldn't ask him to clarify. Not now. Maybe not ever. Instead, she repeated the last words he'd said to her the day he left the Amish: "There's a consequence for every choice you make."

He nodded and held her gaze. "You remembered."

She remembered everything about that day. But she wouldn't tell him that. Wouldn't bring it up. That would only open a whole well of hurt.

"Look, I'm sorry I kissed you like that today," he said. "If you want, consider that the kiss I owed you."

Leave it to him to bring it up. She sighed. That fateful nacht flashed through her memory. He'd refused to participate when the other youth played spin the bottle. At least, after they told him to go into the closet with her and shut the door.

Instead, he shamed her by outright refusing, then got up and strode out of the haus.

Leaving the community. The Amish.

For years.

Chapter 2

Josh fell silent. Greta stayed beside him, maybe a foot away, but close enough that he caught the scents of vanilla, from all the baking she did. Every time he smelled the sweet aroma, he thought of her. With longing and regret.

He swallowed the lump in his throat and kicked at a rock in the dirt road. If only they could skip the conversation and he could just take her in his arms and kiss her soft lips, as he had done only hours earlier. He wanted to hold her close to his heart. *Ach, Greta.* But that wasn't an option.

"So, what happened to your daed?" Andy wouldn't tell him, but maybe Greta would. It might be an icebreaker. Besides, Josh was concerned. Anything that caused her pain injured him, too. He hated that her family situation forced her to do things she wouldn't have chosen for herself.

Greta frowned. "I wasn't home when it happened, but they told me he slipped and fell. He'd been standing on the hay wagon. His feet got caught in the reins, and he was run over by the thresher, then dragged several feet by the Belgian horses before our Englisch neighbor rescued him. It injured his back so badly that he can't work anymore. Sometimes, he can't even stand without help." She paused for a moment, her bottom lip quivering. "I know some people are saying he's lazy, but you can *see* he hurts. The doctors have him on strong pain medicine, but I think the drugs affect his thoughts. He says crazy things sometimes, sees things that aren't there, and sometimes he seems to live in the past." She sighed.

"He hasn't been going to church because he can't sit through the services."

"I could see his pain," Josh agreed, remembering Andy's haggard expression. Perhaps the pain pills were the reason he thought Josh and Greta were still a couple. "What do the doctors say regarding his chances of recovery?"

She scuffed her feet, looking down. "He needs some sort of surgery. They told us what it was, but I don't remember the exact medical terms. But the church fund is depleted. Lena Schultz needed chemotherapy and multiple surgeries, and then Bishop Joe's barn burned this past summer, followed by the fire at Onkel Samuel's, landing two of his buwe and David Lapp in the hospital. The church leaders said Daed has to wait until they've replenished the reserves. They're hoping the annual quilt auction will help."

Josh nodded. He knew Rachel's mamm had made dozens of quilts for the event. He'd helped set up the frames in her sewing room. "So, you were supporting your family by working at the Amish Country Store."

She shifted, putting more distance between them as they walked. "Joel could only afford to keep me on part-time. Mamm can't leave Daed to work outside the home, and William is taking care of the farm and going to school." Greta shrugged. "We talked about my selling baked goods and jams and such at the farmers' markets, but I didn't know it would be a full-time arrangement."

Josh ached to wrap his arms around her and let her cry on his shoulder. He almost reached for her again. It took great effort not to.

She bit her bottom lip. "I don't really mind that Gizelle is going to take my job, but I would have liked to have been consulted."

"You should've been."

She eyed him askance. "What was it you wanted to discuss? So far, I'm doing all the talking."

And he liked it that way. Saved him from having to say…he still didn't know what. He pulled in a breath. And sent up a silent prayer for the words Gott would have him speak.

"I'm sorry for all the hurt I caused you," he began. "The way I left. For not keeping in contact. Coming back without warning. Everything." He wanted to ask if they could be friends again, but maybe the fact that she was walking and talking with him indicated they could be. "And I wanted to ask a favor from you."

She huffed. "I should've realized your apology would kum at a cost."

He blinked and shook his head. "What? Nein. Not at all. It's unrelated. I've regretted my actions for a long time. I'll share that story, if you want to hear it."

She shot him a glance that he couldn't decipher. "I'm not interested."

Right. That clarified the look. He pressed his lips together.

"The favor?"

"I need a proofreader."

Another look he couldn't interpret. Incredulity, perhaps?

"I thought of asking Esther or Rachel, since they're avid readers, but I think…." He unwrapped a piece of peppermint candy and popped it in his mouth. "I need to ask you." At least, Gott had seemed to indicate as much when he'd prayed about it. "Esther is busy with her new family." He held another piece of candy out to her. "Want one?"

"Nein." She barely glanced at it. "Why do you need a proofreader?"

"Ach." He was afraid of that question. Terrified at how people would react, mostly. Especially since his project was being pursued without permission from the bishop or the prechers. "I'm, um, writing a book."

"A book? You?" Greta stopped walking and stared at Josh. She never would have expected that from him. He'd barely picked up a book during their years in school together.

He didn't look at her as he pulled off his hat, slapped it against his leg, then returned it to his head. "Jah, a book." His voice held a tone of reverence she'd never heard him use before.

"On what? Growing up Amish? I think it's already been done." She cringed at the derision in her voice.

"I have a contract." He spoke so quietly, she had to strain to hear him. He still didn't look at her.

"A contract. For what?"

A muscle jumped in his jaw. "For writing a book. Sort of. They're talking about using my Appalachian Trail journals for most of it."

"What? Who? Why?" The one-word questions tumbled out and lingered between them, then fizzled when he finally looked up and met her gaze with his blue eyes.

"Ach, Greta." Her name came out as a groan.

For a second, something sizzled between them. His eyes darkened as they settled on her mouth. He moved toward her, raising his arms, then dropping them as he stepped back without touching her. He jerked his gaze up to meet hers once more.

Her lips parted, suddenly burning with an inexplicable need. Odd, since the first—and the only—time he'd ever kissed her like a man had been at the Amish Country Store earlier that day.

"I...uh...." He shut his eyes, then opened them and cleared his throat. "In October, there was a message on the machine in the phone shanty from a publisher. We played phone tag awhile before finally setting up a time to talk. Had several conversations. I got the contract today. That's one of the reasons I went into town. I needed to sign it and send it back. They want me to write a book about...my life as ex-Amish."

One of the reasons he went into town? Was another to kiss her? "Your life. As ex-Amish."

"Jah. Well, sort of. I just can't…." He exhaled loudly. "I can't explain it. But you'll see. If you agree to proofread the manuscript."

She'd never been able to resist a mystery. And Josh definitely was one.

"I'll do it." Maybe the project would help her to figure him out. She needed to understand this new, different Josh Yoder.

"Danki, Greta. I appreciate you." His smile still made her knees weak and her stomach flutter. Then he stepped back again, his smile faltering. He glanced down the road, in the direction of her haus. "I…I guess I better go."

But instead of going, he stood still. Looking at her. Studying her, as if intending to memorize her features.

And instead of agreeing and turning toward home, she remained motionless. "I…I think I'll walk a little farther. You're welkum to join me. If you want." She knew that she spoke against her better judgment. How many times had they done this before he'd left? She would have to be careful where she allowed this road to take them.

His mouth quirked. "It's gut to be back, Greta."

Back. With her. As they fell into step together, Josh dared a glance at Greta. Maybe she thought he was referring to being back in the community. And, in a sense, he was. Because even though he was with her, he wasn't *with* her.

Maybe someday.

Hopefully, this visit meant she would stop avoiding him. She wouldn't be able to, if she'd been serious about agreeing to proofread his manuscript.

They walked in silence down to the end of the lane, then turned around and started back. Not touching. Not talking. Just together in a comfortable quiet that he didn't feel obligated to fill with words. Apparently, neither did she.

While he was gone, he'd missed the hours they used to spend walking together, just like this. But he hadn't been worthy of her attention due to his poor decisions.

If only he could forget the look in her eyes when— Nein. He wouldn't go there.

Awareness of her put all his senses on alert. He heard the swish of her skirts, the skid of her white tennis shoes along the gravel road. Saw her kapp strings fluttering in the light breeze. Could almost feel the tiny curls at the back of her neck. Smelled the lavender....

He'd been a fool, leaving her. Leaving their relationship, their courtship, in the dust. Blowing her off in an effort to escape his mistakes. His sins.

There'd been no escape. His poor decisions, and their repercussions, had followed him to the ends of the earth.

As they neared the driveway to Greta's haus, she stopped and looked up at him.

But it'd been worth it because....

"Joshua, I appreciate your offer to have the driver transport my goods to sell and to help William around the farm. And I don't mind repaying you by proofreading your book. But I don't want you to think I'm going to let you court me again. Because I won't."

Wow. The girl who disliked drama had somehow found her voice. In spite of himself, he smiled. "I wouldn't dream of making that assumption."

The way her eyes narrowed, he knew she doubted him.

"And I don't want you writing about me."

He couldn't keep his grin from spreading. He leaned nearer, a slight invasion of her personal space, and resisted the urge to reach for her hands.

As if sensing his temptation, she buried her fingers in the folds of her apron.

"It's not all about you."

Her cheeks reddened. Maybe with a flash of anger.

It's about Him. Josh stepped backward.

"See you tomorrow, schnuckelchen." *Beautiful girl.* "The usual driver is busy, so her sohn, Stan, is helping out and driving for her for a while. We'll be by after breakfast to pick you up." He winked. "If you're going tomorrow, that is."

"I'll have some things prepared."

He nodded. "Tomorrow, then." Then he turned and jogged to his buggy.

He looked forward to the next day more than he had a right to.

Chapter 3

Greta smothered a yawn as she loaded several plastic crates with an assortment of fresh baked goods: breads, cookies, muffins, and pies. She'd already wrapped and packed up a crate of jams, jellies, preserves, pickled eggs, and home-canned salsas while Mamm and Gizelle fixed breakfast. It seemed Mamm and Daed had made an exaggerated estimation of what she could sell in one day. But the leftovers might sell another day. Or get eaten.

She'd intended to make doughnuts, too, but she'd run out of time. As it was, she and Mamm had stayed up working hours after the rest of the family had gone to bed. After they'd finished, she'd carefully slid into the full-size bed she shared with Gizelle, so as not to wake her. But Greta hadn't been able to sleep. Instead, she'd relived every moment of her interactions with Josh that day—especially the kiss. She wouldn't mind a repeat performance. Not that it would happen. After several sleepless hours, she'd finally given up on slumber and gotten up—long before the rooster crowed.

Tires scattered gravel as someone sped into the driveway and stopped. Probably the Stan Josh had mentioned. Two doors slammed, and then a single set of footsteps pounded on the creaky, rotten porch stairs. Something cracked. Hopefully, he wouldn't fall through.

Greta moved toward the entrance, but before she could reach it, the door opened. Josh stepped into the kitchen.

His eyes met hers. "Morgen, Greta. You ready?" His gaze lingered a moment, sweeping over her, before moving to the table. "Morgen, Andy."

"Morgen, Josh. Pull up a seat and join us for breakfast. My frau made scrambled eggs, toast, and oatmeal." Daed's smile was tight. His pain pill waited beside him, since it was supposed to be taken with food.

Josh shook his head. "Danki, but I already ate. We are here to pick up Greta. We have a lot to do before the farmers' market opens." His gaze flickered to her. "Do you have a cash box?" He bent over the stack of crates of canned goods and hefted them both up, his muscles bunching and flexing.

She marveled at his strength. One of the crates was so heavy, she'd had to slide it across the floor. She couldn't imagine lifting it and the other at the same time.

"Jah. I packed it in with the baked items. At the bottom." She didn't know where Mamm had gotten all the bills, fifty dollars' worth. Possibly from cashing Greta's latest paycheck.

"Be careful, Greta," Daed warned her. "Don't take any personal checks. You don't know what you're dealing with."

"Don't worry," Josh assured him. "I'll keep an eye on her."

Daed nodded. "Glad you're staying. I wondered."

Josh had told them last nacht that he sold birdhouses at the market. It seemed Daed's memory was getting worse by the day.

"Jah, I'm staying. See you later, Andy. We need to go." Josh nodded at her. "Get the door for me, please, Greta?"

She opened it, and as Josh moved past her, his nearness stirred strange flutters in her stomach. She swallowed hard and looked away as Mamm came in from hanging laundry with Gizelle. "Bye, Mamm and Daed."

"Don't forget your lunch, Greta." Mamm handed her a bag.

"Danki." She accepted it, not taking her eyes off Josh's muscular frame.

"Hey, Stan—would you run in and get the other crates? Thanks. Ach, I forgot about these steps." Josh set the crates on the edge of the porch, then jumped down as a young Englisch man gingerly made his way up the stairs. "Greta, tell your daed I'll get these fixed after we bring you home to-nacht, if that's okay."

"I heard." Daed lifted his hand, still clutching his spoon. "And you'll join us for supper, too."

Josh didn't respond. Maybe he hadn't heard.

Stan approached the door. He was probably around Greta's age. His brown hair curled just below his collar. He wore jeans, a black T-shirt, and cowboy boots that thumped when he walked. The rotten porch boards shifted and cracked even more than usual under his heavy steps.

He winked as he walked past Greta but didn't acknowledge either of her parents as he lifted the two remaining crates and tromped back outside. He opened the back door of the white van, then helped Josh load all the crates before slamming the hatch shut.

"You can sit up front, babe." Stan held the passenger door open for her.

Babe? Greta hesitated. This stranger thought she was a boppli? And she'd never ridden anywhere but the backseat before.

Josh reached for the handle of the sliding side door. "She'll sit back here, Stan." There was a hard note in his voice. Maybe he'd sensed her discomfort.

Stan blinked. "Is it against the rules for women to sit up front?"

"No, but it's discouraged." Josh held out his hand to Greta. "Do you need help getting in?"

She shook her head. Climbing into the middle seat of a van was easy after plenty of practice getting in and out of buggies. She ducked inside. To her surprise, Josh climbed in after her. "Scoot over."

For a brief moment, his left leg pressed against her right thigh. Even through the thick material of her dress, her skin tingled. She pressed herself against the left armrest and clasped her hands primly in her lap.

Josh closed the door with one swift, easy move. Why hadn't he sat up front with Stan? Half a foot away from her was entirely too close.

Stan inserted the key in the ignition and gave it a turn. "I wanted to bring my convertible. I think your stuff would've fit, between the trunk and the backseat. But Mom said I *had* to use the van." He shrugged. "I guess it would've been tight. Maybe I'll drive that the next time I give you a ride. Tonight."

A convertible? Greta wiped her sweaty palms on her apron. She was already out of her comfort zone. She aimed a sideways glance at Josh. His concerned gaze met hers for a moment, and then he looked away.

He seemed to be in a protective mode, the way he hovered and kept stealing glances at her. His hands were bunched in fists at his sides. What did he think she needed protecting from? Was Stan dangerous?

She stole another glance at him. At his steel-blue gaze resting steadily on her. At his curly blond hair, a little too long, touching the collar of his shirt. At his suspenders, stretched taut over his muscular chest.

Her heart pounded as her mouth went dry. She hastily averted her eyes.

Nobody could be more dangerous than Josh Yoder.

Josh strained as he lifted the crates of Greta's baked goods from the back of the van. It'd been nice to sit beside her on the ride to the farmers' market. If only they could've cuddled—his arm around her shoulders, their legs touching—the way they did when he was courting her. When they talked of marriage. Planned their future together.

His stomach clenched. Best not to think of that.

Especially since she made it clear they were *not* courting now.

Josh glanced down at the crate and eyed the delicious-looking cookies on top. Red velvet, with white chocolate chips. "If these cookies don't sell, I'll buy them at lunchtime," he told Greta, setting the crate on the table she'd been assigned.

She lifted them out of the crate and went to stash them under the table.

"Nein, don't hold them for me. I'll purchase them only if they don't sell."

She looked up at him. "Are you sure?"

"I'll take my chances." He winked at her.

A becoming shade of red colored her cheeks. She glanced away.

Stan started to set up the tent canopy Josh had brought to protect them the sun. It was big enough to cover both her table and his.

Leaving Stan to his work, Josh returned to the van and unloaded the items he'd brought to sell. It was gut that he'd secured a table next to Greta's, not only so they could share the canopy, but also so he could look out for her on her first day at the farmers' market. She'd sold homemade goods plenty of times before at her family's roadside vegetable stand, but never here.

He noticed her unusually pale skin. Her wide eyes. The way she kept smoothing her hands over her dress.

"Relax," he told her. "It's not so bad. You might even have fun." He resisted the urge to touch her upper arm.

Maybe he should offer to pray for her. With her. If it were anyone else, he would. Instead, he walked away. What made her different? He hesitated and turned around. "I'm praying, liebling," he told her. "If you need me, I'm here." And he would be. Both there and praying.

If it were possible, her skin paled even more. He'd intended his words to be comforting. Instead, they seemed to scare her. Or maybe it was the endearment he'd used. His shoulders slumped with deflated hope.

While she unpacked her goods and arranged them on the table, he went to set up his own display. He'd brought three baby quilts made by Rachel's mamm, Elsie—one in variegated blue, the second in yellows and greens, and the third in shades of pink. He also carried a handful of business cards—some for Elsie, others for David Lapp, and his own, just in case someone wanted to place a custom order. He placed them in his cash box.

After arranging the quilts, Josh set up a display of the colorful fly-fishing ties David had made, along with a few of his baskets—some made of pine needles, the other of reeds. In the middle of the table, he placed several bird feeders and birdhouses—just enough samples to pique interest, but not so many as to create a cluttered look. The rest he kept under the table to put out when the others sold or to offer as an example of an alternate design.

Once he'd put the final touches on his display, he stood back to study it. He reached out to adjust the angle of a birdhouse. Not that it would stay that way. Customers had a tendency to pick things up and put them back wherever they pleased.

He eyed the other vendors setting up their tables. Greta was the only one selling baked goods. Most of them had brought home-grown vegetables. A few had crocheted or knitted items for sale, and one older lady sold paintings. And a couple women in hospital scrubs were offering blood pressure screenings. *Odd.*

When the first customers of the day stopped at Greta's table, she played nervously with her kapp strings as she spoke to them. Selling at an open-air marketplace was probably overwhelming compared with working part-time in a grocery store stocking shelves and answering only an occasional question. This new venture would involve a lot more interaction with Englischers. Josh kept watching, ready to assist if she needed him, but not close enough to make it seem that he wanted to take over.

Not that he'd be a lot of help. As much as he loved eating jam on his breakfast toast, he didn't know the ingredients or how it was made. Mamm and his sisters handled that sort of thing.

A large woman wearing a floppy straw hat picked up a jar of strawberry jam and asked the price. Greta answered. The woman handed her a twenty-dollar bill. "I'll take four. These will make excellent gifts. And I love the way you tied red ribbon around the lids."

Glad to see her sale going so well, Josh turned to assist a customer who'd picked up the pink baby quilt. She made loud oohing and aahing noises, which attracted the attention of several of her friends. They gathered around her. "This is so beautiful," she said to Josh. "Did your mother make it?"

"No, ma'am." At least she hadn't asked if his wife had made it. He'd heard that question a time or two. Not everyone knew that if an Amish man was clean-shaven, it indicated he was unmarried. He couldn't resist a glance at Greta. "Another woman in the community made them. Her quilts have won blue ribbons at the county fair dozens of times." Not that Elsie Miller would ever share that information. It would be considered prideful. But it was common knowledge in the community.

"Does she make full-size ones, too?" the woman asked. "I've always dreamed of owning a log cabin quilt in shades of browns, tans, and ecru." She peered more closely at the pink quilt. "Just look at those tiny stitches...." She held it out to the woman who'd bought jam from Greta and had now joined her at Josh's table.

Ecru? Josh pulled out one of Elsie's business cards, glad that he wasn't responsible for recording the specifications for any custom orders. To be in compliance with the Ordnung, her cards were printed on plain white paper with no personal name or address.

"Quilts," hers simply read, along with the phone number for the shanty at the end of the Millers' driveway.

Josh handed it to the woman.

"Thank you." She closed her fingers around the card. "I'll take this quilt, for now. It'll be perfect for my new grandbaby. I still can't believe my daughter's having a girl of her own." She checked the price tag, then handed him the quilt to wrap as she dug around inside her bulky purse for her wallet.

One of the woman's friends picked up a bird feeder. "*This* would be perfect for my back patio. Does it keep out the squirrels?" She eyed Josh with a look of skepticism, as if he were one of the mischievous critters.

"Yes, ma'am. Unless they are more determined than most." He finished wrapping the quilt, packed the bird feeder in a bag, and accepted cash payment from both women.

The day continued in a similar manner. Josh glanced over at Greta from time to time, and her complexion appeared to improve as the hours went by. Her baked goods sold out before noon—including the cookies he'd wanted to buy. Just picturing them made his mouth water. He forced his mind away from them. They were gone and shouldn't be a source of temptation.

Just like Greta. Gone. And by his own doing.

But, unlike the cookies, she was still a source of temptation.

He watched her pocket some cash, pushing it deep inside her apron, which pulled the material tight against her curves. He swallowed and glanced away. Why wasn't she adding it to her cash box? He could see it sitting under the table. Maybe she was waiting for a less busy time. Hopefully, she was earning as much as she'd hoped to.

He'd looked forward to picnicking with her at lunch, but that didn't end up happening. The crowd of customers peaked, and her table was a major attraction.

At least he'd have this evening. Maybe they could go on another walk once he'd repaired the porch steps.

Around five, they started packing up. Stan returned, driving a convertible with the radio blaring. He parked and turned off the car, silencing the music. Then he got out and approached them. "Almost ready?"

"Yep. Just closing up shop." Josh put away the few remaining birdhouses and woven baskets. The feeders, quilts, and fishing items had sold out fast. He'd need to restock before tomorrow morgen.

Stan collapsed the tent as Josh went to help Greta. She'd brought four full plastic crates, and three of them were empty; the remaining one was only halfway full of jams and jellies. She set the cash box on top, and then Josh carried everything to the car.

Stan put the empty crates in the trunk and collapsed Josh's cardboard boxes while Josh set the canned goods on the floorboard and his other boxes on the backseat, where Greta would sit alone on the drive home.

Unless Josh was a gentleman and offered to let her sit up front.

But the way Stan looked at her, and his habit of calling her "babe…." Josh's stomach knotted. Maybe it didn't mean anything. But he'd been around enough men to know that some of them would hit on any available female.

Josh sighed. He'd have to give Greta the option, at least.

She approached, wiping her hands down the front of her apron again, and eyed the car with distrust.

"Busy day, ain't so?" Josh's fingers itched to smooth the weariness from her face. He refrained from reminding her that they would be at it again tomorrow.

He smiled at her. "Front or back?"

Her chest rose and fell as she studied the vehicle. "Is it safe?"

Probably safer than being alone with him in a closet after playing spin the bottle.

Not that she ever had been in that position, thanks to him.

He sighed and glanced at her soft lips. Swallowed. Then looked up and met her eyes. "Jah, I think so. If you're buckled in."

Greta climbed into the backseat of the convertible and pulled her black bonnet over her kapp, tying the strings in a loose bow. As she fastened her seat belt, she glanced at the pink plastic crate on the floorboard. Mamm and Daed hadn't been as off as she'd thought when they'd tried to anticipate how much she would need to take. She hoped they'd be happy with the money she'd earned. She didn't have any idea how much it added up to. She hadn't had any spare time to count cash. But the busyness had been a blessing. She'd feared having to fend off attention from Josh all day as he tried to worm his way back into her heart. Instead, he'd been just as busy with customers.

She leaned back wearily. If only she could go to bed early tonacht. Instead, she faced another long evening of baking—unless Mamm had done a lot of that today. Maybe Greta could set aside a few extra cookies just for Josh....

Nein. She wouldn't do that. He didn't deserve any special favors from her.

Stan started the car, and the radio blasted yet again. She cringed, wishing he'd turn it down. Or that Josh would ask him to. He didn't.

They pulled out into traffic with a burst of speed that pushed Greta back against the seat. The wind tugged at her black bonnet, loosening the strings. She grabbed for it. Stan went around a curve so quickly, she fell sideways into the box on the seat beside her.

After straightening herself, she removed the bonnet and stuffed it in the crate on the floor, cramming it in between two jars so it wouldn't blow away. If only Stan would put the roof up. But he didn't offer to, and Josh didn't ask. But he did remove his straw hat.

She hoped the wind wouldn't prove stronger than the straight pins holding her kapp in place. Her hair was coming loose at it was, with several loose strands blowing in her face.

When they finally arrived at her haus, Stan left the car idling while he and Josh unloaded everything, including a box full of Josh's birdhouses and another of David's baskets, and put it on the back porch. How would Josh get his leftover items home? Maybe he planned to leave them there over-nacht and pick them up in the morgen.

It didn't matter. What did matter was the overwhelming task ahead of her: staying up late baking more things to sell at the farmers' market, wherever it would be tomorrow. Once again, she felt a tiny flare of hope that Mamm had managed to do the baking that day.

She climbed the stairs, careful to avoid the weak planks, and entered the kitchen. She stumbled to a halt. Bishop Joe sat at the table with Daed, a steaming mug in front of him.

The bishop shot to his feet, bumping the table. Tea sloshed over the rim of the mug. "What have you been doing out, looking like that?" His tone overflowed with condemnation. "Your hair all out of—"

Josh came in, carrying two of the empty crates.

The bishop's eyes narrowed as he turned to him. "Joshua Yoder. I should've known you were involved." Then he frowned at Greta. "You should know better, Greta Miller. With your father as ill as he is, you go and do something like this...." He pulled in a sharp breath. "I've half a mind to force you two to get married."

Josh reared back. "Wh—"

"Married?" Daed sounded confused. Was he about to defend her?

His gaze, clouded by the pain medicine, moved to Josh. "Married would be gut, jah."

Josh shook his head, backing away. "Nein. We spent the day at the farmers' market, and the driver brought us home in a convertible. I'll get your last two crates, Greta." He avoided her gaze as he turned and stepped out on the porch.

Even though she didn't fancy the idea of marrying Josh, it hurt to realize he didn't want her.

"A convertible." Bishop Joe snorted. "Does the bu think I'm daft? Nein driver uses one of those. They all drive vans." He eyed Greta with distrust. Disapproval. And Daed didn't defend her. Of course, he had probably missed half the conversation. Greta didn't like for him to be on those pain pills. She looked forward to him having his surgery, so he could finally go off them.

She glanced back at Bishop Joe. His glare pierced her. Despite Josh's denial and explanation, he'd judged her and found her guilty. How dare he accuse her of lying? Trying to force her to marry Josh.... Was the man blind? Couldn't he see the crates? But he didn't have a track record of compassion and understanding. The one time Greta had dared approach him, regarding her cousin Esther, he hadn't listened. Nein reason for him to start listening now.

But she would *not* marry Josh. She would fight that sentence with everything in her.

Josh came back with the final two crates. "Here you go, Greta. I'll fix the steps now." He went back outside, shutting the door behind him.

Greta nodded with a belated "Danki." Then she looked at Daed. "Where's Mamm?" She should have started supper by now, but it didn't appear that anything had been prepared.

Daed merely shook his head. Maybe he didn't know.

Bishop Joe sat down again. "She'll be mighty ashamed of you, for sure. She went to pick up your sister from work and to buy a few groceries. Since I was here, she asked me to stay and visit with Andy until she returned."

Greta didn't ask where her brother was, or why he couldn't have watched Daed or gone to pick up Gizelle. Instead, she got some potatoes out of the pantry and started peeling them at the sink. Did the bishop intend to join them for dinner, too? She thought of telling him that he could go, since she was there now and could keep an eye on her daed, but that would be rude.

"I'll be back, Andy." Bishop Joe scooted back in his chair and got to his feet once again. "I need to have a talk with that bu about marrying your dochter." The door shut behind the bishop.

"Marrying?" Daed repeated.

Greta pursed her lips and continued peeling potatoes with more vigor than usual.

She. *Peel.* Would. *Peel.* Not. *Peel.* Marry. *Peel.* Josh. *Peel.*

Ever.

Chapter 4

Josh went into the Millers' barn and looked around. Did Andy still keep his tools and lumber in the lowest loft? He should've thought to ask before coming out here. He hadn't, in his haste to get away from the bishop.

Something moved in his peripheral vision, and he turned toward it. Thirteen-year-old William came out of a stall. Dark circles shadowed his eyes, and his shoulders showed a pronounced slump.

Josh's heart went out to him. He was far too young to be running the family farm on his own.

"Hallo," Josh said. "I promised your daed I'd fix the porch steps. Where would I find the wood?"

William straightened with a smile. "I'll show you. Thanks, Joshua. I can't keep up. And the bishop won't let me drop out of school to get things done." He turned and started for the back of the barn.

Josh followed him to the tack room. "I'll help as much as I can. I spend the morgen working with Daed on our farm and the day manning a table at the farmers' market, but I can kum here in the evening, if you don't mind." When he would find time to write his book, he didn't know.

"I don't mind." William lifted a hammer from a hook on the wall and handed it to Josh. "Everything you should need is in here. Nails are in that cabinet. Put things back when you're finished. I need to get back to work." Without specifying what he'd been working on, he went out, leaving Josh to gather the supplies he needed.

As Josh crossed the yard toward the haus, the bishop stood on the porch, hands planted on his hips, and watched him approach. It didn't surprise Josh that he'd waited for him. Once Bishop Joe got an idea stuck in his head, it took a miracle of Gott to get it removed. And right now, he seemed fixated on seeing Josh and Greta married. All because she'd kum home with messy hair.

Josh blew out a frustrated sigh. If he'd had anything to do with it, the white prayer kapp would've been removed, too, and the pins holding her long, beautiful hair in place would've been pulled out, displaying her crown in all its glory. Giving him access to tangle his fingers in it. But he hadn't so much as slid his finger over a strand of the silky softness since before he'd left the Amish. And since his return, she'd avoided him. Almost a whole year of hiding or running from him. Thankfully, the farmers' market and craft festivals would bring them together, with nein way of escape. Maybe, Gott willing, he could win her back.

The bishop shifted, reclaiming Josh's attention.

"Joshua Yoder. What have you to say for yourself? You're already on shaky ground around here, leading those unauthorized Bible studies. Don't think I don't know about them. I know all. They need to end." His glare intensified. "You're signed up for baptism classes. And with Greta having been baptized already, she needs to kneel and confess."

The bishop didn't know as much as he thought he did. Including the full story behind the Bible studies. David Lapp led them. And Preacher Samuel had been attending them, as had another baptized Amish man. But Josh wouldn't spill their secrets. Instead, he straightened and met the bishop's gaze. "She'll need to kneel and confess for a sin she didn't commit?"

"The evidence is there, plain to see."

Josh gestured to the unsold birdhouses and baskets sitting on the Millers' porch, waiting for the next day. "As I said, we were at the farmers' market. The regular driver wasn't available, so her son filled in. He took us there in the van but brought us home in his convertible. With the roof down." Hopefully, that wouldn't happen again. In addition to payment for the transportation, Josh had given Stan a few firm words while they unloaded the boxes and crates from the vehicle.

Bishop Joe eyed the boxes. His stance relaxed. "I'm keeping my eye on you two."

Josh nodded. At least a forced wedding wouldn't happen for this "sin." Not that he'd object to marrying Greta; but he wanted her on his terms. Wanted her to be as crazy in love with him as she'd been before.

He expelled another forceful breath and turned his attention to the steps.

Without apologizing for the false accusations, the bishop pivoted and stomped inside. Josh doubted Greta would hear an apology, either. Instead, just another warning: *I'm keeping my eye on you....*

Sure enough, through the open window came those very words.

Greta made no response—at least, none that he could hear.

Josh stuck the claw of the hammer under a nail and yanked it out. As he repeated the action along one plank, his anger built. He probably should've held his tongue and not talked back to the bishop, but seriously....

He blew out another puff of air, releasing some of his pent-up frustration, and bowed his head. *Lord Gott, I'm sorry for losing my temper with him. Please help me to be a positive witness for You, and to do everything You're asking of me.* Right now, the list seemed overwhelming. There were his home and work responsibilities, the help he'd promised Greta's family, the book he needed to write, the witnessing he was called to do, the wrongs he had to right. And Greta. *Ach, Lord.*

My grace is sufficient.

A horse and buggy turned into the driveway, and Josh looked up as it neared. Greta's mamm, Martha, and Gizelle. Martha stopped the buggy in front of the barn, and William came out to assist. Josh put the hammer down and went to help. If he'd known they weren't home, he wouldn't have been so hasty in tearing the steps apart. But they could go in through the rarely used front door, instead.

He approached with a nod of greeting. "I'm fixing the steps, but I'll carry your groceries in if you want to go around to the front."

Martha smiled. "Danki, Josh. We appreciate it. We'll feed you supper, for sure. Is Greta here? I told her we'd have dinner going when she got home, so we could get started baking right away. But this trip took longer than I expected. Groceries are in the back."

Eighteen-year-old Gizelle gave him a slow, flirty smile as she grabbed a bag. "Danki, Josh."

He nodded again, then lifted two bulk bags of flour and sugar as William unhitched the horse.

"Whippoorwill?" Josh raised his eyebrows at William. "Isn't that Greta's horse?"

"Daed sold the other horses and buggies," William said quietly. "Greta's horse was the oldest. Worth the least." He dipped his head as if ashamed.

This family needed help now. Not after the next quilt auction. Josh had been saving up for his future home and farm. The one he hoped to share with Greta someday. Maybe he should start putting some of it toward helping the Millers now.

But they wouldn't accept money from him. Not knowingly.

He would stop by Preacher Samuel's haus on the way home. He needed to give Elsie the money she'd earned that day, anyway, and pick up a few more of her boppli quilts. And Preacher Samuel needed to know about the dire straits his brother's family was in. Maybe he'd have some idea of how to help.

He carried the groceries to the porch, set them down on the edge, and hoisted himself up. Martha opened the door as he hefted the bag of flour.

"Where do you want this?" he asked as he entered the kitchen.

"Just put it on the floor over there." She pointed to the far wall. "We need both the sugar and the flour for our baking to-nacht."

The kitchen smelled delicious. Josh couldn't quite identify all the aromas, but garlic was one. His stomach rumbled in response. Greta stood at the stove, stirring something in a large pot. She'd fixed her hair and resecured her kapp. Probably at the bishop's insistence. And he still sat at the table, glaring, his eyes fastened on Greta. As if he expected her to...what? Say or do something inappropriate, for sure.

Greta glanced at Josh. She looked stressed. Had Bishop Joe made additional comments about her appearance? Had he told her mamm?

None of his business. Josh brought in the rest of the groceries, then got back to work on the porch steps.

He'd just finished pounding in the last nail when the door opened. Greta came out and crossed the porch to him. "You've done a great job, Josh. Danki. Mamm says to tell you dinner's ready. Would you let William know when you return the tools to the barn?"

Josh stood. "I'll tell him, but I'm not staying."

She looked away, but not before he saw the sheen of tears in her eyes. "There's plenty. And Daed insists."

He scratched his chin. "I have other plans. Do you mind if I leave those birdhouses here over-nacht?"

Greta glanced at them briefly. The corners of her mouth turned down. "Jah, that's fine."

She sounded suddenly deflated. But he wasn't conceited enough to wonder if it was because she'd wanted him to stay for the meal. Besides, he knew better. It was probably due to what the bishop had said. Josh wouldn't blame her. He felt frustrated, too. But he couldn't think of a way to reassure her, except by taking her in his arms—and that would make matters worse. Especially when anything he might say would be overheard through the open window.

Josh picked up the tools and turned away. "See you tomorrow, Greta."

"Jah. Danki, again."

He headed for the barn. "William?" he called out once inside. "Your sister said supper's ready."

"Be right there."

He couldn't see William, but he could guess what he'd been working on. The barn floor near the entrance had been swept clean, and an empty feed bag waited by the door.

Josh put away the tools, retrieved his cash box from the porch, and started the walk home.

He'd just reached the end of the driveway when he heard footsteps pounding behind him. He turned around as Greta ran to him. "Don't tell anyone. Please." Desperation colored her tone. "My parents don't want anyone to know. They already think Daed's lazy. They don't need to know how the pain medicine affects his brain. Or that my parents are selling things off to pay the bills."

Whether he told anyone or not, such things rarely went unnoticed in close-knit communities like theirs.

Either way, he couldn't fulfill her request. For if he didn't tell, how could he help?

Greta stared at Josh, her eyes silently echoing her plea.

He scuffed his feet, then slowly met her gaze. "What about Bishop Joe? He's seen the reality for himself. The truth is plain."

She scowled. "Bishop Joe sees only what he wants to see. And he doesn't *want* to know how we're really doing. Because then he'd be obligated to place a call in the *Budget* for financial help from other communities. And he sure doesn't want to do that. It's a matter of pride, I think."

He hesitated a moment, then shook his head. "Bishop Joe needs to do what is necessary to help your family. That's what the fund is in place for, Greta. You know that."

Tears burned her eyes. She didn't know what else to say to make him agree to keep the gravity of her family's situation a secret. But maybe she could kum up with something during the course of dinner, if she could convince him to stay. "I didn't poison the food, you know. You should join us. Please."

He made a move toward her, then pulled back. A muscle worked in his jaw. "I'm sorry. I really can't."

"Hot date with another girl?" she asked, then pressed her lips together. That wasn't her business. She ought to apologize for overstepping her bounds.

He chuckled. "Nein." He didn't elaborate further. Nor did he accuse her of being jealous, as he had done once upon a time.

Truthfully, she was. Greta swallowed the lump in her throat and forced the green-eyed monster into submission. "I'm sorry. I shouldn't have said that. None of my business, really."

His steady gaze met hers. "You're right. It's not."

So, he was courting someone else? Then why had he kissed her yesterday? Simply because she was there and available? The green-eyed monster reared its head again. "Fine. I won't keep you from her. Gut nacht."

Josh rubbed his jaw. "I'll swing by later. After dinner."

She turned away as the tears she'd been holding at bay began to escape her feeble control. "Nein. I'll be busy. See you tomorrow." Her voice caught.

"I'll say hallo to your aenti Elsie when I drop off her day's earnings."

She hesitated, then faced him again. "Please, don't tell."

"I'm sorry, Greta." His voice was quiet but resolved. "Preacher Samuel—"

"Onkel Samuel is okay." He'd be a safe person for Josh to talk to. After all, he had kum by the haus multiple times, offering help—physical and financial. And he'd been sent away each time with a firm refusal. He would tell Josh as much, and advise him to back off.

Why hadn't Daed refused Josh's offer of physical help? Was it because of his medication-induced belief that Josh still courted his dochter?

If he hadn't left the Amish in the first place, they would've been married by now.

Pain knifed a fresh wound in her heart.

If only he'd never left.

~

When Josh got home, the dawdi-haus screamed silence. Mamm was probably still working at the cheese store, and Daed was likely out in the fields. Josh carried the cash box upstairs to his room and separated out the money he needed to deliver.

After he pocketed the cash, he hitched Sea Grass to the buggy and drove out to Preacher Samuel's. The place bustled with activity—the way Josh's home used to when his older brothers and sisters still lived there. Now they were all married and had homes of their own, except for his brother James, who lived in the main haus with his frau and their kinner.

The two smallest girls, Jenny and Mary, ran out to meet Josh. "If you're looking for Rachel, she's over at Esther's haus."

Josh grinned. "I'm not. Is your daed home?"

"He's in the chicken yard, preaching to the rooster," Jenny said, pointing.

"Danki." Josh handed each of them a peppermint, then turned toward the small building enclosed by chicken wire.

As Josh approached, he saw Preacher Samuel filling the water feeders. He wasn't delivering a sermon, unless he'd lost his train of thought due to the chickens' apparent engagement in active praise, judging by the noise level.

The preacher looked up with a smile as Josh approached. "Hallo. What brings you by?"

"I wanted to deliver the money Elsie's quilt sales earned today. I also wanted to talk to you about your brother, Andy."

His smile faded. He silently regarded Josh.

"Greta says they don't want anyone to know how bad things are, but Andy desperately needs help. Did you know they sold all the buggy horses but one? They needed the money to pay the bills. And he's so drugged with pain medicine, he doesn't seem aware of reality."

Preacher Samuel nodded. "I know. I've offered to help in any way I can, but they've declined. I tried arranging for them to receive boxes of food that are collected for the needy. They refused the charity. 'Gott will provide,' they say. And He does, but sometimes it's through other people, ain't so?"

Josh nodded. "What about asking for assistance through the *Budget?* It'd help build up the financial reserve so Andy could have the surgery he needs." *And get off the drugs.*

"I already talked to the bishop about it, but I don't know if he took my advice. I'll bring it up to him again." Preacher Samuel came out of the enclosure and put his hand on Josh's shoulder. "Danki for your concern. Are you and our Greta…back together?"

Josh sighed. "Nein." He couldn't even claim friendship with her anymore. If only things were different.

"Anything I need to add to my prayer list?" Preacher Samuel raised his eyebrows.

"Ach, just…I have a lot on my plate. And I promised to help William with the farm chores as much as I can."

Preacher Samuel's eyebrows hitched even higher. "Andy agreed to let you help? Wonders never cease. As I said, he's rejected all my offers."

Josh kicked at a rock. "He thinks I'm still courting Greta. Guess he forgot all the years I spent away."

"I see." Preacher Samuel nodded. "He views you as a member of his immediate family, hence his acceptance of your help." He paused a moment. "I'll make a trip to Bishop Joe's to-nacht and have a talk with him about Andy. I agree that something needs to be done." He glanced toward his haus. "My frau is in her sewing room. Go on in to make your delivery. She probably has some more quilts for you to sell."

Josh nodded. "Danki."

"Did you ever apologize to Greta for hurting her? For leaving?"

"I said I was sorry. That's it. Nein discussion, nein resolution. She's not ready to hear more from me." He shrugged. "I did ask for her help with proofreading the book I mentioned at our last Bible study. But remember, this is just between us. Please don't mention it to the bishop."

Preacher Samuel nodded. "He asked me to keep an eye on the Bible studies, to see if any baptized church members were going. But…." He lifted one shoulder. "I already know, since I'm going. And I think it's needed. I'm tempted to invite the bishop to join us. Maybe things would change."

"Or you could be excommunicated."

The preacher's lips settled into a flat line. "Perhaps." He climbed the porch stairs and opened the door. Josh followed him into the kitchen. "My frau made a couple snitz pies today. Want a slice?" Without waiting for an answer, he set out two plates.

Josh went to the sewing room, took the money from his pocket, and laid it on the table.

Elsie looked up from her work and smiled. "Danki, Josh."

"Do you have any more quilts ready? I'll take whatever you want to give me."

"Jah." She nodded toward the cabinet in the corner as she started working the needle through the material again. "Take all the boppli quilts you think you can sell. I can have the girls start putting together more. Ach, wait. I need to keep one." She stood up, leaving the needle sticking out of the quilt, and pulled out a cream-colored quilt, beautiful in its simplicity. "For Esther."

Josh rubbed his neck. "Is that why Rachel's over there? I hadn't heard."

"Jah, in the wee hours of the morgen, the little bu was born. Named him Michael."

"I'll need to stop by sometime." Maybe Greta would like to see the boppli. He could offer to take her.

"I'm going tomorrow, when Rachel's at work, to help Esther," Elsie said. "But Rachel is staying with her as a mother's helper for a while."

Josh lifted the pile of remaining boppli blankets. "I'll bring the earnings by."

"Danki. It's all going toward the emergency fund for Andy. I'm hoping the quilt sales will bring in enough so that he can have the surgery he needs. Really tragic, the way he's suffering."

"Jah, it is." An idea sparked. Josh carried the quilts into the kitchen, where Preacher Samuel had served the pie. He laid the quilts on the edge of the table and sat in a chair. After the silent prayer, he raised his head. "Do you think it'd be worth it if I moved into Andy's barn? That way, I'd be there to help with the chores in the morgen and nacht. I could still go home for meals, so I wouldn't be an extra mouth to feed." Unless he somehow provided his own food or gave Martha money toward the groceries if she fed him.

Spoken out loud, the idea sounded ridiculous.

Preacher Samuel frowned. But then he nodded. "Andy needs more help than just his only sohn. And since he accepts you, you're the logical choice. But what about that book you're supposed to write?"

"I don't know." Josh forked a piece of the pie into his mouth. "I guess there's nacht-time, after chores."

"On the other hand...." The preacher winked. "Living there would get you closer to Greta. Perhaps you could have that long-overdue conversation. And maybe we'll be able to plan on another wedding this fall."

Chapter 5

Greta woke with a start in the middle of the nacht. She lay in bed for a few moments, listening, but she didn't hear anything out of the ordinary. Moonlight filtered in through the leafy branches of the tree outside her window, casting soft shadows around the bedroom. Beside her, Gizelle slept, her breathing shallow.

It must've been a dream.

Greta rolled over and shut her eyes, but the sound came again. Pebbles tapping against her bedroom window. *Josh?* For a second, time rolled back, and she sat up, a smile forming. But then it faded. *Nein*. It wouldn't be Josh. He was no longer courting her. She blew out a puff of air. Maybe it was Gizelle's beau, and she was only pretending to sleep.

Gizelle didn't move. When the tapping sound resumed, Greta slipped off her covers and peeked out the window. Josh stood beneath the tree, his face illuminated by a flashlight.

Her mouth went dry. What was he doing here? She waved at him, then stepped away from the window, peering down at her white nacht-gown. What now? Back in the days when he'd kum courting, she always knew in advance and would go to sleep in her day dress. But now....

She grabbed her robe and shrugged it on, loosely tied the belt around her waist, and padded barefoot down the stairs.

Josh was waiting on the porch. Greta stepped outside and shut the door behind her, then opened her mouth to demand what he was doing there. But she bit back the question. It would be rude. Instead, she stared at him. Silently.

His gaze rested on her uncovered head, on the long braid dangling over her shoulder. A muscle worked in his jaw as his gaze skimmed over her robe and stopped at her bare feet. He looked up again and raised a trembling hand to her cheek. "Greta." His voice was a hoarse whisper.

She shied away from his gentle touch, her heart skittering, as if filled with crickets dancing to a lively tune.

Josh shook his head and dropped his hand to his side. "I.... You're.... Uh...." He cleared his throat. "Preacher Samuel was already aware of your family's situation. He's already spoken to the bishop about it."

Greta smirked. She'd known it wouldn't do much gut to talk to Onkel Samuel. Yet she resisted saying, "I told you so."

"We discussed my sleeping in your barn."

Sleeping in...what? "Nein!" The word burst from her mouth without conscious thought. She lowered her voice to ask, "Why?"

"So I can be here early in the morgen to help William before he goes to school. Or just in case you need help with your daed in the middle of the nacht, and—"

"Go home, Josh. We don't need you here."

Josh's fingers still tingled from the too-brief contact with her soft cheek. They ached to touch the long rope of hair hanging over her shoulder. To pull her to him before he kissed her senseless.

He had nein right.

Josh took two steps backward—literally and mentally—putting her out of reach. "Preacher Samuel thought it made sense." He cleared his throat. "My folks were in agreement. I already stabled Sea Grass in your barn. Just wanted to let you know. I'll help William with the morgen chores before heading home to do my chores and have breakfast. Stan and I will be by at the usual time." He swiped his hand over his chin and turned away. "Gut nacht."

"Wait. Why?"

He thought he'd already answered that question. He glanced over his shoulder. Swallowed. "Gott told me to do this, Greta."

"Gott told.... What?"

Josh could guess what she'd left unspoken. *You imagine Gott speaks to you?* He waited for her to say it but heard only the chirrup of crickets.

After a long silence, she exhaled a quiet sigh. "I won't argue with Gott. He knows our needs."

Josh hadn't expected acceptance. He smiled. "I brought what I needed with me. I'll bed down with my horse. Gut nacht, liebling. Sweet dreams." He knew his would be, with the vision of Greta engraved in his mind.

To help himself resist touching her again, he gathered the flattened cardboard boxes he'd left on the porch earlier, filling his arms with a bulky unyieldingness instead of her softness. He'd load the boxes into his buggy to take home in the morgen.

"Gut nacht, Josh." She turned with a swish of her robe, opened the door, and disappeared into the darkness of the haus.

Leaving him alone to wrestle with his sinful desires.

Long before Greta was ready to get out of bed, the rooster crowed. Sitting up, she forced her eyes open, rubbing away the blurriness. Gizelle was already gone, her side of the bed straightened as much as it could be.

Greta staggered over to the window and looked out. Josh stood near the shadowy entrance of the barn, hitching Sea Grass to his buggy.

So, his late-nacht visit hadn't been a dream. He really had tossed pebbles at her window to lure her outside. She backed away from view and hurriedly dressed.

When she entered the kitchen, the teakettle was whistling. She turned off the burner and heard soft voices coming from her parents' bedroom. Mamm was probably helping Daed dress, which he could no longer do on his own. *Ach, Lord Gott, please provide the surgery he needs. Soon.*

Greta slipped her shoes on, grabbed a wicker basket, and went out to the chicken coop to collect the eggs. She also thought she might catch Josh before he left.

He looked up as she neared the barn. His blue eyes brightened with his smile. "Gut morgen, schnuckelchen. Did you sleep well?"

The endearment from their days of courting made her stomach flutter. "Jah. Danki, Josh." Did he notice the huskiness in her voice? She held up the basket. "I'm going to collect the eggs." *Obviously.* "And feed the chickens."

He nodded. "William is almost finished with the milking. I'll see you in a few hours." With a wink, he swung himself up into the buggy and clicked his tongue at Sea Grass.

Greta watched him go, then shook herself as he turned out of the driveway. When had Josh started working his way back into her affections? Well, she wouldn't let him get any further. She deliberately turned away from him to the chicken coop. Gizelle stood amid the squawking birds, looking toward the road.

Did Gizelle desire Josh? Had he encouraged her affections?

She could have him.

The thought produced a strange prick of pain in Greta's heart. She squared her shoulders, determined to ignore it.

Yet he still called her "beautiful girl" and had summoned her with pebbles.

Maybe Gizelle simply wondered why Josh had slept in the barn.

"I already fed and watered the birds," Gizelle told her.

Greta nodded. Gizelle had refused to collect the eggs ever since a hen had pecked her when she was a child. "How was your first day of work?"

"Fine. I think I'll enjoy working there." Gizelle shrugged. "I'm off today, so I'll be weeding the garden and doing laundry."

"I'll help you when I get home," Greta told her.

When she returned to the haus with the eggs she'd collected, Daed was seated at the dining room table. Mamm was straining the milk, separating the cream to make butter. Gizelle stirred a bubbling pot of oatmeal with raisins on the stove.

William came into the kitchen, his hair still damp from washing up. He glanced at Greta as she set the table. "Why did Josh Yoder spend the nacht in the barn? He left his blanket folded in the stable."

Greta glanced at Daed.

He frowned, apparently clear of mind right now. The pain pill waited on the table. "He stayed over-nacht?"

"He, uh, wanted to be close, in case we needed him," Greta stammered.

His gaze narrowed. "You weren't bundling, were you?"

In the barn? Greta shook her head. "Nein. I know better, Daed." And Gizelle had been in bed beside her. Did her sister know she'd left the room wearing a robe and with her braided hair uncovered?

Gizelle carried the oatmeal over to the table.

Mamm took the cinnamon out of the spice cupboard. "Is everything packed and ready for the farmers' market today, Greta? Your driver should be here soon."

Greta glanced at the wall clock. "Just need to replenish the canned goods." She slid into her chair and bowed her head for the silent prayer.

She couldn't whip her thoughts into submission enough to pray. They whirled out of control, with Josh in the midst of them.

Had Gott really told him to take care of her family? Did Gott do that—care so much as to take active steps to provide for them?

If He did, maybe she could entrust the scheduling and payment for Daed's back surgery to Him.

But Josh? If Gott talked to Josh, then he'd really changed—somehow—in the years he was gone. Either that, or Josh was drunk.

She frowned as she considered that possibility, then quickly dismissed it. She'd seen him drunk. This Josh was totally different. In a gut way.

"Amen." Daed's spoon clattered against his bowl.

Greta opened her eyes and hurriedly ate. After bowing her head for the final prayer—*Danki, Gott, for the food. Please provide for our family*—she went down to the cellar to replenish the inventory of home-canned goods.

As she carried the crate upstairs, she heard gravel scatter outside. Josh was here.

Her pulse increased as she hurried to the door, the crate still in her arms. Gizelle beat her to it and swung it open wide. "Morgen, Josh-u-a." She drew his name out in a singsongy way.

"Morgen, again, Gizelle. Is Greta ready?" When his gaze lit on her, he grinned. "Let me take that for you, liebling." He stepped past Gizelle and reached for the crate.

Gizelle slumped.

And Greta gave him a warm smile.

Liebling.

She liked that. A lot.

Too much.

Chapter 6

Josh handed his latest customer the aqua birdhouse covered with a discarded license plate and decorated with bottle caps, buttons, and a broken ruler. The woman had gushed over it, saying she loved all the "bling"—whatever that was.

He thanked the woman with a smile, then glanced over at Greta. An elderly Englisch man was stooped over her selection of baked goods. He held up a loaf of bread and a paper plate full of cookies to the white-haired woman next to him, giving her a big, toothy grin. Just like Grossdaedi had looked whenever he was trying to cajole Grossmammi into something.

"You don't need cookies." She shook her head but smiled as she reached into her purse and handed Greta some money.

After they moved on, Josh took a few dollars from his cash box and made his way to Greta's side. "You doing okay?"

"Jah. It isn't even noon, and I'm already out of strawberry jam." Her green eyes sparkled. It was a refreshing sight, after the bedraggled air she'd had about her the day before. "Raspberry doesn't sell so well. People say they don't like the seeds." She shrugged. "And some don't know what rhubarb is." She pointed to a jar of strawberry-rhubarb jam. "I'll leave those varieties at home next time and bring apple butter and peach jam, instead."

So, she could talk to him about jam—but not about his past. At least it was a start.

Josh picked up a paper plate holding half a dozen oatmeal raisin cookies. "For lunch." He winked as he held out the money.

She held her hand up. "Nein. You don't need to pay. You do so much."

He shook his head. "Take it."

"You can't make me." She backed away with a teasing grin.

He could, and he would. His heart rate increased in anticipation of the wrestling match that would inevitably end with her in his arms. His gaze dropped to her lips, and he advanced toward her. Then he stopped himself, glancing around. *Oops. Not alone.* Suddenly, there was a throng of people meandering from booth to booth, pausing to examine crocheted afghans and fresh-picked vegetables as they moved in the direction of his table.

He'd get her to take his money later. If the cookies were still available. He set the plate back on the table while Greta, with her head bent to hide her flaming cheeks, fussed over rearranging the jars of jam that some customers had jumbled. She looked flustered, as if she'd sensed where his thoughts had taken him. He regretted the intrusion of customers, but the interruption was probably a gut thing. They needed to talk before any wrestling/kissing occurred.

A woman picked up a jar of jam, checked the price tag, and handed Greta a five-dollar bill. Over at his own display, a man browsed the assortment of fishing flies David had made. Josh didn't like to assume the worst, but small objects were easy to pocket. He returned to his table to keep an eye on the man, engaging him in meaningless chatter about the weather.

Once they'd completed their latest sales, Josh returned to Greta's table. To Josh's dismay, the cookies had departed. He studied the few sweets she had left. Brownies. Zucchini bread. He should've held the cookies back, but he didn't want to stand in the way of paying customers. And nothing else appealed.

Wait. She had some blueberry pie left. His mouth watered, and he snagged two pieces. He put them beside her money box. "For later."

"Okay." She nodded.

When she wasn't watching, he would slip some money in the box.

Maybe he should approach her table as a customer rather than as a friend. He'd do that Monday. Tomorrow was Sunday, the Lord's day. Maybe he would take Greta home from singing. If she went.

And if she didn't accept a ride from someone else first.

His shoulders slumped. Why hadn't he considered that? He'd kum striding into her life again with every intention of stepping back into the role of beau. Never once stopping to consider that she might be taken.

Though he hadn't noticed any one particular bu consistently taking her home afterward. And he'd watched. Closely.

Her cousin Sam had taken her home a few times. So had Rachel's beau, David Lapp. And maybe a few other men. But none regularly.

Josh cleared his throat. "Are you and Gizelle going to the singing tomorrow nacht?"

Greta's glance was wary. "Gizelle might be."

"Not you?" He had no interest in Gizelle.

She shrugged. A non-answer.

He met her eyes and took a deep breath for courage. "If you go, may I take you home?"

Greta swallowed as his gaze searched hers, seeing she didn't know what. Hopefully, it wasn't obvious she still loved him. Had never stopped. Even though she'd fought it, he alone still occupied her heart.

But she couldn't give in that easily. He'd had no problem leaving her before. He might do it again. This time, she wanted to make him work for her affections.

She pulled in a breath and shook her head. "I really shouldn't go. I need to...." She couldn't say that she had baking to do. Nein working on Sundays.

Wait. She had a legitimate excuse. "Esther just had her boppli. I promised to go there Sunday afternoon and stay with her and Viktor's grossmammi, in case they need me, so Rachel can go to the singing with David."

He nodded, frowning slightly, then turned away without offering to go to Viktor's to spend time with her.

Though maybe he would just show up. He and Viktor were best friends, after all.

A woman approached the table. She set down her bags of purchases from the other vendors and reached for a jar of jam. "I just love strawberry-rhubarb."

Greta smiled at the woman. Maybe she could get her to buy more than one jar. "It's one of my favorites, too, but it seems a lot of people either don't like rhubarb or aren't familiar with it. I probably won't bring that variety again, since it doesn't sell."

The woman glanced at her. "Really? Maybe I should buy a couple jars so you'll bring some back. And those brownies look good, too." She patted her wide hips ruefully. "Unfortunately, I'll have to stay away from those."

Greta was warming toward the woman. "Didn't I tell you? These are special brownies. We bake them in a special oven that eliminates all the calories."

The woman laughed, then handed Greta the exact amount for two jars of jam. "I'll still pass on the brownies, but thanks anyway."

Greta slid the money into her apron pocket, to transfer to the cash box when there weren't any customers around. It made her nervous to open it, though she had to do so whenever a customer needed change. Cash was such a valuable commodity for her family, she didn't want to flaunt the box's content to strangers.

The woman bought a birdhouse from Josh, then made an about-face and came back to Greta's table. "I want those brownies, after all. They were calling to me. We'll see how well that special oven works." She grinned. "Oh, and I'll take a loaf of zucchini bread, too."

The brownies were calling to Greta, too, but she'd ignored the chocolatey deliciousness tempting her. Just as she tried to ignore the bu manning the next table. If you ignored a temptation long enough, it went away, ain't so? A quick glance at Josh made her wonder if that were true.

She accepted the woman's money, sent the last loaf of zucchini bread and the brownies on their merry way, and then busied herself rearranging the remaining jars of jam. Nein point in adding more to the display, since what she had left was more of the same: strawberry-rhubarb and raspberry. She loved both; so, even though she would have appreciated earning money for them, it didn't bother her that they didn't sell. Her family would enjoy them during the fall and winter months.

Josh picked up the small cooler he'd brought and carried it over. "Ready for lunch?"

She glanced at the sky. The sun wasn't directly overhead yet.

He followed her gaze. "Close enough. And it'll probably get busier during the noon hour."

"Jah." It had been that way yesterday, though the market had been in a different town. She reached for her brown bag, which contained half a peanut butter sandwich, a thin slice of cheese, a handful of black grapes, and an embarrassing, Disney-themed, child-size thermos of ice water. Well, it had started as ice water. It was probably lukewarm by now.

Josh settled on the grass behind their tables and patted the spot next to him. "Join me?"

Greta clutched her bag tighter, ashamed to reveal the meager contents of her lunch compared to what he'd brought. She should be grateful for what she had. Instead, she lusted over the contents of his cooler as he lifted them out: a hearty roast beef sandwich, a giant dill pickle, a shiny red apple, and a glass bottle of Coca-Cola.

She dropped beside him and bowed her head for the silent prayer. *Lord Gott, forgive me for the sin of envy. Help me to be satisfied with what You've provided for me. Danki for sending Josh to help my family. Protect my heart from being broken again. Heal Daed.*

At least the last part didn't reek of selfishness.

She swallowed her pride and pulled out the peanut butter sandwich. *Did I ever mention how much I hate peanut butter, Gott?* But she took a bite. In her mind, peanut butter was gut only in baking. She loved peanut butter cookies. Any cookies, really. Especially chocolate chip. And miniature cheesecakes with cherries on top.

Okay, this wasn't helping. Now she craved cheesecake.

"Is that all you have? Half a sandwich? Is that…peanut butter?" Did he have to sound so incredulous? "But you don't like…. Hmmm. Want to trade?"

"What is this, school?" She'd responded with sarcasm to conceal the fact that his offer tempted her. Josh knew she hated the icky, sticky, gooey stuff. "I already took a bite."

He shrugged and held out his sandwich. "I don't mind."

She shook her head. "It's okay." She took another bite of her own, just to prove it.

"How about we share our lunches? I'll take half of yours, and you'll take half of mine." He pulled out a pocketknife.

"Is that clean?"

Josh chuckled. "Brand-new. Never been used."

She frowned. How many people had touched the blade, testing its sharpness, before he'd bought it?

He reached in his bag and pulled out a moist towelette, the antibacterial kind. He ripped it open and used it to wipe off the blade. "Feel safer?"

"Jah." And a bit foolish.

He sliced his sandwich in half, then reached for hers.

"You can just have the rest." The two bites she'd taken were two too many. She opened the childish thermos and took a swig of water to wash the stickiness out of her mouth. The liquid was still cold, thankfully. She counted out her grapes—ten—and popped five in her mouth. She held the other five out to Josh.

"You keep those, Greta. In payment for the sandwich." He handed her half of his roast beef, then finished hers off in three bites. "Want half the pickle and the apple?"

She shook her head, even though she did. It was enough that he'd shared his sandwich with her. It filled a long-empty spot in her stomach. She offered him half her slice of cheese, but he declined.

"Monday, I'll bring enough for both of us," he told her. When he'd finished off his lunch, he got up and grabbed the two slices of pie he'd set aside. "Please let me pay for these, Greta."

She shook her head. "It's enough you're helping my family."

"One's for you." He held it out to her. "May I at least pay for that one?"

"I don't want any." Another lie.

Josh studied her a moment, then set one of the small plates down beside her. "Jah, you do. Be right back." He walked over to her booth, opened her cash box, and slipped something inside. She didn't see how much.

But, knowing Josh, it was more than enough for both slices.

And with that kindness, on top of all the others, he purchased her heart.

Josh ate supper at home with his family, then returned to the Millers' and helped William with the evening chores. After they finished, Josh settled down on a hay bale in Andy Miller's barn, his laptop balanced on his knees. He pressed the power button and reached for a reusable bottle of water as he waited for it to boot up. He had just a few hours of battery life left, so he'd have to charge it soon.

He opened Microsoft Word and spent a few minutes staring at the blank page in front of him. He'd thought this would be so easy. He bowed his head. *Lord Gott, I have nein idea what to say, much less how to say it. But You gave me this opportunity, and I'm thankful for it. Please give me the words You would have me write.*

He swallowed the lump in his throat and started typing.

> *Some people take to the woods because they want to get close to nature. Some plan to hike the Appalachian Trail just to say they did. And some want to escape. I guess I fell into the last category. I wanted to escape the demons chasing me.*
>
> *That night in the back field started out as harmless fun. Shooting off fireworks. Drinking with my friends. Laughing and acting silly. And then it turned into a terrible nightmare. I'll never forget the glow on the horizon as the flames raged high in the air, as the smoke plume rose toward the clouds. I'll never forget the nausea that overcame me when I realized I'd had a part in destroying the life of another.*
>
> *Along with most of the other men in our community, I hurried to respond to the emergency bells that sounded the alarm. But I never dreamed it would be my best friend's house. My best friend's family.*
>
> *Gone. All gone.*
>
> *And I never dreamed it would affect me the way it did.*

Josh paused to swipe at the tears that burned his eyes.

> *I tried to forget—but how can a person forget something like that? Staying drunk dulled the pain some, but not enough. Not*

when my best friend lost everything—his home, his family. Not when I realized it would cost me as much.

I realized I had to go, to get away, long before I acted on that realization. It was too difficult pretending everything was normal. Going on as if nothing had happened. Planning marriage to the girl of my dreams. And seeing the pain and anger in my friend's eyes as he tended to the needs of his grandparents. Making sure they had someplace to live. Burying his immediate family.

Meanwhile, I attended church and went to singings. Joined the baptism classes.

And then came that fateful night when I was offered the opportunity to spend time in the closet with my girl during a game of spin the bottle.

She looked at me with expectation, knowing I would willingly participate. Knowing we would soon be kissing for the first time—and maybe more. Not that there was much risk of doing more, in a house filled with friends and relatives. Still, my blood heated as I looked at her beautiful face. At the loose strands of strawberry blonde hair peeking out from under her kapp, where the rest of it was tucked, the way it should be. My fingers itched to take off the kapp and tangle themselves in the full length of her tresses. There was just a hint of naughtiness in her green eyes. I dropped my gaze to skim her curves, partway obscured by her modest dress.

I burned with desire for her. I wanted all that she would allow me to have. Probably more.

Now it was shame that burned inside Josh, recalling his impure thoughts. Granted, they'd been planning to marry soon; but that didn't make it any better.

For some reason, I couldn't do it. I couldn't even go into that closet of temptation with her. Instead, I got up, left the party, and walked out of her life. I wasn't good enough for her. Not good enough for anyone. Not good enough for God.

I walked away from the guilt that pursued me. And left my home. My family. My Amish community. My God.

I told myself it was for the best. My girl would be better off without me. Still, it hurt.

I started walking. Hitched rides when they were offered. I ended up in downtown St. Louis. The Arch was in plain view from the window of my pay-by-the-week motel room. So were flashing lights advertising a chance to forget reality.

He shut his eyes to relieve the burn. This would be a hard book to write.

Forgetting reality was harder than promised. Sure, there were moments when I forgot. But the memories always came back, and in excruciating detail.

I went from job to job. City to city. State to state. Always on the run. Always trying to escape.

There was no escape from what lived within me.

Josh hit "save" just as a warning flashed on his laptop screen that the battery was almost dead. He powered it off and snapped it shut. He figured he'd rehashed enough drama for one day. And people actually wanted to read this stuff?

He zipped the verboden device into its carrying case, then slid it under the seat of his buggy.

"Josh?" Greta called. "Are you out here?"

She'd kum. Out to the barn. To be with him.

His blood heated.

A slow smile formed on his lips as he straightened and started in the direction of her voice. "Jah, liebling. I'm here. I promised—"

Her alarmed expression silenced him. Her wide eyes. Her pallid skin.

Panic hit. His smile died.

"Ach, nein. What's wrong? Is it your daed?"

Chapter 7

Greta struggled to catch her breath. She'd never run so fast. "Daed fell. Can you help William lift him and get him in his bed?"

"In bed?" Josh frowned. "We should probably call for an ambulance."

She gave her head a vigorous shake. "We don't need an ambulance."

"Did he hit his head?"

She hoped not. "I don't know. He's conscious, but he's moaning and complaining about a Belgian horse standing on his chest. William said to get you. And to hurry."

"Belgian…chest? Ach, nein." Josh took off at a run toward the haus.

What wasn't he saying? Could it be worse than she thought? Greta hurried to catch up.

"Where is he?" Josh called over his shoulder.

"On the floor."

Josh glanced back at her. "More specifically?"

Her face heated. "The bathroom." At least he was wearing his pajamas.

"Greta, run to the phone shanty and call for an ambulance."

"Why? You haven't seen him yet."

"Just go. Wait—your Englisch neighbors are closer than the shanty. Have them call. Tell them probable heart attack. Go!"

Heart attack? Nein, nein, nein.

Josh burst into the haus and ran down the hall to the bathroom. William stood in the open doorway, while Martha knelt on the floor by her ehemann.

Josh edged into the closet-sized room. "What's going on, Andy?"

The man looked up at him, tears glittering in his eyes. His right hand gripped his left shoulder. "A team…of Belgian…horses. Hurt."

This was the last thing this family needed. *Gott, please intervene.*

Josh looked up at Martha. "Do you have any aspirin? We need one tablet, crushed, to put on his tongue."

Martha stood, opened the cabinet, and pulled out a bottle. She shook one tablet into her hand and moved past Josh. "I'll be right back."

Josh moved further into the bathroom as a pounding sound came from the kitchen. "Andy, did you hit your head when you fell?"

"Nein." Sweat beaded on his brow.

"Let's get your head elevated." Josh eased behind him and assisted him to a semi-upright position.

William shuffled his feet. "What can I do?"

"You could get a pillow to prop his head on. A blanket would work, too, if we folded it."

Martha returned, her palm cupping the powder of a pulverized Aspirin tablet.

"Andy? Open wide." Despite the gravity of the situation, a grin threatened to form on Joshua's lips. "Martha? Dump it in."

She brushed the contents of her hand into his mouth. "What was that for?"

Andy grimaced.

"It's supposed to minimize the damage of a heart attack."

Greta appeared in the doorway, looking even more disheveled than before. "Mrs. Bailey is calling for an ambulance, and for the driver to take the rest of us to the hospital."

Josh frowned. "Where's Gizelle?"

Greta's gaze caught his, and something flickered in the depths of her green eyes that he couldn't quite identify. "She's out."

Out with a beau, nein doubt. Someone needed to find her and tell her about her daed. But Josh didn't know where to begin looking for her. She and her beau might be merely walking down the road. Or they might've gone on a buggy ride to one of the sparking places. They weren't in the barn—that much he knew. He would've seen them.

William returned with both a pillow and a blanket. Josh gently slid the pillow under Andy's head.

"Danki, William." Josh glanced at him. "Could you look for Gizelle, maybe?"

"Jah." William vanished again.

Josh looked at Andy. He didn't know what to do for the older man, other than what he'd already done—pray, administer aspirin, and elevate Andy's head. How long before the ambulance would arrive? He bowed his head again. *Gott....*

As if on cue, a voice called out. Josh didn't hear what was said, but Martha left, and Greta disappeared from view.

"Help is on the way," he murmured to Andy.

Two uniformed men entered the bathroom. As Josh moved out of the way, he peered over them, hoping he hadn't made any mistakes that might cost Andy his life. He answered their questions about what he'd done, then backed into the hall and headed toward the kitchen, hearing voices coming from there. But before he had taken two steps, someone behind him sniffled. He turned around.

Greta sat against the wall at the end of the hall, clutching her knees to her chest, her forehead pressed against them.

Josh sat down beside her and draped an arm over her shoulders. She turned to him, burrowing her head in his neck and gripping his upper arm as if he were a lifeline. As if he alone could save her from this latest source of despair.

But he had no words. Nothing. He could only hold her, as her tears soaked his shirt, and pray. *Ach, Gott....*

Greta heard the low rumble of male voices in the bathroom without understanding their words. One of the men exited, returning a few minutes later with a stretcher. He parked it in the hall, then disappeared into the bathroom again.

Though Greta knew she should, she didn't have the strength to move away from Josh. She fought to control her tears, but they turned into gulping sobs that shook her body as she gasped for breath.

The men reappeared, carrying Daed. They laid him on the gurney and fastened the straps over his chest and hips. Then they raised the contraption until it locked into place at waist height before wheeling him quickly down the hall and out of sight.

"You going to be okay?" Josh asked softly.

Nein. Never. Daed was her rock. Her source of stability. When Josh had left, Daed had been the one to hold her, to comfort her, to whisper that Gott had someone better for her. She couldn't bear to think of him dying from a heart attack, like the former bishop. "I...I think Gott must be punishing my family."

Josh stilled. "Nein. Not true." His hand slid down her back, then moved slowly up again. Over and over, soothing her inner turmoil. Her gulping sobs slowed to hiccups, her tears from a deluge to a trickle.

"Wasn't Daed's injury enough?" she sniffed. "Where was der Herr then? Where is He now?"

"Shh, Greta." Josh's chest rose and fell with his sigh. "You're not alone. Never alone. Gott will be with you every step of the way, even if you can't sense His presence."

She sniffed. They still had plenty of the unpaid hospital bills from Daed's hospitalization following his tumble from the hay wagon. Then, there was the surgery he needed. And now this.

Sirens wailed, quickly fading into the distance.

Hot tears burned Greta's eyes again.

Mamm cleared her throat. "Greta."

Caught in Josh's arms. Greta tried to pull away, but his grip tightened. She relaxed against him again. Maybe it'd be okay, just this once.

"The driver just arrived." Mamm's voice cracked. "William and I are going to the hospital. I want you to stay here, so when Gizelle comes home, she'll know what's going on. You can prepare a meal for tomorrow."

Josh shifted slightly. "My mamm will fix something. Don't worry about meals."

"Joshua Yoder, you can't volunteer your mamm," she scolded him softly. "It's late. She's likely in bed already."

"The news will spread quickly through the grapevine," Josh told her. "I guarantee more than one family will be arriving soon with a meal. And Mamm will be among them. She loves Greta. You know this."

Mamm opened her mouth and then shut it, apparently remembering that, once upon a time, Greta had almost become Lizzie Yoder's dochter-in-law. She nodded. "We loved you, too, Josh."

Did she intend to use the past tense? Maybe she was merely hesitant to accept him back into their life after the heartbreak his departure had caused Greta.

Greta could understand her trepidation, even though he'd proven to be trustworthy. So far.

"Pray," Mamm said.

"I will," Josh said as she retreated down the hall. "We will."

Greta shuddered against him. Pray? To a Gott who seemed intent on destroying her family? She couldn't. She wouldn't. Ever again.

Josh resumed stroking her back. But this time, when he moved upward, his fingers traveled even further, grazing the bare skin of her neck. They stopped there a moment, then slowly traveled to the side, his calluses scratching her skin.

Greta's breath caught. Her stomach fluttered. And everything about the tender gesture changed from comforting to supercharged. Every one of her nerve endings sprang to life.

People would be arriving any moment. She needed to pull herself together. Needed to be strong and stoic, like a gut Amish woman. She broke away from him and got to her feet, her legs wobbling like cooked spaghetti noodles. Holding on to the wall for support, she made her way into the bathroom. She avoided looking at the spot of the floor where Daed had lain. The discarded pillow and the used medical supplies. She'd have to clean everything up. Later.

She splashed cold water on her face, but it wasn't enough. She held both hands under the faucet, cupped them till they were filled, and buried her face in the icy pool of water for several seconds. Then she blindly reached for a towel. She was startled when someone pressed the rough line-dried fabric into her hand. She mopped her face, dropped the towel on the counter, and turned around.

Into Josh's arms.

Chapter 8

Josh eased Greta close against his chest. If only he could shield her from this heartache. Fix it like he'd fixed the porch steps. But he didn't know how. All he knew to do was pray. So, he did. Nonstop. He'd never seen Greta fall apart like this, and it scared him. At the same time, he was glad he could be there for her. To hold her. To try to comfort her as best he could.

Who had comforted her when he left?

The seventeen-year-old Greta had been crazy in love with him. She'd made her infatuation more than clear. He'd felt the same way about her, and even though they were young, they'd planned on marriage.

And now, three years later, he still felt the same way.

But he'd killed everything she'd felt for him.

Or maybe it was still buried inside her somewhere. Waiting for him to thaw her heart.

A door banged.

She stiffened and pulled away from him, then picked up the towel and started folding it.

Josh backed into the hall. It wouldn't do for any of the neighbors to find them alone.

He reached the living room just as his mamm arrived. Relief filled him. He wouldn't be alone with Greta any longer. Alone with the temptation to try to comfort her in a way he shouldn't. "Mamm. I'm glad you came."

"Ach, Josh. You're still here. I knew you were sleeping in their barn, but…." She released a sigh. "I don't suppose there's any news yet?"

"They just left for the hospital." His throat was as raw as if he'd been the one doing all the crying.

"Did they all go? I brought over what I'd fixed for our lunch tomorrow."

"Greta's still here. And Gizelle is…around somewhere."

"Where's Greta?"

Josh gestured down the hall. As if on cue, Greta came out of the bathroom. Her shoulders still shook. She still wobbled when she walked. But Mamm was there. She'd be the one to hold her now. Not him.

His arms felt the loss.

Mamm made a strange keening sound and rushed at Greta as though they'd been apart for years, even though she'd seen her routinely at the grocery store. She held her against her chest. "Ach, you poor child. I'll stay with you as long as you need." Over Greta's shoulder, she shooed Josh away. "Go make her some chamomile tea."

Josh dutifully went to the kitchen and started going through the cabinets, looking for boxes of tea. Then it struck him that instead of tea bags, they might have the herb hanging up to dry. Or stored in plastic baggies.

He went to the small room off the kitchen where the wringer washer was kept. There, on the line used for drying clothes on bad-weather days, was an assortment of dried herbs. Most of them, he didn't recognize. But he knew chamomile.

He took some down off the line and then went to fill the tea-kettle. As he was putting it on the stove, the door opened, and Elsie Miller came in. "Making tea, Joshua? I'll do it. I know where Martha keeps things." She set a covered dish in the gas-powered refrigerator, then moved to the stove.

"Danki." Josh was adept with outdoor fire pits. Not so much in the kitchen.

He glanced outside and saw another buggy rolling in. Followed by another. It warmed him to see the community members turning out in force. Showing they could be counted on when needed.

But he wanted to be the one to comfort Greta.

Pray for Andy.

The urge was too strong to ignore. Josh opened the basement door, descended the stairs, and found the darkest corner, where he dropped to his knees and bowed his head.

Time dragged by endlessly as Greta sat on the couch, shivering under an afghan and sipping chamomile tea, while Lizzie Yoder held her close, whispering platitudes and prayers that Greta doubted were making it past the ceiling.

Aenti Elsie had just delivered them two steaming mugs of chamomile tea when the kitchen door squeaked open and slammed shut. Seconds later, the bishop's frau, Barbie, appeared. "A van has been called to pick up anyone who wants to go to the hospital to sit with Martha," she told them.

Greta wanted to go, but Gizelle still hadn't kum home. She supposed one of these other ladies could stay in her stead. She looked around, wondering whom to ask.

When her gaze alit on Barbie, the woman was studying her with a frown.

"Poor child is in shock," Lizzie said.

"She needs to be with her family," someone murmured.

"Gizelle still doesn't know." Lizzie tucked Greta closer against her. "But I agree. She needs to go to the hospital. Where's Josh?" She looked around.

Aenti Elsie shook her head. "I thought he went outside about the time you arrived." She glanced at Barbie.

"I haven't seen him."

"Hmm. I was going to send him with Greta, but I guess I'll go instead."

Voices continued to rise and fall around her. Greta wanted to tell everybody to go away. She wanted to be left alone to rage at Gott for abandoning her family. Instead, she allowed Lizzie Yoder to hold her against her side, while she focused on forcing breaths past her swollen throat. In. Out. In. Out.

The hot tea soothed it a little.

Finally, Greta leaned away from Lizzie. "You should go home and care for your family."

Lizzie waved the suggestion away. "Don't you worry about us."

Headlights flashed through the window. "Here's the van," someone said from the kitchen.

"I'll stay and wait for Gizelle," someone else said, pressing a black bonnet into Greta's hands. She numbly got up and went outside to the van. "Hi, babe," Stan said quietly as he helped her into the passenger seat. She didn't respond. And nobody objected to her sitting up front. Probably because the van was full. Where had all these people kum from?

But even though men were in the back of the van, she didn't see Josh among them. She longed for his presence, for his support.

He'd vanished.

Typical.

Minutes later, they pulled into the hospital parking lot. Greta blinked as her eyes adjusted from the darkness of the vehicle to the sudden brightness of the streetlight they'd parked under, and then to the interior lights of the van.

Greta stumbled out of the vehicle and merged with the other members of her community as they filed into the waiting area outside the emergency room. She found a seat and bowed her head, so she'd appear to be praying—though that was the last thing she intended to do. Nein, she would abandon Gott, as He'd done to her family. Give Him a taste of His own medicine.

Then again, maybe He wouldn't care.

Someone sat beside her. Someone with denim-clad legs. She lifted her gaze. Stan pressed an ice-cold can of Coke into her hand. "I thought you shouldn't be alone."

She wasn't exactly alone. Mamm and William were there, too, though they were busy talking with the other friends and family members who had arrived in the van. She'd overheard enough to know they'd taken her daed back for surgery.

She forced a smile and popped the tab. "Thank you. This is a nice treat." And it was. Coke wasn't exactly in her family's budget.

"How are you holding up?" Stan leaned forward a bit as he opened his own soft drink.

Greta shrugged. "Fine." A lie, but it was the expected response. Nobody who asked ever really wanted to know.

Stan eyed her dubiously. "When my grandpa had a stroke, I was a mess. He was my fishing buddy. He also had this awesome toy train collection that took up the whole basement. Then suddenly, he was gone. Gone. And I had no one to fish with. My dad doesn't have time for that stuff. And my grandma packed up all those toy trains and sold them on eBay. Gone. Everything was gone."

Greta studied Stan as a trickle of compassion coursed through her. She could identify. Her grossdaedi hadn't owned any toy trains, but he had often taken her and her siblings fishing. And she had spent hours in the kitchen with her grossmammi, helping make sugar cookies. Greta's job had always been to press the top of a cup into the dough to get the right shape.

But losing them was nothing compared to what it would be to lose Daed.

"I like to fish, too," she finally said. Fishing was a safe topic.

"I'll be your fishing buddy." Stan leaned closer. "Go ahead. Tell me how you really feel about this."

~

Josh prayed until a sense of peace settled in his spirit. After a time of praise for answered prayer—though he wasn't yet sure how they would be answered, or when—he made his way out of the dark basement into the lantern-lit kitchen, where a dozen or so women were milling about, some wiping already-clean counters, others rearranging the items in the refrigerator to fit more food in there.

It seemed everyone from the community had shown up. Too bad they hadn't made such an effort in the months following Andy's back injury. They probably had, immediately; but such efforts always dwindled as time passed.

He went into the living room—vacant, except for one woman, an old maud named Eve, wielding a feather duster. Where were Greta and Mamm? He eyed Eve, wondering whether she would notice if he went upstairs to check Greta's bedroom.

Eve looked at him with raised eyebrows, as if guessing his thoughts.

Jah, she would notice. He grimaced. "Have you seen Greta?"

"She went to the hospital with a group of others. The van left a couple hours ago."

Really? He'd been praying that long?

"Has Gizelle kum home yet?"

"I haven't seen her."

He stared at Eve long enough that she averted her gaze to the wind-up clock on the end table. It was almost mid-nacht. "I'll check upstairs."

Everyone had stayed up late due to this emergency. And tomorrow was church Sunday...unless they decided to cancel the service. That had happened a time or two. But it was likelier that they would still gather together, tired, weary, and worn, to hear a sermon about how Gott allowed calamities to befall His children in order to teach them a lesson. To hear how the sick or injured must have had unconfessed sin in their lives. As if Gott looked for a reason to punish His people. Any reason.

They were wrong.

"For by grace are ye saved through faith...."

That was the main reason Josh had kum back. He needed to share that message.

Chapter 9

It seemed an eternity before the emergency room doors opened and an unsmiling nurse strode into the room. "Miller family?"

All the Amish in the waiting room got to their feet. Greta went to stand with Mamm. After a moment, Stan joined her, even though he wasn't family. He stood too close, almost in her personal space. Greta frowned and stepped away from him.

The nurse blinked at the crowd. "Immediate family only." When only Mamm, William, Onkel Samuel, and Greta stood before her, she led them to a smaller waiting area, then left through a different door. The four of them stood there in a cluster.

Minutes later, a surgeon and a different nurse carrying a clipboard came into the room. "Miller family?" the surgeon verified.

Mamm nodded.

"I was told Mr. Miller coded in the ambulance, but they revived him. I was able to clear the blockages with an emergency angioplasty and some stents. He will need to have bypass surgery later, after he's had time to recover. For now, he's stable and in recovery. Someone will come to get you when he's been assigned a room. Any questions?"

Jah, Greta thought. *For starters, how much will this cost? And who will pay for it? Does this mean the back surgery will have to wait? Or will this expense finally motivate Bishop Joe to ask for help from other communities?*

"How long is recovery expected to take?" Mamm asked. "And what about his diet?"

The surgeon frowned. "Recovery varies by individual. His doctor will discuss any dietary modifications with you." He glanced at his watch, then turned and left the room.

Onkel Samuel rested his hand on Mamm's upper arm. "We should pray. Let's gather in a circle and hold hands."

Greta rolled her eyes. Praying was a waste of time. Still, she supposed a preacher would be obligated to say something like that.

But his suggestion that they hold hands and pray together was completely unconventional. She blinked in surprise as Mamm took one of her hands, her onkel the other. How long had he been bucking the system?

"Lord Gott, danki for saving my brother's life today," Onkel Samuel began. "We ask that You would take it and use it for Your service. Help him to be a light to those around him. Let him—and let us, his family—be receptive to the changes that will be coming, in life and in heart alike. Help Josh and me to minister to them and to supply their needs, according to Your will. We give You all the glory, honor, and praise, forever and ever. Amen."

Greta pursed her lips. She'd never heard anyone pray out loud before. It wasn't their way, and she didn't know quite what to think of it. Part of her liked hearing someone treat prayer as a conversation with Gott, while another part of her found the idea intimidating. And what was with the "Josh and me" stuff? Onkel Samuel hadn't helped.

Then again, it wasn't as if he hadn't offered.

Daed had refused to accept help. From anyone.

Except Josh.

~

Josh gave up searching for Gizelle at one a.m. He'd checked all the hiding places he knew of, hollering her name until hoarse.

Now, back at Andy Miller's haus, he made himself at home in the living room with the somber old maud who wore black. Her attire matched her grim expression, as if she expected the worst.

News came with the return of the van, albeit in bits and pieces: "Died in the ambulance…needs bypass surgery." Had Josh's prayers been instrumental in bringing Andy back to life on the ride to the hospital? It was a blessing if Gott had used him in that way.

Neither Greta nor any member of her immediate family had returned in the van. Everyone else left soon after, except for Eve.

At two a.m., Josh rubbed his eyes and stood from the hard wooden chair at the kitchen table. He was tired of waiting for Gizelle. And he *needed* to know what was going on with Andy. How Greta was holding up. But it was too late to call a driver for a non-emergency.

Unless Gizelle had snuck in through an open window on the second floor, she hadn't kum home. That scenario would've been easy enough—she could have climbed the trellis. But Eve didn't go upstairs to check, not even when Josh suggested it. He didn't dare do it himself, even with someone else in the haus.

Yawning, Josh went into the living room, removed his socks, and stretched out on the couch, hoping to catch some sleep. He figured the van's headlights would wake him when it returned the second time with Greta. Eve followed him and collapsed in the lopsided recliner, raising the footrest. She was asleep and snoring within minutes.

But it was the rooster's crow that jarred Josh from sleep. He lay there a minute, processing his whereabouts. Had Greta returned during the nacht? If so, why hadn't someone awakened him? He peeked over at the recliner. Eve was gone.

He stumbled into the kitchen, blinking the fatigue from his eyes, and found Gizelle cracking eggs into a sizzling frying pan. Eve was buttering a stack of toasted bread. She looked up with her permanent scowl firmly in place. "Gut morgen. Breakfast will be ready soon."

He rubbed his eyes. "How's Andy? Any news?"

"What do you mean?" Gizelle turned to him. "What happened?"

Hadn't the old maud told her?

"There, there." Eve patted her arm. "He's in the hands of der Herr."

Josh thought maybe he had better find out the prognosis before he said anything more. "Did Greta kum home last nacht?"

"Jah...." Gizelle eyed him warily. "She didn't stir when I got up this morgen. Why? And you still haven't answered my question about Daed."

Josh spun on his heels and left the room. He would let Eve answer her. She should have explained the situation already.

He went to the foot of the stairs and peered up. Did he dare? He glanced toward the kitchen, hearing the rise and fall of conversation, then carefully made his ascent, hoping no steps would creak and give him away.

The first bedroom door was ajar. Josh peered in. Greta lay there, her back to him. She'd kicked off the covers, exposing her bare legs beneath the twisted fabric of her nacht-gown. Her strawberry blonde braid was splayed across the pillow. He glanced downstairs. Still clear. He nudged the door open wider and stepped inside.

He shouldn't be there. Warning sirens wailed in his mind. But he didn't move away from the doorway. Didn't approach the bed. He just stood there in silence. Willing her to wake up.

Even talking in her bedroom would be taboo, especially with her state of dress. Her uncovered hair. If the bishop got wind of it....

She stirred, then rolled over to face him, her eyes still shut. The movement pulled her nacht-gown taut against her, accentuating her curves.

Something burned inside Josh. He trembled. Dangerous territory here. Better leave fast.

Her eyelids fluttered open. Shut. Then snapped open again. Her lips parted as she sat up and sucked in air, as if she might scream.

Josh hurried over, pressing his palm against her lips. "Shhh."

She jerked the thin bedsheet up to her chin. Not that it did any gut. The image of her body was already etched in his mind.

Her lips moved against his palm as she spoke, but whatever she said got lost in the sensation of her mouth against his skin. His toes curled.

"Ach, Greta," he whispered. He lifted his hand and trailed a fingertip across her lips.

She sucked in a sharp breath, her gaze lowering to his mouth.

He wanted to kiss her. Wanted to crawl into bed beside her and hold her tight. He leaned closer to her. He wanted—

"What are you doing?" William demanded from behind him, interrupting his musings.

They needed interrupting.

He forced his mind to recall his reason for coming upstairs. At least, the acceptable reason. "I wanted to see if Greta had any news about your daed." He backed away and turned sideways, so he could see both Greta, sitting up in bed, and William, standing in the doorway, hands clenched at his sides.

The latter vision was enough to make him leave. He gave Greta one last look, probably showing her the unbridled desire in his eyes, then walked out and pulled the door shut.

William relaxed his posture once they were in the hallway, probably since there was now a closed door between Josh and the girl who haunted his dreams. "You shouldn't have gone in there. But I'll tell you what you want to know. They're keeping Daed at the hospital for a few days to keep an eye on him. Hoping he'll heal enough to undergo bypass surgery."

"Danki." Josh nodded. "I was really concerned. I'm praying for him. For the whole family."

William set his jaw. "Maybe Greta was right. Maybe you shouldn't waste your time. The prayers aren't going any higher than the ceiling."

"William, that's not tr—"

"I don't want to hear it. You can tell us Gott cares when our prayers start getting answered." He gave Josh a hard look. "See you at breakfast."

Josh hurried back down to the living room and sat on the couch to pull his socks on again. He needed to get started on the necessary Sunday chores before going home and doing the same there.

He entered the kitchen, ignored by Eve and a sniffing, tearful Gizelle, and slipped into his shoes before heading to the barn. He fed Whippoorwill, milked the cows, and carried the full buckets to the haus. Back at the barn again, he hitched Sea Grass to the buggy and started for home. Instead of going to church and subjecting himself to a sermon he'd be sure to disagree with, maybe he'd kum back to the Millers' to see Greta.

He swallowed the lump in his throat. In her mind, they weren't courting. But in his mind, jah, he was courting her.

After helping his brother and their daed with the chores, he found Mamm in the kitchen, setting a platter of warm cinnamon rolls on the table. His stomach rumbled.

"Gut morgen, Josh. Any more word on Andy? And did you see their bare cupboards? I'm planning on taking over a box of food later and leaving it on the porch. Hopefully then, they won't refuse it."

"That's sweet, Mamm. They need it. About Andy…nein news, other than that the hospital is keeping him a few days for observation. Give me a minute to clean up, and I'll be back for breakfast." He started for the door.

"Are you going to church?"

Josh paused and glanced back. "Nein. I thought about visiting Viktor and Esther, and maybe Greta, too, to see if…. Her. To see her." Might as well be honest about it.

"It's wunderbaar you two are back together."

Josh looked down. "We're not."

"But…."

"I would love to be with her, Mamm. But she'd made it plain that our relationship was in the past. Not the present."

"Maybe, Gott willing, it will be in the present and the future, too."

He prayed so. But, as she'd said, *Gott willing.*

Greta lay back down, closed her eyes, and daydreamed about Josh. In her bedroom. Giving her *the look.*

She awoke with a start to Gizelle shaking her by the shoulders. "Why didn't you tell me?" she demanded. "He's my daed, too. I had the right to know. You should have told me when you came to bed."

Daed. Reality came crashing in. Tears stung Greta's eyes, and a heavy load of depression settled over her. "We tried to find you."

Gizelle's eyes flashed. "I was with Josh."

"Nein, you weren't. Josh was with us." Except not at the hospital. He'd disappeared before Greta had left.

He'd also been sleeping inside the haus when she got home. With a chaperone. And Gizelle had been upstairs. Nein, Gizelle and Josh hadn't been together.

"Joshua Yoder isn't the only Josh in the world." Gizelle released her.

Nein, he wasn't. He was just the only Josh who mattered.

As much as she wanted to stay in bed and sink into despair, letting the tears flow freely, Greta sat up and fluffed her pillow.

Outside the window, the pink of the dawn was fading. She'd overslept. She needed to get over to Esther's.

"Eve told me that Daed had a heart attack, and that he died on the way to the hospital, but they revived him. She also said that he needs bypass surgery to survive."

Greta nodded. "They did say something about bypass surgery…after he heals." She didn't remember the words "to survive." And how would Eve have known? She hadn't been at the hospital. And all the family had stayed until Daed was out of recovery and in a room. So, the information Eve had relayed had been secondhand. Not entirely based on fact.

"The first people Joshua Yoder asked about this morgen were Daed and you," Gizelle told her. "That was my first clue that something had happened."

"Didn't you wonder why Eve was in the kitchen this morgen instead of me or Mamm?"

Gizelle passed over her point. "Why didn't you wake me?"

"It was mostly over by then. Daed was already at the hospital, the stents were in, and now he's in a hospital room. Mamm's going back to visit today. She'll probably take you, if you want to go." Greta glanced out the window again. If only she could go along and see for herself how Daed was doing. But she couldn't. Duty first. She sighed and swung her legs over the edge of the bed. "I need to get going. I promised Rachel I'd fill in for her as a mother's helper to Esther today. And I'll be paid for it." She would have preferred filling in for free. It was awful taking money from a friend. It smacked of charity, which dealt a blow to her pride.

Gizelle nodded. "We need the money, for sure. I'll have your breakfast waiting on the table."

"Danki." Greta wiped away a tear that she'd failed to hold back. Then she took off her rumpled nacht-clothes and picked out a dress in a shade of green that Josh used to say made her eyes look even greener. She pinned it shut, then fastened her apron over it.

Would she even see Josh again today? It shouldn't matter, but it did. Maybe he'd stop by Viktor and Esther's haus, since Greta had told him she'd be there.

When Greta went downstairs, Mamm was just coming out of her bedroom. She had dark circles under her eyes, as if she hadn't slept well. Or at all.

"Gut morgen, Mamm."

"Morgen. I'm sure Rachel will understand if you don't go over to relieve her this morgen, in light of your daed and all."

Really? Then she could go with Mamm and Gizelle, after all.

But nein. Greta smoothed her hands down her apron. "We need the money," she murmured. "That has to kum first. Tell Daed I'll stop by tomorrow." Except that she was supposed to spend the day at the farmers' market. Which meant that, despite its being Sunday, she would have to do some baking today. Either that, or just sell canned goods tomorrow. Of course, she could get up extra early and bake a few dozen cookies. Her thoughts whirled as she tried to plan it out, all the while trying to justify taking a trip to see Daed—what she wanted to do more than anything else.

If only she could dump all her cares and concerns on someone else for a while.

"Gizelle is coming with me today. The driver will be by in a while to pick us up. William has already left for church. He needs to give an update. Maybe then, Bishop Joe...." Mamm sniffed. "Well, hope springs eternal."

Jah. It would take a tragedy of epic proportion to get the bishop to help. Evidently his ruined barn was of bigger importance than her daed's health. The likelihood of Bishop Joe's doing anything was about the same as that of Gott. Not at all.

If William had gone to church, it meant he'd taken the buggy. Which meant Greta would have to walk to Viktor and Esther's. Gut thing it wasn't too far.

On the kitchen table, as promised, she found a plate of eggs and toast at her place. A dirty dish occupied William's place. He must have left in a serious haste, to have neglected taking it to the sink. She'd say something to him later.

Eve sat at Daed's place at the table, her sour expression turning the day on its side. The one person who'd volunteered to stay and help this family with meals and cleaning....

Greta should be grateful, she knew. But she wanted to tell Eve to go home. She and Gizelle could handle the haus and still work their regular jobs. Hadn't they—well, she—been doing it for a while?

But dismissing Eve was Mamm's prerogative.

Once Greta finished her breakfast, she started to carry the dishes over to the sink, thinking she'd wash them quickly.

Eve cleared her throat. "Leave them. I don't like dishes piled in the sink."

It's not your sink. "But—"

"Go on, Greta," Mamm told her. "You're running late." Her unspoken but clearly communicated message was, *We'll do it Eve's way.*

She wouldn't let this ruin her day. A day that already seemed dark, gloomy, and depressing. She had to function. Nodding, Greta returned the dishes to the table, then put on her shoes and headed out.

As she walked, she tried to find a smile to greet Esther and Rachel with. But her ability to put on a cheery face seemed to have died sometime during Daed's heart attack. Probably nein hope that it would be revived anytime soon. Maybe she should be more realistic and hope for nein more tears. After all, crying was a boppli thing. Not something grown women did. She cringed as she remembered soaking Josh's shirt with her tears.

The clip-clop of a horse's hooves sounded someone's approach from behind her. She glanced over as a buggy pulled alongside her.

"Going my way, liebling?"

Chapter 10

Greta's cheeks turned a becoming shade of pink. "I told you yesterday, I'm working as a mother's helper for Esther today."

"Jah, I remember. I didn't know if that had changed, though, with your daed being in the hospital and all."

"We still need the money. More so now." Greta looked away.

"I could still give you a ride." If only he knew of something more to do.

She turned back and approached the buggy. Josh held out a hand to help her up, closing his fingers around hers. They were warm. Dainty yet strong. Capable.

She climbed in and dropped onto the narrow seat beside him. Her shoulder brushed against his, then she moved aside.

Josh reluctantly released her as she settled her skirts around her. She finally stilled. Clasped her hands in her lap.

"Ready?"

"Jah."

Josh grasped the reins with both hands. Safer than leaving one of them free. There was too much temptation to hold her hand. To pull her against him and hold her tight.

"About this morgen..." he began. "I shouldn't have gone into your room. I'm sorry for that."

The pink in her cheeks deepened. "I wasn't sure I hadn't dreamed it."

"It was gut that your brother came when he did." His gaze swept her features. "I might have overstepped my boundaries." *Might have?* Talk about an understatement.

She shrugged. "I trust you."

She shouldn't trust him. He was a man. And she was the woman he'd been in love with since before he could remember. They'd known each other as boppli. Grown up together. Somewhere along the way, they'd become so much more than friends.

Too soon, they reached the Petersheims' haus. Josh pulled the buggy into the driveway and parked. Viktor came out of the barn and took the reins. He nodded at Greta. "Go on in."

Josh reached over and helped her out of the buggy.

"Danki." She smiled up at him, then turned to Viktor. "Is Rachel still here?"

He nodded. "Waiting on you."

She hurried up the wheelchair ramp Viktor had built for his grossmammi, her skirts swaying.

Viktor unhitched Sea Grass and led him into the barn. Josh followed him.

"So, what's it like being a daed?"

Viktor's dark gaze shot to him. His eyes misted. "It's nothing short of a miracle. That Gott can make this tiny person so perfectly, and…." He started filling the water trough. "It's scary. I'm responsible for his every need. I'm the one accountable for raising him right." He frowned, glanced around, and lowered his voice. "I need to make a decision soon on which side of the Amish fence he's going to grow up. Unfortunately, this is one issue I can't avoid indefinitely."

Viktor and Esther were supposed to kneel along with Josh for baptism at the end of the summer—if they agreed to take the vows to give up the ways of the world and join the church.

"Is Esther all right?"

Viktor raised an eyebrow. "With the boppli or the decision?"

Josh shrugged. "Both."

Viktor's grin was slow. "Esther is…awesome. Simply awesome. You can't imagine."

Actually, Josh could. He, too, loved an awesome woman.

Greta took the boppli swaddled in a blue flannel blanket from Rachel. "He is so tiny," she whispered. "So cute."

"He's the most beautiful bu ever." Anna Petersheim, Viktor's grossmammi, wheeled herself into the room and stopped next to Esther. She reached for her hand and gave it a pat.

Esther smiled at her. "Jah, he is."

Greta exchanged glances with Rachel. "Just think…maybe next year, it'll be your turn."

Rachel blushed. "David and I plan to get married around the middle of November. But don't tell anyone. The community will find out when the banns are read at church two weeks beforehand." She looked at the wind-up clock on the mantel. "Speaking of church, I need to go, or I'll be late for the service. Gut thing it's being held right next door. I'll be back later to-nacht. After the singing." She opened the door and stepped out. A moment later, she opened it again and peeked inside. "I'm praying for Onkel Andy, Greta. So scary." She shut the door again, then opened it yet again. "Dinner is in the refrigerator. Just put it in the oven at three-fifty for a half an hour." The door shut for the third time.

Esther giggled. If only Greta could brush off her depression and worry as easily as her bossy cousin barked orders.

Anna rolled her wheelchair back and forth in a slight rocking movement. "I'll take the boppli when you're done holding him, Greta." She beamed at her. "Any hope for you and your young man working things out? It sure took the community by surprise when he up and left like he did. Leaving at the same time as our

Viktor...." Her mouth settled into a sad line, and she shifted slightly in the chair. "But Gott brought him—them—back to us."

Greta didn't feel it necessary to address Anna's question. Besides, she didn't know the answer. She supposed that, if Josh were to ask, she might consider letting him court her again. But he hadn't asked. And they had mountains of issues to discuss before they made any type of commitment.

And they hadn't made any effort to do so.

Well, that wasn't true. He'd brought it up. Once.

And she'd shot it down with the precision of the bow and arrow Daed used every deer season.

"He really is the most beautiful boppli I've ever seen." Greta gently laid the boppli in Anna's arms, then looked at Esther. "Should I go clean up the kitchen from breakfast?"

"Already done," Esther said. "Rachel took care of it."

"Make the beds?"

Esther laughed. "That's done, too. All that's required is sitting here and keeping us company. Honestly, I'm quite capable of handling things myself, but the midwife doesn't want me doing anything strenuous for a few days."

"Meaning she isn't supposed to be taking care of me." Anna rocked the wheelchair a little faster. The boppli gurgled. "She doesn't want her getting me up and helping me when I need it. I'm such a bother." She sighed.

Esther smiled at the woman, love shining in her eyes. "You aren't a bother, Anna. Ich liebe dich."

"I know, süße. And ich liebe dich. But that doesn't change the facts, ain't so? You know as well as I do what the midwife meant." She looked at Greta. "That's why Reuben and I told Viktor to hire a mother's helper. But I don't need anything right now, so your job is nothing more than to sit and talk with us. And, while I may be old and confined to a wheelchair, I'm not daft. I noticed the way you evaded my question. So, sit. Visit awhile."

Greta sat in a hard wooden rocking chair.

Silence fell, except for the sounds of the wheelchair rolling forward and back, set in motion by Anna's feet, and the wooden rocker creaking back and forth.

Anna looked at Greta. "Well?"

Greta shook her head, playing dumb. "I'm sorry. What was it you asked about? Daed?" Guilt ate at her, even as a fresh wave of grief washed over her. How was he doing?

"A tragedy, to be sure. A heart attack was the last thing that poor man needed. But I was thinking of Josh. And you. Are there any hopes of you getting back together?"

Greta opened and shut her mouth a couple times, but she couldn't kum up with a generic enough response.

Esther wasn't any help. She looked expectantly at Greta. "I wondered, too. Last I heard, you were still avoiding him. Hiding in the shadows when he went over to Rachel's haus, less than six months ago. And now he's taking you on buggy rides?" Esther stood slowly and made her way to the kitchen. "Want some red raspberry tea? It should be finished steeping by now."

"I can get it." Greta jumped to her feet. "That's why I'm here."

"Nonsense." Esther waved her off. "I told you, I can take care of myself."

Just then, the door opened. Viktor walked in, followed by Reuben, his grossdaedi. And Josh.

"Talk to Anna," Esther told Greta. "She needs a gut romance to keep her mind occupied. Especially when the man in question is in the haus."

Greta's face flamed as she caught Josh's smirk. She turned to Anna. "You should've told me. I would've gladly picked one up at the library."

In the kitchen, Viktor chuckled. "Sounds like you and Greta are the next target of my grossmammi's matchmaking, now that Rachel and David are together."

Josh shook his head. "I wasn't aware Anna played a part in it. Neither David or Rachel ever mentioned it."

Reuben hung his hat on a wall hook. "Doubt they knew. She prayed for them to get together. Just like she did with Viktor and Esther. And she's already started praying for you and Greta. Started the day you returned—as soon as she heard you were back."

"Gott is taking His time, then." Josh hung his hat beside Reuben's. Not that he minded the prayers. He and Greta each had much to work out.

He more so than she, probably. Except for the not-so-minor-problem of her lack of faith in Gott. Would she ever forgive him for his mistakes?

The cry of Viktor's newborn sohn split the quiet. Josh glanced in the other room. Greta took the boppli from Anna and started walking, gently bouncing him, as she made some cooing sounds.

Esther filled three cups with tea, then looked at Viktor. "Do you want koffee?"

"I'll get it," he said. "I don't care for the instant kind so much as the stuff brewed in a koffeemaker. Daedi, do you think Bishop Joe—ach, never mind."

Reuben chuckled. "Do I think he'll allow electric just so you can have your automatic twelve-cup koffeepot plugged in? I think not. But there's no rule against having wires run to the barn. Or using the generator to run the koffeemaker." He headed into the living room and said a few words to Anna that Josh couldn't discern.

The next several minutes were silent, save for Greta's voice speaking soft gibberish to the boppli. Josh watched as she carried the newborn next to her heart. The boppli looked so content, so right, in her arms. Wouldn't it be wunderbaar if she carried his kinner someday?

"Speaking of barns," Viktor said, "did you ever consider taking Greta behind one?" He winked. "Solves a world of problems."

Esther swatted her ehemann. "Viktor!"

Josh glanced at Greta. Her cheeks flamed red, and her gaze shot to him. He was sure his own face burned hot enough to match hers. He wanted to deny having done so, but that would be a lie. And she'd know it. "Uh...I might have considered it a time or two."

It would have been only slightly better than locking himself in a closet with her during a game of spin the bottle.

Judging by the way her eyes widened and the color fled her face, her thoughts had gone there, too. She turned abruptly and carried Michael quickly in the other direction.

"I didn't realize she was in earshot," Viktor murmured. "Of course, going behind the barn creates a few problems, as well." He held out a cup of koffee. "I'm sorry."

"Jah. Me, too." For more than just the words.

He was sorry for his actions, too.

And for the fact that it'd take nothing short of a miracle for Gott to work things out between Greta and him.

Chapter 11

Greta dipped her head when Esther and the men returned to the living room. As Esther set a full teacup on the table beside her, Greta watched Josh's stockinged feet pass within inches of where she sat, holding the boppli. He paused.

If she and Gott had still been on speaking terms, she would've prayed that Josh would go on by without acknowledging her. *Take me behind the barn, indeed.* Like she would agree to go. The scenario was too similar to the opportunity in the closet that he'd passed up, to her shame. Nein, she wouldn't go. Not in a million years.

Josh moved past her rocking chair and lowered himself to the floor by her feet. Close enough that, if she'd wanted to, she could have reached out and touched his blond hair. He was finally letting it grow back into the Amish style.

Truthfully, she wanted to touch it. She clenched the boppli's swaddle blanket to alleviate the temptation.

He sat close enough to send the message to the others in the room—including her—that they were a couple.

The notion sent a guilty thrill shooting through her.

But they couldn't be a couple. Not with so many unresolved issues standing between them.

Besides, who was to say he wouldn't leave again? She couldn't trust him to stay.

So then, why was he…?

Nein. She didn't want to know.

She expelled a forceful breath.

Fine. So maybe she did want to know. And a tiny part of her wanted to know what she might find behind the barn....

Every fiber of her being was aware of him. She studied the breadth of his shoulders, the strong muscles bulging beneath the long sleeves of his shirt, the way the suspenders stretched over the length of his back. Would his bare chest be as defined as those she'd seen depicted on the covers of some secular romance novels at the library and at various garage sales?

She shouldn't dwell on such things. She forced her attention away from him—but it only went as far as the thick black stuff in the mug that he drank from. She'd never developed a taste for koffee. Probably a gut thing, since her family couldn't afford it.

They couldn't afford much of anything these days. One glance at Esther's full pantry was a painful reminder of that fact. But at least they hadn't gone hungry, thanks to an ample supply of home-grown fruits and vegetables, wild meat, and dried beans. And Joel had been gut about letting her purchase produce that was a little past its prime at a marked-down price.

She reached for her tea.

Josh shifted a little, his arm bumping against her shin, then the side of his chest coming to rest there. Her heart rate pounded as a wave of heat flowed through her. Her hand trembled, causing a few drops of hot tea to slosh over the brim of the mug onto her fingers. Thankfully, none of it landed on the boppli.

Around her, the conversation continued, but she had no idea what was being said. Or by whom. All her attention was focused on Josh. And that small bit of contact with just a layer or two of cloth between flesh....

Maybe going behind the barn wasn't such a bad idea, after all.

Josh settled closer to Greta, knowing full well he pushed the boundaries.

But maybe it was time she noticed him as more than…whatever he was in her mind. Her former beau. If only she'd agree to let him kum courting again.

But then, he hadn't asked to. It was still too soon. And they hadn't talked. Probably better to wait. To go on as he was, caring for her and her family. Then maybe, if Gott willed it, their relationship would blossom and grow once more.

It pained Josh to have to earn their trust all over again.

His own fault, he knew.

If only he could give her his manuscript to read. Then she would understand so much more. He'd asked her to proofread it. But he didn't know if he should wait until it was finished and give her the entire manuscript at once, printed out, or loan her his laptop and let her read each entry as he wrote it. How did other writers handle the editing process? He didn't know of anyone to question on the matter. Nobody he knew wrote anything besides letters.

He finished his koffee and set the empty mug on the floor beside him, regretfully moving away from the improper contact with Greta as he settled a few inches away. She still sipped from the dainty teacup—part of the set Viktor had bought Esther on their honeymoon. Beautiful, but it seemed so out of place on an Amish farm. Kind of the way Josh felt sometimes. He shifted again, looking toward Viktor, as Esther ran her fingers through his too-short-by-Amish-standards hair. If only Greta would do the same to him. Desire ignited. *Time to go.* He stood.

Viktor got to his feet, picked up his own mug, and followed him into the kitchen. "Are you okay?" he asked. "Never seen you so quiet."

Josh shrugged. "Just a lot on my mind. Guess I'm not very gut company today."

Viktor looked into the other room, where Greta sat in plain view, then regarded Josh again with a slight smirk. "Who…uh, what's on your mind? Maybe I can help."

"Too many things to count." Josh shook his head. "Mostly, I'm worried about the Millers. About Andy. The family is relying on what Greta and Gizelle earn to pay all the bills, and with Andy's medical problems…they're having to sell off various things. Almost all the livestock and buggies have already been sold. I don't know how to help, except by doing physical labor. I'm praying for guidance, but Gott hasn't given me any clear answers yet."

Viktor's smirk faded, replaced by a grave expression. "The whole community knows. Andy refuses anything that even remotely resembles charity. He still has his pride. Not much you can do when the situation is like that."

"Just seems like there should be another way." Josh sighed. "Well, I really just stopped by to offer my congratulations on your new sohn. I should get going."

Esther peeked into the kitchen, holding little Michael. "You're welkum to stay for dinner, Josh. There's plenty to share. And we hardly see you anymore."

Greta came up behind her. "You're leaving?" Her voice trembled. "But I thought…." She pursed her lips.

"See me out, Greta? Please?" She needed to know. To understand.

She nodded. "I'll be right back, Esther."

Josh shoved his feet into his boots, then gestured for Greta to precede him out the door. He avoided Viktor's gaze, afraid of what he'd see there. He'd kum back when he felt more himself. Not the confused replica that had been impersonating him since he'd walked into Greta's bedroom that morgen. Or maybe since even before that. Because he knew better than to go upstairs. He knew better than to go into a girl's bedroom.

Especially since he'd been consumed with guilt ever since. A sense of guilt similar to the one that had sent him running from home the first time.

Greta stopped on the porch and turned to look at Josh. "What's going on? I thought you...." She wouldn't complete the statement. *I thought you were going to spend the day with me here. Courting.*

Josh's neck reddened. His gaze dropped from hers and landed somewhere in the vicinity of her feet. "I'm sorry for coming into your bedroom this morgen."

She frowned. "You apologized already. And I told you that I trust you."

"That's just it. You shouldn't." He raised his eyes briefly to hers, then looked past her. "Quite honestly, what I'm feeling right now rivals what I felt that day years ago when we played spin the bottle."

She tried to keep from sagging. "Repulsion, then. Gut thing we never married." She bit her lower lip to keep it from trembling.

Josh shook his head. "Not repulsion, liebling. Lust." His eyes met hers again, their blue depths shining with earnestness—and shame.

Lust? She opened her mouth, but nein words would kum. Her brain went numb. She stared into his eyes, unable to look away. *Why?*

"Because I wanted to go behind the barn with you. I wanted to go in that closet with you. I wanted to do a lot of things I'd never done. I wasn't worthy of you then. And now...now...." He swallowed, his Adam's apple bobbing. "I'm sorry. That's all."

"You ran away from home—left the Amish—because you... you wanted to go into that closet with me?" She shook her head. "Are you leaving again?"

He blinked, breaking the magnetic hold his blue eyes had on her. "What? Nein. I'm not going anywhere."

"But you just said...." She held up her hands, silently begging him to fill in the blanks. Or maybe subconsciously desiring to grab his suspenders and yank him into her arms. A glance toward the open window alleviated that desire. They had nein privacy here. Her face heated.

"I said I wanted you. I want a lot more than I have a right to. And I'm going to respect you. So, I'm temporarily removing myself from the temptation. And, liebling, you are overwhelmingly tempting."

He didn't seem to notice the open window. Or their audience. She wished he'd just give in. Take her behind the barn. Take her in his arms. Kiss her until her knees turned to Jell-O. Hold her and never let her go. If he knew how many times she'd mentally rewritten the spin-the-bottle incident, so that the outcome matched the desire she'd seen in his eyes that nacht…the passion that she'd wanted, before it was replaced with a hardness she'd never seen, and anger, and a complete withdrawal….

She still wanted that passion.

"You…? Me…?" She still couldn't form a coherent statement.

He didn't respond. At least, not verbally. Instead, his gaze wandered to her lips. Lingered there long enough that they began to tingle. She parted them.

He took a big step backward. Then a wide one sideways. "I'll see you tomorrow, liebling." He jumped off the porch and hurried to the barn as if he couldn't escape fast enough.

The haus door opened, and Viktor stepped out. He looked back at Greta. "Yep, he should've taken you behind the barn." He started down the steps, then paused on the bottom one and glanced over his shoulder. "You've got a choice here, Greta. You can let him go, or you can go to him. I'd suggest the latter."

Chapter 12

Josh took the long way home from the Petersheims' to give his thoughts time to settle before he faced his family. Thankfully, neither Greta nor Viktor had followed him into the barn after he bolted. He'd knelt in the stable beside his horse, praying for Gott to relieve him of his sinful thoughts and to give him guidance on how to help Greta's family. No immediate answers came to mind, other than to give them all the money he earned selling birdhouses. He'd do it in a heartbeat, but he knew her family wouldn't accept the charity.

And he'd be delaying his dream of owning a farm.

He wouldn't spend the nacht at the Millers' barn anymore. Not while Andy was in the hospital and Greta was within easy reach. Too much temptation.

When Josh walked into the kitchen shortly before noon, Mamm looked up from the table, her eyebrows rising as her gaze rested on the black laptop he carried, freshly charged thanks to the generator in the barn. Daed pushed his glasses up, pinched the bridge of his nose, and frowned. But neither one said a word about the verboden electronic device.

Mamm rose to her feet. "I thought you were spending the day with Greta. Is everything okay there? And her daed...he's all right?"

"Last I heard, he was stabilized." Josh shrugged. "You didn't go to church?"

"We should have," Mamm said. "But with the late nacht we had, it just seemed like too much effort. And Greta? Is she with her daed?"

"Ach, nein. With Esther. She's working as a mother's helper for the day." Josh clutched the computer closer to his side.

"On a Sunday. Tsk, tsk. Poor child." Mamm shook her head. "Do you want something warm to drink while I start lunch?"

"I'm fine, danki. Just call me when lunch is ready."

"I hope you're not intending to work on that...."

Josh left her muttering and headed upstairs, but the guilt pursued him. He may not have Wi-Fi at home, but he needed to get some more words down on paper—on screen, rather. Even if it was Sunday.

At least it would help to take his mind off Greta.

He opened the document and read the last entry he'd made.

There was no escape from what lived within me.

Again, the enormous task threatened to overwhelm him. Josh bowed his head. *Lord, I ask You once more to guide my words.*

He positioned his fingers on the keyboard. Gut thing he'd learned to type during his time away from the Amish.

After a few dead-end jobs in St. Louis, I found work across the river, on an apple orchard in Illinois.

At least I was more suited for that line of business.

The job didn't last long, and the lodging wasn't ideal. I lived among migrant farm workers who didn't speak much English in a small shack that let in more of the elements than it kept out.

I had never met any migrant workers before. They aren't common where I grew up. I soon figured out they moved from state to state, farm to farm, going wherever there was work. Nomads, of sorts, but hardworking people.

Kind of appealing, in a way.

I did good work at the orchards. I learned how to drive a tractor, and since I spoke English, and the owner trusted me, he allowed me to start taking groups of people on hayrides during their busy season. I think it was mostly because I wasn't the typical migrant worker, being ex-Amish. He also tasked me with driving the self-pickers out to the designated orchards.

It was all good.

Except at night, when I couldn't sleep. When I turned to the bottle to help me forget.

I joined the migrant workers, moving from farm to farm, each time going further south, as growing seasons in the north ended.

I picked peaches in Georgia. While there, I met an older man by the name of Dan. He said I reminded him a lot of himself at my age. He put up with my rages, discouraged me from drowning my sorrows with drink (that didn't work so well, anyway), and shared about a life-changing experience on the Appalachian Trail. He never finished hiking it, due to an injury he sustained on the trail that prompted an unexpected medical diagnosis. His words followed me as I spent hours doing backbreaking work in cotton fields in Mississippi, then moved on to picking oranges in Florida.

After those jobs were over, I returned to Georgia and looked Dan up. He gave me all his hiking equipment and even drove me to the starting point. Told me he'd be my first follower on the trail journals.

And that he'd be praying I'd find my way.

Praying. I scoffed and told him not to waste his time.

Josh had heard the same sentiment recently, from both Greta and William.

"Josh?" Mamm appeared in his bedroom doorway. "Lunch is ready."

"Coming." He hit "save," put the laptop in hibernation mode, and went downstairs.

Daed came in from the barn. "I need the bu to help out there," he told Mamm. "Cow's having a troublesome late birth, and Stephen and his family are still at church. We'll eat after a bit."

"After a bit" turned into hours later, since the stubborn bull-calf took its merry time making its way into the world.

Josh washed up, ate his meal quickly, and went to bed. He woke up to the sun shining through his window—the promise of another hot day. Was it too much to hope for rain? The gardens certainly needed it. But that would shut down the open-air farmers' market for the day, to the detriment of Greta's family.

How had Greta gotten home from Esther's last nacht? Probably walked. Or maybe Viktor gave her a ride.

Josh finished his chores, showered, shaved, then hurriedly ate a bowl of Mamm's homemade granola cereal. Mamm didn't cook breakfast on the days she was scheduled to work at the cheese shop, so Josh usually fended for himself. Daed, on the other hand, would eat a hearty home-cooked breakfast in their old home, which now belonged to Josh's brother.

As Josh ate, he studied the wall calendar they'd received from the local bank. This month featured a photo of bicycles parked among colorful flowers. It brought to mind the time he and Greta had strolled hand in hand through a local garden center. He'd been looking for the perfect rose bush to give Mamm for her birthday. He couldn't remember the name of the type he'd finally chosen, but the blossoms were an orange-red. Greta had picked out a pink one for her own mamm, whose birthday was around the same time; but she never bought it, as far as he knew. She'd said she would kum back later, closer to her mamm's birthday. Had her family's finances been in tight straits even then?

Mamm came into the kitchen, carrying the grater and a bar of lye soap. She put them away, then washed her hands. "I got a load soaking in the wringer washer. Going to be a scorcher out there today. Must be close to ninety already. I need to get the laundry on the line before I head to work." She sat across from him to drink a cup of koffee. "What are your plans today, Sohn?"

Josh swallowed the last bite of granola and set his spoon in the empty bowl. "As soon as I can, I'm going over to Andy Miller's. Would you mind telling Stan to pick me up there? I have the boxes loaded in my buggy."

"Are the birdhouses selling well?" Mamm stirred a spoonful of sugar and a glug of cream into her koffee. "I noticed your supply is going down."

"Jah. I was surprised, since it's late in the season. I think they're selling mostly to collectors who want them for strictly decorative purposes." He shrugged. "I'll make more during the winter, when the farm work is done. And I got the message Daed left on my door about needing my help with the berries. I'll plan to stay home from the farmers' market tomorrow."

"It might be more than one day's worth of work," Mamm said.

Josh nodded, then bowed his head for the silent prayer before rising to his feet. "See you to-nacht. Don't forget to tell Stan I'm at Greta's."

At the Millers', Josh unloaded his boxes on the edge of the porch, then parked his buggy beside the barn and let Sea Grass out to pasture. Josh went into the barn's dim interior, down the short hallway that led to the cow barn, and descended the concrete steps.

William stood at the trough, filling it with water from the pump. "Wasn't sure you were coming."

"I told you I would. Sorry I didn't kum last nacht. We had a heifer birthing, and she had some problems."

"I need to leave for school as soon as we finish milking the cows. Bishop Joe says I can't miss any more school unless it's an emergency. And Mamm isn't sure if Daed's hospitalization counts."

Josh frowned. "I think it should. But who's to say what Bishop Joe thinks? Probably best to assume it doesn't. I know they ran school several weeks longer than usual last fall due to the absence of a teacher. It's letting out the end of this week, I heard. Is Greta going to the farmers' market or to the hospital?"

"Farmers' market. She's filling crates now. Mamm's real happy with the income she's brought in so far."

"Gut." Josh reached for a bucket and a three-legged stool. "Guess we'd better get busy. You go ahead and leave whenever you need to. I can finish up."

A little while later, after William left, Josh carried two full buckets of milk to the haus and knocked at the door with his foot.

Gizelle opened it. "Gut morgen, Josh-u-a." She moved out of the way so he could enter.

Greta glanced at him, her cheeks flushing. Then she looked shyly away.

Josh set the milk pails on the table.

"Did you have breakfast yet?" Gizelle asked. "Greta made cinnamon rolls to sell, but some of them got burnt."

"They aren't that bad," Greta almost growled. "But they are a little too brown to take to the market." She started spreading icing on a tray of rolls.

Josh's stomach growled. "Where's your mamm?"

"She got a ride to the hospital," Gizelle replied. "She's spending the day with Daed. I get to drive the horse and buggy to work." She grinned. "Want a burnt cinnamon roll?"

"Uh, jah. Danki." Josh glanced at Greta, then accepted a roll from Gizelle. "Smells fine to me."

"They don't taste bad," Gizelle conceded. "But Greta is making mistakes like crazy. Mamm said it was because she started baking as soon as she got home from Esther's yesterday evening, and Gott's punishing her for working on Sunday. She messed up a batch of cookies, too. Too much salt. And the brownies were so hard, I don't think a stray dog would eat them. Now, the cinnamon rolls are passable...."

Greta's back stiffened.

Josh frowned at Gizelle. "I don't think Gott's punishing her. He understands the situation. Something else is bothering her. She's probably distracted by her concern for your daed."

Greta swatted at something near her face. A fly, maybe. Or perhaps she was close to tears.

"I think it's you, ain't so?" Gizelle chirped with a nasty look at her sister. "She's been muttering under her breath about you all morgen, and she did the same yesterday evening, too. Probably thought nobody noticed."

"Gizelle, please," Greta snapped.

So, he was the distraction. The "something else" that bothered her.

And not in a gut way.

Greta brushed away the pesky tear that lingered on her lashes. She didn't need her know-it-all eighteen-year-old sister spilling her secrets to Josh. Especially since he already threatened to turn her world upside-down. Best he think she was upset about Daed. Truly, she was. When Mamm and Gizelle had returned from their hospital visit the day before, they'd reported that he was improving but very grumpy, demanding to be allowed to go home and recover there. The doctor hadn't acquiesced.

Greta peeked at Josh out of the corner of her eye. Her stomach did a couple flips. She didn't know how to act around him since hearing his confession that he lusted after her. Lusted, not loved. Or since listening to him discuss the boundaries he was setting up—boundaries she couldn't force herself to step over, even though Viktor had shaken his head with disbelief when she'd refused to go to the barn. As if she'd go out there when she knew they had an audience. Besides, she wasn't sure she wanted to disregard the imaginary lines. She didn't want to be the one pushing Josh over the edge of whatever cliff he teetered on.

She'd wanted him to talk to her, but she hadn't expected the raw honesty that had boiled out. It'd bothered her to the point that she probably should've stayed out of the kitchen and not attempted to bake anything. Her mind wasn't on measuring ingredients and keeping an eye on the oven but on Josh and his revelations, spoken and unspoken. Her poor decision had resulted in wasted ingredients—which meant wasted money.

Almost against her will, her gaze wandered to Josh again. If it wasn't repulsion that had prompted him to leave, then what? And how, exactly, had he spent his time away from the Amish?

He'd changed so much.

She couldn't be in love with the old Josh, because he no longer existed. And the new one? They didn't know each other.

Or did they?

In the driveway, gravel crunched beneath car tires. Josh shoved the last bite of the overbaked cinnamon roll in his mouth. Despite its being a little brown, it tasted great. After wiping his sticky fingers on the damp washrag Gizelle had left within reach, he opened the door, lifted Greta's crates of goods, and carried them outside to the van.

Stan opened the back door and helped Josh load the crates, then his boxes.

Greta came outside, looking downcast. "I don't have a wide variety of baked goods to sell this time. Hopefully, the extra jars of apple butter will help make up for it."

"You just had an off day," Josh told her. "You'll do better to-nacht. I could...."

What was he doing, offering to help? He didn't know a single thing about baking.

"I don't think that would be a gut idea." She didn't meet his eyes.

"I'll help." Stan stepped forward. "I'm really a great cook."

"Ach, sure." She sounded dubious.

But Stan seemed oblivious. He beamed. "Great. I'll be back after supper."

Josh opened his mouth to object, then shut it without saying anything. It was Greta's place. But if Stan would be there, then so would he. And he'd try to help however he could.

"I'm not going to need a ride tomorrow, and possibly not on Wednesday, either," he told Stan. "Daed needs my help on the farm."

Stan gave him a playful punch in the arm. Pretty presumptuous, considering they weren't friends. Not in Josh's eyes, at least. "No worries, man. I'll keep my eye on the babe for ya."

Josh scowled as Stan wrapped an arm around Greta's shoulders and gave them a quick squeeze.

Right. And *that* didn't worry him in the least.

Chapter 13

Greta tucked several loose strands of hair back under her kapp and tried to keep from fidgeting with her apron. Stan stood beside her, talking a blue streak about the college classes he took on Tuesdays and Thursdays—stuff she cared nothing about. She wished he wouldn't keep hanging around, though he had been a welkum source of support at the hospital.

Josh stole intermittent glances at them as he conversed with several men perusing David's fishing flies.

A pickup truck she recognized as Viktor's pulled into the parking lot. What was he doing here?

Viktor adjusted his sunglasses and nodded at her as he approached Josh's table. When the customers moved on, he stepped up. "Hey, Josh. Your brother Stephen sent me here to bring you home. Your daed decided to get started on the berries today, since Wednesday's forecast calls for rain."

Josh frowned, glancing briefly at Greta. "Okay. Let me get packed up." He bent down to begin retrieving his boxes from under the table. First, though, he grabbed his cooler and brought it to Greta. Her stomach rumbled as she imagined another wunderbaar roast beef sandwich and a pickle. And a Coke. "I packed enough food for both of us," he told her, then glanced at Stan. "You staying?"

"Oh, yeah." Stan grinned. "I don't have anything else to do, other than look for a real job. Or study for my quiz tomorrow. But I can do that later."

"You can share it with Stan, if you like. You'll be okay, Greta?" An emotion she couldn't read flashed in Josh's eyes.

Greta eyed her table. She wanted to pack up and leave, too, since his comforting presence would be gone. But she needed to try selling off the items she'd brought in order to buy more ingredients for baking. She forced a smile. "I'll be fine. Stan's here."

Josh balled his fists for a brief moment, then relaxed them with a nod. "If you're sure, then." He turned away and picked up a beautiful birdhouse. Greta couldn't believe it hadn't sold yet. She would have bought it, if she had money to waste on frivolities. It looked like a traditional haus with a white picket fence around it. Her dream haus, only in miniature. Bird-size.

"Hey, Josh," Stan called. "I'll manage your table, if you want."

Josh hesitated a long moment. He glanced briefly at Greta with a look of concern before addressing Stan again. "Thanks. I'd appreciate it. Keep the price tags from any items that sell, so I'll know how to distribute the earnings at the end of the day. And watch the fishing flies. They tend to wander off if left unattended." He put the birdhouse down and faced Greta. "I'll kum over later to-nacht, as we planned." Then he nodded at Stan, walked around the table, and followed Viktor to the pickup.

Greta watched him go. Farm work had to kum first. In mid-June. Viktor had mentioned berries. Blackberries, raspberries, and blueberries would be ripe about now. And Josh's family maintained several large berry patches. Some of them were available for customers to pick themselves. Handwritten signs were posted along the road nearby, drawing large groups of Englischers every June.

"You planning to go to the hospital after we leave here?" Stan asked Greta.

She nodded. Her worry over Daed had eased some, since hearing Mamm's report that he seemed better, but Greta still wanted to visit him. Though she'd imagined going with Josh by her side, being her rock. Instead, she would go alone.

Not alone. Stan would be there. But it wouldn't be the same. Daed would eye Stan with distrust and wouldn't be as open in his conversation as he would have been if Josh were there.

The same distrust had flickered in Josh's eyes as he'd left Greta with Stan.

It made her feel loved and protected.

"I'll treat you to dinner afterward," Stan told her. "There's this nice little café near the hospital."

"Sounds good." It would be after supper by the time she got home, and it would be nice to have a hot meal, instead of one warmed over or eaten cold.

Stan winked, then ambled back to Josh's table as several customers approached. He had the same easy way with people as Josh. Talkative. Smiling. Greta didn't interact well with strangers, except with the ones who were openly friendly toward her.

She squared her shoulders and forced a smile as a woman picked up a loaf of bread. "Baked fresh this morning," she told her. "Goes well with...." She reached for the nearest canning jar and glanced at the label. "Peach preserves and home-churned butter."

The woman looked at the jar. "I *love* peaches. Do you sell home-churned butter here?"

Greta blinked. "Nein—no. But it's easy to make. All you need is some heavy cream and a glass jar with a lid. Add a little salt, then shake it vigorously until it forms a ball, and you have butter."

The woman arched an eyebrow. "Seriously? I didn't realize it was so simple."

Greta nodded. "Don't expect it to be yellow, like the kind you buy in the store. That's because of the food coloring they add. It'll be white."

"Thanks. I'll have to try that." The woman dug in her purse and handed Greta a ten-dollar bill. "I'll take a loaf of bread and the peach preserves. And I'll try to make butter sometime. How much salt did you say?"

"A pinch. Not too much." Why did Englischers always ask for exact measurements? She handed the woman her change, along with a bag of her purchases. "Thank you."

Josh would be proud of her for conquering her shyness. She couldn't wait to see him this evening and tell him what she'd done.

But first she would see Daed and go out for dinner. It wouldn't be a date, though. What if Stan thought it was? They were just going to visit the hospital and then grab a quick bite to eat. Perfectly innocent.

Except it made her insides twist in weird ways. From fear, maybe. Apprehension. She had nein clue why. Stan seemed nice enough.

Just before five, Stan took down the canopy tent covering both tables and loaded it in his van, then returned and started packing up the few items that were left on Josh's table. Mostly baskets, and few birdhouses—unbelievably, still including the pretty one she loved.

Greta's leftover goods didn't even fill an entire crate. She loaded it into the back of the van, then climbed into the front seat beside Stan. It reminded her of when she'd ridden through the darkness, filled with worry and fear, after Daed's heart attack.

The hospital was in the same town as the farmers' market—a much larger town than Jamesport. There weren't any horses and buggies here, and cars zipped up and down the narrow streets. Stan turned at a green light and drove into the hospital parking lot. He found a parking space, and once they'd gotten out of the van, he clicked a button on the key ring, automatically locking the doors.

"Come on, babe. Do you know what floor your old man is on?"

Greta cringed inwardly as she told him the room number. Stan strode confidently down a hallway and around a corner to the elevator, then pushed the button to summon it. Gut thing he knew his way around. The door slid open, and Stan held out his hand, motioning for her to get on first. When the doors shut again, he pushed another button, and they were jerked into motion.

He stood beside her. Too close, really, but she didn't move away. That would seem rude.

The elevator shuddered to a stop, and Stan let her precede him through the door once again. He glanced at a sign on the wall. "This way."

When they entered the room, Daed lay in the first bed. A beige curtain was partially drawn, dividing the room in half. On the other side, the television blared, and three people stood at the end of the bed, competing with the TV for the patient's attention. One of them glanced at Greta. He did a double take, his gaze sliding over her navy blue dress and black apron. Taking in her sensible white tennis shoes. Then rising to her black bonnet. He said something to the person beside him, then laughed.

The room started swimming. It felt unbearably hot. Greta tried to focus on Daed. She moved behind the curtain to get closer to him, as well as to hide from the gawking strangers.

Daed grinned at her. "Hallo, dochter." His gaze shifted to Stan. The smile dimmed. He turned his attention back to Greta. "Your mamm said you might be by. I'm glad you came."

"How are you?" She touched his hand, careful not to disturb the IV needle stuck in his vein.

"They changed my medications."

Probably wise, seeing that he seemed to be in his right mind, not drugged. "Are you feeling better?"

Daed shrugged, his gaze going to Stan again. "Ready to go home. You'll take me, right?" He sat up straighter and leaned to the left, as if he was about to get out of bed, but his knees hit the railing that was locked into place.

Stan moved a little closer. "Either my mom or I will. Depends on when they release you, sir."

Daed grunted. "Not to-nacht, then." He craned his neck toward the door. "Josh didn't kum with you?"

"Nein, he left the farmers' market early to go home and help pick berries," Greta told him.

"I thought he said he'd stay with you." Daed grimaced as he settled back in bed.

"No worries, sir." Stan beamed. "I stayed with her. And I'm taking her to dinner, since we're getting home so late."

Daed grunted again, and the worry Greta had seen in his eyes too much lately reappeared.

Josh peered out the Millers' kitchen window while Gizelle assembled ingredients, the open recipe box on the counter behind her. Where was Greta? Stan should've brought her home hours ago. His mother had driven Martha and William to go the hospital to see Andy.

Gizelle started getting out bowls and spoons. A crank-style hand mixer. "Do you know what Greta sells out of the fastest?" she asked him. "Seems she ought to make more of whatever that is." She carried the bottle of vanilla and the can of baking powder to the table. "Can you get the flour and sugar?" She pointed to the twenty-pound bags she and her mamm had brought home from the store.

Josh dutifully hefted them up on the kitchen table. "Greta didn't call and leave a message, did she?"

"I haven't gone to the phone shanty to check." Gizelle collected some more ingredients. "What did you say sold the best?"

"Cookies. Definitely cookies. But bread, cinnamon rolls, and pies sell well, too. She's usually out of all her baked goods before noon." He paused, thinking. "Should I check the shanty? Or I could just call Stan on his cell phone."

Gizelle rolled her eyes. "Whatever would make you feel better. If you get ahold of Stan, tell him I could use Greta's help with the baking. As long as she promises not to burn anything to-nacht." She released a heavy sigh. "What's the most popular cookie? Chocolate chip?"

Josh nodded. "As long as there aren't any nuts in them. Oatmeal cookies without raisins are a close second." He turned toward the door. "I'll let you know if I reach them."

He went down the porch steps and glanced toward the barn. Should he take Sea Grass? The bishop might frown on him riding it without a buggy. If he saw.

He'd take that chance. The faster he could get to a phone.... *Lord, let Stan answer.*

Josh led Sea Grass out of the barn, swung himself up on his back—sans saddle—and nudged him into a gallop down the driveway. As they neared the end, Josh saw headlights approaching. He slowed Sea Grass to a stop, his heart pounding. The van pulled up alongside him.

Stan rolled down the window. "I thought you were helping with the baking this evening."

Josh glared at him. "I thought you were bringing her home right after work."

Stan smirked. "We went out for supper. And then I treated her to ice cream and we took a walk through the park."

Greta seemed to shrink in the passenger seat.

A date? Stan took her on a date? Josh's hand formed a fist. He pressed it against the horse's neck to keep from planting it in Stan's face. Though part of him was just as angry with Greta. Why had she gone along with Stan when she had so much work to do at home?

"We'll meet you at the house, if you're staying." Stan rolled the window up and continued toward the haus.

Josh remained where he was, listening to the car tires crush gravel as they rolled away. Crushing his heart. It wasn't unheard of for Amish girls to fall in love with Englisch buwe, but somehow....

He spun Sea Grass around and hastened her back to the barn. Greta was too smart for the likes of Stan. And her demeanor when Stan was boasting about their date might've indicated that she'd been bullied into staying out with him.

After stabling Sea Grass, Josh strode into the Millers' kitchen.

"You need to make pretzels," Stan was saying. "I can make some great ones. Basic pizza dough, with sea salt, and...." He scanned the array of ingredients on the table. "You have everything I'd need. I'll do a double batch. You'll love them, and I bet they'll sell well. They're best straight out of the oven—'in all their warm, buttery goodness,' as my mom says—but they're still good the next day."

"I never thought to make pretzels." Greta glanced at Josh. "A hidden talent, ain't so? Do you have one, too, Josh?"

He startled, staring at her a moment. *Not in baking, but....* He allowed his gaze to lower to her lips. "I might."

Greta controlled a shiver and turned her back to Josh as she sorted through the recipes Gizelle had set out. At the other end of the table, her sister stirred milk chocolate chips into cookie batter. Stan ripped open a packet of yeast.

She could feel Josh's gaze on her as she picked up the recipe for oatmeal cookies. After a few moments' hesitation, she selected the card for peanut butter cookies, too, then turned to face him. She held out the card. "Here. Make yourself useful."

Josh hesitated a moment before taking the recipe.

She admired his bravery. Like most Amish men, he was likely uncomfortable in the kitchen. That was a woman's place. But he could read. And if he paid attention to what he was doing, he'd find that baking wasn't hard.

Or maybe it was. Hadn't she burned the cinnamon rolls that very morgen? She frowned. "If you need help, just ask."

Josh's gaze shifted to Stan, then returned to Greta. "I got this, liebling."

He had his pride, too. Greta nodded as he studied the recipe. She preferred Josh's way of calling her "liebling" over Stan's more abrasive "babe."

"Can't be that hard," he muttered. "But maybe you could stay nearby. One half cup peanut butter and one half cup butter, softened…."

Greta nudged the dry measuring cup and the glass jar of butter toward him.

He grinned.

Her heart flipped.

"Are you staying here to-nacht?" she whispered. "In the barn?"

"Jah. I think I let William down when I didn't. He took it as a personal betrayal, as if Gott Himself abandoned him." Shadows filled Josh's eyes. "I…." He hesitated, his gaze searching Greta's.

She knew, without being able to see her own expression, what Josh saw there. Knew by the sadness that turned his lips down and furrowed his brow. The belief that Gott *had* abandoned them. Their whole family.

"'*The Lord, he it is that doth go before thee; he will be with thee, he will not fail thee, neither forsake thee: fear not, neither be dismayed.*' Deuteronomy thirty-one, verse eight. And again, in Hebrews thirteen, verse five, it says, '*Let your conversation be without covetousness; and be content with such things as ye have: for he hath said, I will never leave thee, nor forsake thee.*'"

She glanced at him. The old Josh never quoted Scripture.

His words stirred something inside of her. She *wanted* to believe that Gott had her in His hands. Had them. Had *this*. Her very being cried for it. Longed for it.

Tears burned her eyes.

If only....

But Daed still lay in the hospital, unable to work, needing not one but two surgeries. Her family was buried under a mountain of debt. She didn't see as much as a drizzle of blessings, let alone a shower.

Nein. Gott *had* abandoned her and her family.

Greta hardened her heart and turned away from Josh. Away from the hope that his words had attempted to instill in her. And focused on trying to measure ingredients accurately through the sheen of tears blurring her vision.

Josh's finger grazed across her neck. Fire followed in its wake. Her stomach flipped in response. He leaned nearer, his breath tickling her ear, as he whispered, "Be still and know that He is Gott, liebling. He is able."

Chapter 14

Josh ached to take this burden from Greta. To restore her trust in Gott. He would have willingly handed over the money he'd saved for his future—*their* future—but it would be a mere drop in the bucket. And, on the tiny chance she accepted it, she might put her faith in *him,* a mere man, instead of the all-powerful Gott of the universe.

He bowed his head. *Gott....*

Wait.

A still, small voice calmed Josh. He could wait. Wait on the Gott who had this. Somehow.

A vehicle turned into the lane. Josh peered out the window. A white van similar to Stan's came to a stop at the bottom of the porch steps. He watched as the back passenger door slid open, and Martha and William climbed out.

Just then the wind-up timer buzzed, alerting them that it was time to check the final batch of cookies.

Josh slid the last bite of fresh-baked soft pretzel into his mouth and wiped his hands on a napkin. "You didn't exaggerate, Stan—the pretzels are wunderbaar." His mamm never made pretzels. Maybe he could buy the whole batch of buttery-salty goodness to take home for his family to enjoy. Or maybe he'd wait until Greta made some, since the gleam in her eyes indicated she wanted to.

"They really are," Gizelle agreed. "Mamm and William will want to taste them, for sure."

Greta started carrying the dirty dishes over to the sink. She set them on the counter, put the dishpans in, and ran some water.

"I can't wait to sample the cookies." Stan rubbed his stomach. His gaze shifted toward the window. "Guess I'll have to wait. Looks like my mom is here. I should probably go. See you tomorrow."

He headed toward the door as Josh glanced outside. Martha dug in her purse for money since the driver would need to be paid. Gut thing he'd paid Stan in advance for this week's trips. But he should compensate him for his help.

Josh cleared his throat. "Hey, Stan? Can I offer you something for manning my booth today?" He reached for his wallet.

Stan shook his head. "Nah. Gave me something to do other than get into trouble. Besides, I'm getting paid for driving you."

"Maybe a little something?"

"Honestly, no. But thanks." Stan stepped outside.

Josh followed him. "Really appreciate it. More than I can say."

Stan nodded. "Yeah. If she were my girl, I would, too."

Josh let out a breath. Boundaries had been established and settled. That was a blessing. "Danki, again." He went back inside.

Greta had started the dishwater going in the sink, so Josh began collecting the dirty bowls, measuring cups, and utensils. He might not be adept at women's work, but he would do as much as he could.

"Ach, Josh-u-a?" Gizelle used the flirty, singsongy voice again. "The sandwich baggies are out of reach. Would you mind getting them down for me?"

As he handed them to Gizelle, he noticed Greta studying his bare arms. He'd rolled up his shirtsleeves before the baking marathon had begun. When her gaze rose to his, he grinned. Her cheeks flamed red.

"I'd like a sample of cookies, too." Josh glanced at Gizelle. "But I'll buy them and take them home in the morgen." He laid some cash on the kitchen table. "Six of each, please." Mamm would pretend to scold him, reminding him that she knew how to bake. But she would understand that he was trying to support Greta's family.

As both vans roared out of the driveway, Martha stepped into the kitchen. "It smells wunderbaar in here. But, Greta, I wish you hadn't...." She hesitated, her gaze going from Greta to Gizelle to Josh. "I guess you had plenty of help. We'll talk about this later." She took off her black bonnet and hung it on a peg by the door.

"Is William starting the chores? I'll get my shoes on and go help." Josh carried the last dirty dish over to the sink, then leaned close to Greta's ear and whispered, "If you bring my cookies out to the barn later, I can show you one of my hidden talents. Here's a hint: It isn't pretzel baking."

She lifted her head and she stared at him, her lips parting. Something indiscernible flickered in the depths of her green eyes.

Josh winked, then turned away, trying to slow his galloping heart.

He couldn't wait until his chores were done.

While Greta finished cleaning the kitchen, Mamm sent Gizelle outside to take down the laundry, then poured herself a glass of iced tea and sat in a chair with a soft sigh. "Greta. Turn and look at me, please."

Greta gave the counter a final swipe, then hung the rag up to dry and firmed her jaw as she faced her mamm—and whatever she was about to be scolded over. It undoubtedly had to do with one of four things: baking on Sunday. Burning food. Stan. Or Josh. Maybe a combination of all four.

She pulled in a breath and lowered her head slightly, trying to put herself in a spirit of submission. It wouldn't do to talk back to Mamm.

Mamm sighed again. "Your daed said Stan took you on a date—"

"It wasn't a date." Greta felt her back stiffen. "It was just late, after five, so it was an innocent gesture to get something to eat. Really." The ice cream and evening stroll might have been a bit excessive, but Stan had argued that it was a nice way to unwind after a hot day of hard work, reminding her that her baking endeavors would go better if she wasn't so stressed. Which was true. All true. It hadn't bothered her until she'd gotten home and saw the look on Josh's face.

Mamm's hand shot up. "Don't you interrupt me, Dochter. Stan is acceptable in your life as a driver. But not as a romantic interest. And I certainly didn't appreciate his coming into our haus and making himself at home in our kitchen. He crossed some serious lines there."

"But…he's just a friend. And he offered to help. I thought it'd be okay, since Gizelle and Josh were here, too. Besides, Stan stayed at the farmers' market to manage Josh's table after he left, and to keep an eye on me. And—"

"Are you talking back to me?" Mamm rose to her feet, scowling.

"Nein. Sorry." Greta clamped her mouth shut and looked away.

"Furthermore, Gizelle says that you have been openly flirting with Josh. Don't you know what young men think when girls go outside in their nacht-gown? And for someone who said she'd never talk to him again after he shamed her years ago, you certainly spend enough time chasing him. Did you actually get paid for going over to Esther's? Or was it all a sham to spend the day with Josh?"

Greta nearly choked as she sputtered. "I…I put the money in the jar, Mamm." Chasing Josh? Really? And who was Gizelle to talk? Calling him "Josh-u-a" in a tone Greta had never used? Tears burned her eyes. "I thought you encouraged me to forgive him."

Forgive and forget. Ever since Josh had walked in during the singing on his first weekend back, almost a year ago, that refrain had played over and over. And not just from Mamm, but also the community at large. Guess that went only so far.

"Forgive him, jah. Fall all over him, nein. Even Bishop Joe has complained about your wanton behavior."

Just one time. When the wind had blown her hair out of control.

Josh had "invited" her out to the barn later that nacht. How could she go now, after the talk with Mamm? It was probably wiser not to, anyway.

Lust. Not love.

But how had Mamm found out that Greta had gone outside in her nacht-gown? She'd worn a robe over it. Tied shut. Had Gizelle been merely pretending to sleep?

It wasn't fair. She restrained the temptation to stomp her foot like an impetuous child.

But just barely.

"I'm disappointed in you, Greta. Even more, I'm concerned that your behavior will cause the bishop to refuse to help us."

She scuffed her feet and blinked away her tears. "Sorry, Mamm. I'm…I'll practice more self-restraint." Was that response submissive enough? If Mamm could read her thoughts, definitely not. She swallowed the rest of her pride. "Josh bought some cookies. He…he asked me to bring them out to the barn later so he could take them home in the morgen."

Mamm picked up her glass and took a sip, keeping her eyes firmly fixed on Greta. "Gizelle can do it."

Greta nodded.

"Josh left the Amish once. Who's to say he won't leave again? Until he joins the church, he's unsuitable. Furthermore, I heard he's been involved in a lot of verboden activities. Despite what your daed says, you stay away from him. Do you understand?"

So, it was fine to accept Josh as a helper on the farm, but not okay to accept him as a friend?

"Gizelle will deliver the cookies," Mamm repeated, as if she doubted Greta's ability to obey. "You go on up to your room, get ready for bed, and think about your behavior."

Greta swallowed a slew of words she wanted to say. "Gut nacht, Mamm." She tried to say it as politely as possible.

Mamm didn't answer.

As Greta made for the stairs, she heard the kitchen door open and close. "I got the laundry, Mamm," Gizelle announced cheerily.

"Danki, Gizelle. You're such a gut girl." There was a smile in Mamm's voice.

Greta's tears ran down her cheeks and dripped off her chin as she stumbled up the rest of the stairs and threw herself across the bed.

"Ach, Josh-u-a? Special delivery. I have your cookies."

Why had Greta sent Gizelle? Josh cringed as he closed his laptop. He was tempted to extinguish the lantern and skitter farther back into the dark recesses of the barn.

Instead, he mustered his courage and made his way out of the empty stable where he'd been writing.

Gizelle beamed as she handed him the large plastic bag.

"Danki." He accepted the cookies. "Where's Greta?"

"Ach, she went to bed. Wasn't feeling well."

So much for spending some time with her. Josh swallowed his disappointment as he opened the lid of his cooler, where the cookies would be safe from rodents, and dropped the large plastic bag inside.

Behind him, he heard the sound of scuffing feet. Why was Gizelle following him? Tamping down his discomfort, he turned to face her. "Danki, again. Tell Greta I'll pray she feels better tomorrow."

Gizelle came closer. "Want to go for a walk? The moon and stars are so nice and bright to-nacht."

He'd looked forward to kissing Greta in the moonlight.

The Bible story of Joseph and Potiphar's wife came to mind as Josh took a step back. "Nein, not to-nacht, Gizelle, but danki for asking. I'm rather tired, and I'm sure you are, too. You'll be at the store again tomorrow, ain't so?"

"Jah, but...." She fluttered her eyelashes.

He didn't intend to get caught in a compromising position with Gizelle. Not now. Not ever. When a shadow crossed in front of the barn doors, Josh's nerves went into overdrive. Was it William? Martha? Didn't matter. This encounter was over.

"Go on to bed, Gizelle. I'll see you in the morgen." Maybe. Unless he finished his portion of the chores and left for home before she came out to feed the chickens.

Huffing, she turned around and stalked out. Josh watched her go, then lifted his gaze through the open door to the haus. The window of the room Greta shared with Gizelle was lit.

Josh doubted she was really sick. She'd been fine earlier. Unless something she'd eaten at the restaurant with Stan had disagreed with her stomach.

Once Gizelle had gone inside, he strode out into the dark yard and collected a handful of pebbles, then positioned himself beneath Greta's window and started tossing them, one after another, hoping to catch her attention before Gizelle reached the bedroom.

After almost a minute, Greta finally appeared. Her glorious hair flowed loosely around her shoulders. Her head was uncovered. His stomach did a triple somersault. As she leaned out the window, Josh turned on his penlight, briefly illuminating his face before flipping it off again. "Can you kum out?" he whispered loudly.

"Nein. I'm grounded for chasing someone Gizelle apparently wants."

Josh took a moment to process her statement, then looked up at her again. "I have nein interest in Gizelle. But she told me you were sick, and I wanted to know—"

"Wait there." Greta disappeared from the window. A few seconds later, the light was extinguished. In the light of the moon, he could see her slide the window open a little wider, crawl out onto the porch roof, and close the window almost all the way behind her before creeping closer to the edge. "Ready or not...." There was a note in her voice he'd never heard before.

"Wait a minute. How're you going to get back in?"

Too late. She'd already jumped. She landed on her feet, and Josh reached out to steady her. Then he held her at arm's length, his gaze capturing hers.

His heart pounded.

She pulled away. "Kum on." She took off into the darkness, as they'd done many a time when they were courting. Except that, back then, it was always for a quiet, uneventful stroll down the drive. They'd never even held hands.

Now, the idea tempted him. That...and more.

Greta shifted directions and hurried to the barn...past the barn...toward the woods. Where was she going?

It didn't matter.

He hurried after her as she started down a trail he never would've noticed in the darkness, through the trees to a small clearing at the edge of a creek, where a chorus of crickets and bullfrogs sang. She stopped and turned around to face him. "So, tell me about your hidden talents."

A thrill shot through him. He reached for her, pulling her tightly into his arms. Crushing her against him. "Ach, liebling." Did she hear the tremor in his voice?

She stiffened for a second, and then, with a soft sigh, she snuggled against his chest.

That contented him. For about three seconds. He lifted her chin with his finger. Cupped her face with his hands. And brushed his lips over hers.

Too sweet. Too short. He went back for a second pass, lingering. Her response was tentative at first, then becoming more certain, more passionate. His kisses deepened, and she responded in kind. He worked his fingers through her unbound hair. *Ach, heaven.* His knees went weak. Her hands crept up his chest and traveled over his shoulders as she moved closer, her softness pressed against him.

Kissing her was every bit as wunderbaar as he'd imagined it would be.

And every bit as dangerous. He fought for control.

Her arms tightened around him. Her lips reclaimed his, a hunger in them. A hunger that consumed him, too.

A hunger that would devour them, if he allowed it to.

Chapter 15

Greta wriggled closer to Josh, and his arms tightened around her in response. Their kisses deepened. Who knew kissing would be like this? So wunderbaar. So fantastically wunderbaar. Her toes curled, and her arms left his shoulders to explore their way down his back.

A groan escaped him, and he wrenched away, burying his face in her neck, his fingers in her hair. His breathing was harsh. Ragged. Out of control.

She fought for air, too, even though she didn't want to quit. "Josh…." She trailed kisses down the side of his face, wherever her lips could reach.

"Nein, Greta. Nein." He pulled back a little, then hugged her close, but the hold was different. Less passionate. She trembled in his arms.

"I shouldn't have done that. I'm sorry. So sorry." There was a sob in his voice. A brokenness that scared her.

Filled with regret and guilt for acting this way, after the sinful thoughts he'd confessed just yesterday, she yanked herself completely free of his grasp. "I'm the one who's sorry, Josh. I shouldn't have teased you. Lust, you said…."

Lust. Not love.

She wanted both.

Josh stilled for a moment, then shook his head. He raised a trembling hand to her face and trailed his forefinger down her cheek. "Nein, not lust."

"But you said…on Viktor's porch…." It was hard to compose her thoughts.

"I know what I said, liebling. It was wrong. I was wrong. I do want you. Physically—ach, jah. Definitely. But there are other emotions involved, too."

But he didn't specify what those might be. Instead, he shuddered. And his hand fell away.

His comment left her hoping that it might be something…love, for instance. But maybe it was too soon to say that.

She swallowed. "I stuffed some pillows under my bedsheets." Indicating she could stay out longer, if he wanted her to. She wasn't in any hurry to go back, anyway. Not after being scolded for nein gut reason.

Her life was tattered. Torn. Falling apart. And the only thing that made any sense to her at all right now was being in Josh's arms. She felt safe there.

Strange, since he was Josh—the one who'd hurt her with his sudden departure. The one who'd ripped her dreams to shreds when he'd walked out.

Stranger still, since Josh's embrace was probably the least safe place she could be.

He reached for her again. But instead of pulling her close, he wrapped his fingers around her hand. "Then we can talk awhile?"

She nodded. "I won't be able to sneak in until later, anyway, once everyone else is asleep. And if they see me like this…." She tossed her hair, trying—against the dictates of prudence—to entice him to kiss her again. Right now, that was the only effective distraction from her troubles.

"You're so beautiful." Josh's voice was husky. With his free hand, he touched her hair. Combed through it with his fingers.

"There's…there's a log over there by the creek, where we could sit." William's usual fishing spot. "Or, farther upstream, there's a little waterfall, and…a boulder." She liked to dangle her feet over the edge.

Though maybe her favorite spot wouldn't be a gut idea, if Josh ended up explaining his apology for kissing her. She'd wanted him to. It had been every bit as wunderbaar as her seventeen-year-old self had imagined.

So wunderbaar, it would be worth getting into trouble over, if she was caught.

Definitely worth it.

She tugged him in the direction of the boulder.

Josh's heart insisted his feet follow Greta, even as his brain objected. Not a gut idea. Not at all. The waterfall cascaded over the rocks, showering the boulder with a gentle spray that felt refreshing in the summer heat. The boulder was slippery, covered in soft moss that squished beneath the soles of his tennis shoes.

"The water's not too deep," Greta said. "Only up to my chest, in the deepest part. Sometimes—well, last year, when I had more free time—I'd get in. I always dreamed of a cabin out here, overlooking the falls. Isn't that silly? Not exactly suitable land for an Amish farm."

Nein, it wasn't. But it would be an ideal romantic hideaway.

She released his hand and sat on the boulder, dangling her legs over the edge. A second later, to his surprise, she slid off into the creek. She laughed and looked up at him. "Join me?"

Who was this Greta? Not the prim, proper Amish girl he'd grown up with.

Or maybe this was the only place she felt free to be herself. To be real. To find freedom from forced muteness about the things she couldn't control or didn't like but was forced to accept or conform to.

The woods had a way of doing that.

It was in the forests along the Appalachian Trail that he'd found true freedom from guilt. He needed to talk to her about that, as well.

He sat down and slipped off his shoes and socks, along with his reservations. Then he slid into the water. Cool, not cold. As if it was fed by a hot spring but cooled when it surfaced.

"So...what did you want to talk about?" She cupped water in her hands and let it seep through her fingers.

Her. Gott. Them. But his voice lodged in his throat.

"Tongue-tied? I have a few questions, then. Why'd you say you were sorry after you kissed me? And how did you perfect that hidden talent?" There was a mix of emotions in her voice. As if she were half serious, half flirting.

She had nein idea of the dangerous ground she trod.

Being alone in the dark woods with her—the woman he loved—was a bad idea.

She dipped lower in the water, soaking her dress.

Especially since she seemed to lose all inhibition out here.

She straightened, the dress clinging to her curves. He couldn't help but look.

"I'm sorry...." His throat hurt. But it had to be said. "I'm sorry for being unfaithful while I was gone. That would explain the hidden talent." He looked away. Hopefully, he hadn't ruined his chances of a future with her.

She stilled, and the entire forest seemed to fall absolutely, positively silent. Not even a ripple of water. The animals and insects ceased their tune. Heaviness descended over them, robbing the setting of the peacefulness. Of the romance.

Had he lost all rights to future kisses from Greta? Were the few precious ones from minutes ago be all he'd ever get? His heart threatened to break. *Gott, give me strength....*

"I'm sorry," he whispered again.

Greta nearly felt sick. Never had she considered that Josh, her Josh…. But, really, she should've expected it. "I guess your behavior couldn't be considered unfaithful, since we had broken up." Her voice caught. Hopefully, he hadn't noticed. She stared off into the darkness. "So, let's get this straight. You wouldn't go into a closet with me to steal a kiss at a frolic, but you would sleep with other women?"

"Ach, Greta. You had my love. My respect. My awareness of how unworthy I was of you. And they had…none of the above. Plus, I was drunk. And stupid. If I had to do it over, I never would've touched that first beer. I never would've done a lot of things." His voice was hoarse.

She'd had his love and respect. Past tense. Not anymore?

"I'm not trying to make excuses, liebling. I was wrong. I didn't deserve you. I knew that. And after an entire family died because of some fireworks I'd bought…I had to get away. I needed to forget. To escape. You were the only reason I stayed as long as I did, but I wasn't gut enough for you."

She recalled the anger on his face the nacht he'd left. For the first time, she realized it had been directed at himself. How would she react if she'd been partly responsible for the death of someone she loved?

Sympathy washed over her. She moved closer to him, intending to offer comfort. He sat on a boulder in a shallower part of the water. She lowered herself beside him and wrapped her arm around his shoulder.

He leaned into her. "I couldn't escape, liebling. There was nein escape from the guilt. But…but I've been to the depths. And Gott found me there."

Greta had nothing to say to that. She could identify with the experience of reaching the depths, but she couldn't fathom

Gott caring enough to find her there. Especially since it was His actions—or the lack thereof—that had put her there in the first place.

"And you know what, liebling?" His breath warmed her neck. "Gott loves me. He forgave me. He brought me home. And I hope, maybe, you'll forgive me, too. I'm so very sorry."

She was ever so glad Josh had kum home, whatever the reason. But she didn't want to talk about Gott. He had abandoned her. Not vice versa.

"I forgive you." Did she? It still hurt. But maybe, if she said it often enough, she would kum to believe it, and then it'd be true. "I forgive you," she said again. It came out a little easier that time.

"Danki, Greta." Josh shifted, putting an arm around her. He slid his other arm under her legs and lifted her up, settling her on his lap. She trembled as his mouth found the tender skin of her neck. As the roughness of his stubble scratched her cheek.

She whimpered as Josh pulled her closer, his lips exploring her neck, her ear, and her jaw before claiming her mouth with a passion that reignited the fire deep inside her.

"We." Kiss. "Need." Another longer kiss. "To get you." A third. Longer. Deeper. "Home." Quick. Hard. "Now."

She moaned her objection. She didn't want to go home. She wanted to stay in his arms forever.

Somehow, he untangled himself from her, set her on her feet, and climbed out of the water.

It was a wonder her legs even supported her. She fought for air.

Josh bent to put his socks and shoes back on, then reached for her hand. "Kum on. Everyone should be in bed by now. If not, we'll...go for a walk down the road." He fell quiet for a moment. "Will you consider letting me kum courting?"

"Jah," she answered without hesitation. "But we need to keep it quiet. Secret. After dark, so Mamm and Gizelle won't know."

"Danki."

"I meant to tell you how much I like that one birdhouse you made. The cream-colored one with the white picket fence. It's so pretty."

"I made that for you." His voice caught. "Years ago. You talked about your dream haus…I wanted to remember. To promise to try to supply the haus for you. But it's not for sale. There's a tag on it that says so. It's a sample for custom orders. I couldn't bear to sell what was yours."

How romantic that he'd remembered. He'd loved her enough to build it for her.

He looked away. "Then I kind of gave up on you…on us. It's yours, Greta. Yours, along with all the original promises."

"Danki." Joy filled her. A gift for their future—from Josh.

They emerged from the woods. The haus was dark.

"I'll see you tomorrow nacht, liebling." His hands moved to her waist, and he tugged her near. Bent his head.

She rose up on tiptoe, creek water dripping from her dress onto her bare feet, and wrapped her arms around his neck.

Out of the corner of her eye, she saw something move in the darkness.

A figure emerged from the shadows of the porch.

Mamm.

Chapter 16

Josh glanced up as Greta jerked out of his arms. "What…?" Then his gaze lit on Martha, standing there with her arms crossed. Glaring at him, the way Mamm did when he forgot to shut the gate, and all the cows got loose in the middle of the nacht. His heart stopped for a moment, and he caught his breath.

Busted. Greta had said she was grounded. A surge of panic hit him. Would she continue to be welkum at this haus and in the community? The bishop's harsh accusations the evening they'd ridden home in Stan's convertible replayed in his mind.

But, nein. Martha wouldn't send Greta away. She couldn't afford to. The family depended on Greta's financial contributions. But they could still make her life miserable within the walls of her home.

Martha pointed a shaking finger at Greta. "You. Go. To. Your. Room. I don't even want to see you long enough to scold you."

Greta cringed but didn't move. "Mamm…." She glanced briefly at Josh before looking back at Martha. Her breaths came in rapid succession.

Maybe he should nudge her toward the haus…and obedience. Except that any additional physical contact would only remind Martha of what she'd just caught them doing and probably anger her the more. Josh nodded at Greta, hoping to silently communicate that she should go inside and leave him to take care of things out there. Though he didn't have a clue how he would do that.

"Go!" Martha snapped.

Greta stiffened, then nodded, lowered her head, and started for the haus. In the doorway, he could see the outline of her slumped shoulders silhouetted by the dim light inside.

Josh glanced at Martha, her angry gaze still directed toward Greta's retreat. He began to back away. Maybe he could escape while she was distracted, and avoid the verbal reaming he was certain he'd likely get.

He deserved it, being just as guilty as Greta. He forced himself to stay put. Besides, he'd tried to assure Greta that he'd handle it.

Martha pivoted on her heel and marched toward him. "Didn't my dochter tell you she was grounded? Or have you nein respect for parental authority?"

He averted his gaze, looking toward the barn, hoping for an emergency that would require his attention. Loose cows, for instance. "She did," he finally said, still avoiding Martha's eyes. "I'm sorry. I didn't mean to cause problems."

Weak apology. He hated being reduced to sniveling like a bu. It sickened him. So, he straightened his shoulders, determined to act like the man Gott had redeemed him to be.

"Did she tell you *why* she was grounded?" Martha came closer, studying him closely.

"Uh." Josh hesitated. He glanced up at the dark window of Greta's bedroom, then looked back at Martha. "Something to do with chasing someone Gizelle apparently wants." He pulled in a breath for courage to speak the truth. To defend Greta from this injustice. "If that means what I think it does, then you need to know I have nein interest in Gizelle. I'm in love with Greta. Always have been. Always will be. Even though my actions three years ago would suggest otherwise. And I intend to talk to Andy about it." As soon as Andy was feeling better. And when Josh was sure of Greta's heart. They still needed to talk things through. And he wanted to see her faith in Gott restored.

"Gizelle says you are courting her."

He nodded slowly, confused. "That's my intent." Wait. Gizelle had claimed he was courting *her*? Not Greta? Josh swallowed. "To court Greta, that is," he clarified. "Not Gizelle."

"Gizelle says that she was with you in the barn the nacht of Andy's heart attack."

Josh shook his head. "I was alone in the barn." Typing his recollection of the painful memories he would rather forget than have printed in a book for the world to read, except for the possibility of inspiring even one person to find hope and redemption through a relationship with Gott.

Martha gave an unladylike snort.

She didn't believe him? Anger flared. "Think about it. If Gizelle had been with me, she would've been around for all the to-do, ain't so? Instead, she was off somewhere. And William and I spent hours searching for her."

After a long hesitation, Martha's stance softened a little. "She says Greta is trying to steal you away." There was a smidgen of doubt in her voice. Was she rethinking her decision to believe Gizelle?

"Can't be done." Josh shook his head. "My heart belongs to Greta."

Another long pause. "Why did you encourage her to disobey me?" Martha's voice held a remnant of harshness, even if the bluster had gone out of it.

He hadn't encouraged her disobedience. At least, he hadn't intended to. But.... His stomach clenched as he recalled their kisses. He supposed he could have tried harder to resist the temptation, not that he hadn't enjoyed the result.

"Well?" Martha took to tapping her foot.

"Uh...." He didn't want to get Greta in trouble by telling the truth. But not telling the truth meant lying. Unacceptable. "Gizelle told me Greta was sick. I was checking on her. I didn't ask or expect her to crawl out the window." Or to jump off the roof. "I didn't mean to show any disrespect to you."

"You may go. Home. You had gut intentions in staying here at the barn, and your presence was a blessing the nacht of Andy's heart attack. But it seems you are too much of a temptation for both my dochters."

"But William—"

"I'll explain everything to him."

Hopefully, he wouldn't see this as Josh abandoning him. Again. "Is it okay if I kum by in the morgen to help him?"

Martha nodded. Turned away. Then hesitated and glanced over her shoulder. "Josh, you wouldn't happen to know anything about the two big boxes of food I found on my porch when I left for the hospital today, would you?"

"Nein. I sure don't." Josh fought off the urge to smile. Mamm had said she planned to bring some food by, but it easily could've been someone else. Any number of people had seen the empty cupboards on Saturday nacht. In fact, he suspected the food deliveries would continue until the "culprits" were caught.

He hoped that wouldn't be for a long time.

At least, not until Andy got back on his feet.

Martha frowned. "I guess I can't turn it down if I don't know who brought it. If you happen to find out, please let me know. And convey my thanks."

"I doubt I'll hear much of anything. The Bible says not to let your right hand know what your left hand is doing. Nobody is going to brag about leaving food on your porch."

Martha tugged at her kapp string. "You're right, of course." She sighed. "I still have problems with you courting my dochter, Josh."

He nodded. "I'm sure you do. I jumped the fence. But I also returned, Martha, and I'm going to attend the baptism classes when they start up." Of course, he hadn't reached a decision on whether he would be joining the church. But Preacher Samuel and David Lapp had urged both Josh and Viktor to take that step. And it was easier to influence from the inside than from the outside.

"What about these 'verboden' activities I hear you're engaged in?"

Josh shrugged in a show of nonchalance. "You know how people talk."

Greta threw her pillows across the room, attempting to vent some of her frustration. It was a technique she'd read about in a book. But it was completely ineffective. Her pillows were thin to begin with and needed to be restuffed. They didn't even make an impact when they hit the wall but fell listlessly to the floor. Kind of like her emotions.

She sighed. Her pillows wouldn't be restuffed anytime soon. Someone would have to shoot a goose first.

She had nein idea where Gizelle had disappeared to, but she could guess. Waiting to corner Josh in the barn. It was gut to know he had nein interest in Gizelle. But it still hurt that her sister had designs on him.

Greta retrieved another nacht-gown and some clean undergarments from her dresser, then headed to the bathroom to change out of her wet clothes.

It was so unfair for Mamm to judge her like that. What should she have done to keep Stan from coming in and helping her with the baking? Besides, it hadn't seemed wrong at the time. Josh and Gizelle had been there, too. And the Amish were always organizing frolics involving kitchen work. Granted, the buwe weren't usually involved, unless it was a taffy pull. But it wasn't as if Gizelle was five years old. She should be held accountable for her behavior, as well.

And then there was Josh. Was she supposed to stand by and watch Gizelle pursue him just because she thought she wanted him?

Greta unpinned her soaking dress, peeled it off her skin, then wadded it up and threw it as hard as she could into the laundry basket serving as a hamper. After stripping off her undergarments, she stepped into the shower to wash off the creek water, along with any chiggers that might've found their way past the fabric of her clothes.

Not that she wanted to scrub away the memory of Josh's touch. His kisses.

Someone knocked on the door, and then the latch clicked. "Greta?"

Mamm.

Greta couldn't exactly ignore her. "Jah?" At least any conversation would have to be conducted while separated by the blue shower curtain and plastic liner.

Greta picked up the bar of vanilla-scented soap from the batch she'd helped make earlier in the spring. Soap seemed as effective a distraction as any from whatever it was that Mamm had pursued her into the bathroom to talk about. And whatever it was, it couldn't be gut, because Mamm usually respected her privacy. How would soap sell at the farmers' market? They had plenty on hand, and it was easy enough to make more, even if they would have to ask Rachel to order some of the ingredients online due to legal restrictions governing medicinal substances. Seemed that people could concoct illegal drugs out of the oddest things.

Allowing her mind to ramble was a feeble escape mechanism. She set the bar of soap back on the dish with a sigh.

The door clicked closed. Greta dared to peek around the shower curtain.

Mamm leaned back against the sink, her arms crossed over her chest, and stared Greta in the face. "You are to kum straight home after selling at the market today." She paused. "Actually, if you'd like, you can stop at the hospital to visit your daed. I'll be there. We'll ride home together." Her voice was still lined with steel as she added, "Ich liebe dich, Greta. And I am considering giving Josh permission to court you."

Really? "Danki, Mamm." Though it wasn't her decision to make. Greta had already decided. Given herself permission.

She ducked back behind the shower curtain, hoping to hide any signs of defiance on her face. It would make things easier if Mamm knew and approved of their courtship. Nein sneaking around required.

A seemingly endless period of silence followed. Greta stood there, letting the water rinse the soap away, along with her frustration. Why was Mamm lingering? Did she have something else to say? An apology to offer? Not likely. She'd never heard Mamm admit to being wrong.

Maybe she was waiting for Greta to apologize.

For being falsely accused? Not happening.

Finally, the door opened and closed again.

As the steaming-hot shower enveloped her, all she could think about was spending more time with Josh by the waterfall.

She couldn't stop grinning.

The next morgen, Josh awoke with a start. He'd been dreaming of Greta, of their time by the creek—and in it. He blinked, staring into the darkness. What had awakened him?

Seeing movement in the shadows, Josh sat straight up in bed. "Daed?"

"Jah, it's me. You planning on sleeping all day? I told you, we need to get an early start, with the rain coming in to-nacht."

Josh yawned. "Right. Sorry I forgot." He stretched and climbed out of bed. "But I promised to help William with chores at the Millers'."

"That's right." Daed waved his hand. "Go on and help, then kum home and assist here with anything we haven't finished. We'll have breakfast and then get started picking berries. I'll hitch up Sea Grass for you."

"Danki, Daed. I'll hurry." Josh went into the bathroom to splash cold water on his face and to brush his teeth. He eyed the shower with longing—nein time for that right now. He'd take one when he got home in the evening. He'd showered the nacht before, anyway.

Josh entered the kitchen just as Mamm came inside with a basket of eggs. She set them on the table. Josh took his tennis shoes from the plastic tray by the door and pulled them on, watching Mamm out of the corner of his eye. "Martha Miller said she found two boxes of food on the porch yesterday. Was that your doing?"

Mamm shook her head. "I didn't get over there yet. Planned to, but then I got busy with people wanting to buy berries from the stand. I thought I'd include a special treat for Greta, but then I worried it'd make it obvious who'd brought it."

"Might. Especially since I asked to court her again."

Mamm's face brightened. "You did? And she said jah, ain't so?"

Josh chuckled. "Maybe." He bent to tie his shoes. "I'm headed over there now to help William with the morgen chores. Even between the two of us, none of the repair work is getting done. But maybe in the winter." Still months away. "Or on a rainy day, if it's a sheltered job. At least he's out of school now."

"For the summer?"

Josh reached for the doorknob. "For gut. He'll be fourteen before school starts in the fall."

"Offer him a temporary job picking berries. Or maybe he could take over at the farmers' market for Greta, and she can kum pick them."

The thought of picking berries alongside Greta appealed. "I'll offer. But it'll be up to Andy. See you later, Mamm." He opened the door and slipped outside.

Sea Grass had been hitched to the waiting buggy. Josh untied the reins from the post, then climbed in. Wisps of fog curled ahead of them as the horse trotted down the road. The scent of rain in the air was unmistakable.

William entered the barn as Josh arrived. He moved to take care of Sea Grass, but Josh waved him off. "I'll have to leave right away to pick berries, so don't worry about it. How're you doing today?"

William shrugged and muttered something indiscernible. After the events of the previous nacht, Josh figured it was probably wise not to ask.

"My mamm said to offer you a job picking berries. Or, if you'd rather, you could take over at the farmers' market and let Greta pick berries."

"I suppose you'd rather Greta pick," William murmured. "I'll ask Daed." He turned and looked at Josh. "There was another box of food on our porch this morgen. You didn't pass anyone on your way here, did you?"

"Nein." Josh ducked his head to hide a smile. The community had found a way to help. And he could honestly say he had nein idea who was behind either of the two deliveries.

"Tell you what." William glanced out the barn doors. "It's supposed to stay sunny, so I'm going to work around here today. But I will talk to Daed about your job offer when I see him next." He started up a ladder to the loft. "You can milk the cow."

"Okay." Josh opened the door to the lower room where the cow was kept. He stopped in his tracks. Now there were two. Must have been another anonymous gift.

Another much-needed surprise for the Miller family.

Gott, You are so gut.

Josh delivered the milk to the kitchen, wishing he could stay around to watch Martha's reaction when she saw how much extra milk the second cow had produced. Then he drove his buggy back through the muggy morgen mist. He was almost home when a pickup truck pulled to a stop beside him. Fish and Game Commission. "Whoa." He pulled on the reins.

He recognized the wildlife officer who rolled down his window. "Hey, Josh. Some hunters shot a deer out of season. Can you use it?"

Josh almost laughed at the lavish provision of Gott. "I can't, but I can tell you someone who can. Thanks, Brian." He gave him directions to the Millers' farm.

Would Greta think to give credit to Gott for these gifts? They were plain signs that der Herr had *not* abandoned her family. That they were still wrapped in His loving arms, even in the midst of tough trials.

He should've thought to ask how long Greta was grounded for, but he could find out when he returned in the evening.

Now, breakfast and berry-picking waited.

Lord Gott, please watch over Greta at the farmers' market today. She'd be truly alone. Stan had class.

Not that the necessity of Stan's absence really bothered him.

Greta was his girl. *Danki, Lord, for that, too.*

He couldn't keep from smiling.

Chapter 17

When Greta arrived at the farmers' market, it was already crowded. Two women dressed in hospital scrubs mingled among the customers, passing out health brochures. They said they were nursing students doing community service and would be there until they ran out of pamphlets. A few backyard gardeners had produce to sell, but the real farmers had stayed home to finish their chores before the severe storms that were forecasted showed up.

"I'll need to leave soon for class," Stan told her, "but I'll set up the canopy for you and carry the rest of the crates over."

"Thank you." Greta had forgotten she'd be on her own that day.

She fingered the wad of cash in her apron pocket. She'd decided to leave the cash box at home. It was too cumbersome, and she hated opening it in the presence of customers. Stashing her earnings in her pocket was easier and felt safer.

Stan finished setting up the canopy, then turned to Greta. "My mom will pick you up after she takes your mom to the hospital and runs a few errands."

Greta nodded. "I'll be fine," she said, more to convince herself than Stan. He wouldn't worry about her.

Would Josh? Maybe. Especially since he'd been so protective of her lately.

Greta peeked at the birdhouse he'd made for her all those years ago—and had given her "with all the original promises." So sweet. She'd brought it along and had stashed it under her table, to lift her spirits over the course of the day. She planned to keep it beside her bed and save it for her future home with Josh.

The other gifts he'd given her as a teenager, she'd taken to his mamm after he left. She hadn't known what else to do with them. Lizzie had cried and promised to hold on to them until Josh "came to his senses." Did she still have them? Or had she lost hope and gotten rid of them during Josh's three-year absence? It really didn't matter. They were starting over. Fresh.

Even with the extra baked items she and Mamm had made early that morgen, everything sold out by two in the afternoon. She'd brought five bars of soap with her, too, and sold three. Greta rearranged the soap and jars of fruit preserves, but it did little to improve the empty look of her table. It was better when Josh was there, next to her, with his table loaded with wares. People thought they were a couple.

They were a couple. A thrill shot through her.

She smiled as an old man hobbled up to her table, supported by his cane. He flashed her a toothless grin. "You have any apple butter left? I bought some on Monday in another town. Wonderful on that nasty oatmeal I'm forced to eat for breakfast until I get my new teeth from the dentist."

She'd never thought of mixing apple butter in oatmeal. And she'd never considered oatmeal particularly nasty, either. It was wunderbaar with fresh fruit or maple syrup or brown sugar.... Her stomach growled as she thought of the bananas she'd sliced for their oatmeal that very morgen.

She slid a jar of apple butter toward him. "Maybe some jam would help it taste more palatable, too." She picked up a jar of... blueberry. Made with fruit from Josh's berry farm. Lizzie had brought a bunch of berries over last year, right after Daed's accident, saying they were seconds and wouldn't sell; and that, if she didn't take them, she would feed them to the hogs. Greta had made them into jam. And pie. And muffins.

Her stomach rumbled louder. The peanut butter sandwich and handful of grapes she'd eaten earlier were already wearing off. She missed Josh and his abundant lunches. Mostly, she just missed Josh.

"Ehhh? What's that?" The man leaned nearer. "I'm a bit deaf in one ear."

"I said, blueberry jam might be good on it, too." She held up the jar.

The man frowned, seeming to consider her suggestion. Then he nodded. He peered at the tiny price tags. "I'll take all your apple butter. I know I like that. And one jar of blueberry jam."

She had four jars of apple butter left. He fished inside his wallet and pulled out a twenty-dollar bill—enough for four jars. Not five.

Josh would have given him a special deal, saying something about how Gott had blessed him.

She sniffed at the memory of that morgen, when she, Mamm, and Gizelle had unpacked the three boxes of food they'd received from anonymous donors. The three of them had exclaimed with delight over such unexpected treats as a jar of honey-roasted peanuts. A bag of yogurt-covered raisins. A canister of chocolate powder to add to milk. Cans of tuna and salmon. More baking supplies. It was like Christmas.

And then, William had run in, shouting that a second cow had appeared in their barn. Where had it kum from? How and when had it been delivered? That couldn't have been so easy.

Was Josh behind it? He didn't have a pickup or a trailer to haul animals. Though she supposed he could've tied it to the back of a buggy and led it there.

Mamm had cried tears of joy when an officer from the Fish and Game Commission had shown up with a deer someone had shot illegally.

Greta slipped the bill into her pocket, then loaded all five jars in a bag and handed it to the man. "Thank you."

He shuffled off, clutching his bag close, as if it contained treasure.

Suddenly, she felt warm breaths on the back of her neck. Something hard pressed against her spine.

And a low, rumbly voice whispered in her ear, "Hand over the cash in your pocket, missy, and no one gets hurt."

Josh hauled the pails of berries up to the barn and unloaded them on the tables they had set up. Mamm and his sister-in-law, Linda, sorted through the fruit, putting the gut ones into quart- and pint-sized cartons, and tossing the not-so-gut ones into another pail. Normally, Mamm would use them in baked goods or jam. But last year, she'd given half to Greta's family.

This year? Maybe the same.

Josh's three-year-old nephew, Johnny, emerged from the interior of the barn and ran up to him, arms outstretched. "I help."

Linda nodded wearily, then glanced at her eighteen-month-old twins playing in the playpen. "Go on. His daed can watch him awhile."

"You help." Josh lifted Johnny into the buggy seat, then climbed in next to him. "Hang on tight."

Josh kept his arm around Johnny as he drove out to where Daed and his brothers worked. He glanced at the sky, noting the sun's location—and the black clouds already making their way in. The verboden radio hidden under his buggy seat had forecasted hail as big as a quarter in size. Strong, damaging winds. And frequent lightning strikes.

Discomfort skittered through him. He glanced at Johnny, who obediently gripped the edge of the seat with both hands, his knuckles white.

Josh focused on the rutted road as his thoughts turned to Greta, on her own at the farmers' market. *Gott, keep her safe....*

Tears ran unhampered down Greta's cheeks as she surveyed her overturned table, the broken jars of jams and jellies, and the crowd that had gathered.

It included a police officer, but he was too late.

Her pocket was too light. Too empty.

Why had she been the one targeted? The other vendors had told the officer that they'd thought nothing of the young man who'd kum up behind her. One said she'd assumed he was a friend of Greta's. She remembered him wearing an unbuttoned shirt over a T-shirt and slouchy jeans.

Nobody else reported evidence of a gun.

Except Greta. Her back still hurt from the pressure.

Her stomach roiled, and she turned away, losing her meager lunch. She would've dropped down to the ground if an Englisch woman hadn't pressed a cold water bottle in her hands and gathered Greta in her arms, whispering words she didn't comprehend.

Meanwhile, other strangers picked up the sticky shards of glass and threw them away. Someone else wiped off the few jars that had survived the fall and packed them in the box with Josh's birdhouse.

"Do you need a ride home, honey?" The Englisch woman's voice penetrated the fog clouding Greta's mind.

Greta's throat hurt as she mumbled something in Pennsylvania-Deitsch.

"I didn't understand a word of that, honey. Take a swallow of water and try again." The woman directed one of the men to load Greta's things in the back of her SUV, then gently led Greta toward the vehicle.

Greta swallowed some water, but it only made her nausea worse.

Yet another hardship Gott had allowed her to suffer. Why? Because He didn't care. If He did, He would have spared her from this trouble.

"Where do you live, sweetie?"

Greta shook her head. "My dad…the hospital…."

"Of course. That's not too far." Less than ten minutes later, the woman pulled to a stop in front of the emergency room entrance. "Do you need me to go in with you?"

Greta shook her head. "Nein—no." She pulled the almost-empty crate out of the backseat and propped it on one hip as she shut the door. "Thank you."

"I'll be thinking of you, sweetie."

Greta adjusted the crate to carry it with both hands. It wasn't half as heavy as it had been that morgen, but it was still unwieldy. Gut thing she'd cut back on jams for today and brought her baked items in big brown grocery sacks. This was the only crate she needed to carry.

And she had nothing to show for her efforts.

The tears dripped off her chin.

She stopped in the restroom and washed her face, trying to compose herself, before stumbling into Daed's hospital room.

Mamm, Preacher Zeke, Onkel Samuel, and Bishop Joe stood around Daed's bed. Every face but Daed's showed a blank stare. He looked at her with a smile, but it quickly faded. "Was ist letz?"

She set the crate on the floor near the end of the bed. "I…I was…robbed." More tears threatened.

"Robbed?" Bishop Joe scoffed. "You are full of lies." He scowled as he peeked inside the crate. "Where did that worthless birdhouse kum from? You probably spent all your earnings on it and decided to lie about it. Besides, I know all about you. When I stopped at your haus on the way here, your sister told me you went out in your nacht-gown with a bu and with your hair loose and uncovered. Such behavior. You can be sure your sins will find you out." He stepped toward her and shook his finger in her face. "You will kneel and confess before the congregation for these sins."

"I wasn't...I'm not...I'm telling the truth." Greta's voice trembled as violently as the rest of her. She turned her empty pockets inside out. "See? Nothing."

"Because you spent it all on a worthless birdhouse." Bishop Joe lifted her beloved birdhouse out of the box and slammed it down on the table overhanging the foot of the bed. It broke into several pieces, shattering. Like her heart. "Worthless piece of junk. Don't make matters worse by lying." He turned to Daed. "Andy, you're suffering these inflictions because your very dochter is filled with the evil one. It's her sins that are heaping trouble upon trouble for you...."

Greta's ears buzzed. She turned to Mamm in desperation but saw only censure on her face. Daed's complexion grayed, and he clutched his shoulder, his gaze on her.

She turned and fled from the room.

"Nein," Onkel Samuel said. "Not true. Greta, wait—"

An alarm started buzzing.

Nurses came running from all directions.

Chapter 18

Drops of rain plopped on Josh's arms as he finished his evening chores at home. After loading half of the not-gut-enough-to-sell berries into the buggy, he headed for Greta's haus. If she was still grounded, they wouldn't be able to spend any time alone together. But maybe she would be baking in the kitchen when he delivered the berries, and he could at least see her. Find out how her day had gone.

He'd spent most of the afternoon filling pails with berries while interceding for Andy and Greta. A heavy burden to pray for them both had descended over him. Even after multiple hours of praying, he still didn't feel any peace. But maybe once he reached the Millers' and found out what had happened—if anything—the elusive peace would finally kum.

William exited the barn as Josh drove in, worry lines etching his forehead. "Ach. I was hoping it was Mamm and Greta."

Alarm flickered, then flared. "They haven't come home yet?" They should've been back hours ago. Before supper. At least, according to the schedule they'd been keeping.

William shook his head. "Do you think I should run to the shanty and call the driver?"

"Maybe," Josh said. "I can make the call, if you like."

"I'll do it." William squared his shoulders. "I'm the man of the haus while Daed's laid up."

"I'll go with you, then, if you don't mind. I need to talk to Preacher Samuel, anyway." That, and Josh didn't want to be left alone with Gizelle.

William brightened. "Onkel Samuel might know where they are. He was going with the bishop and another preacher to visit Daed. They stopped here on the way to see the cow that appeared in our barn this morgen, to try to figure out who might've brought it and how. They also talked with Gizelle a bit."

Josh raised an eyebrow.

"They had nein answer. Onkel Samuel said, 'The provision of der Herr.' Preacher Zeke said we shouldn't look a gift horse in the mouth." He shrugged. "Kum on. We'll take your buggy, since it's hitched and ready to go."

Another fat water droplet splashed on Josh's hand. He looked up just as the rain started falling faster and harder. He noticed the pail of blueberries in the back of the buggy as he climbed in. They should be okay to sit there until he brought William back home.

When they reached Preacher Samuel's, the van was parked in the driveway. Stan's mamm sat in the front seat, talking on her cell phone. On the front porch, Martha Miller clung to Preacher Samuel's Elsie, crying on the shoulder of her sister-in-law. A weight settled on Josh's chest. What had happened? Was Andy worse?

As William went to his mamm, Josh headed for the barn, where Preacher Samuel and David Lapp stood in the doorway, waving him over.

Preacher Samuel's expression was grim. "Andy had another heart attack. Gut thing he was in the hospital. They gave him some nitroglycerin and shooed us all out."

"Ach, nein." Josh murmured. He glanced at the haus. Greta must be inside with her cousin Rachel.

David Lapp reached into his pocket and pulled out a few peppermints—Josh's favorite comfort food. He handed them to him. "You might need these for the rest of the news."

Josh tucked the candies in his pocket. He didn't need to pacify himself with sweets. Instead, he braced himself for whatever he was about to hear next.

Preacher Samuel clamped his hand on Josh's shoulder and stepped around to face him. "Greta ran off a few hours ago, after Bishop Joe admonished her harshly. Worse, he blamed Andy's health problems on her 'sins.'"

Josh gasped for breath, his fists clenching. "We have to find her."

"I know. We spent hours searching for her at the hospital and the surrounding areas. She was already upset when she came in to see your daed. Said someone had robbed her at the farmers' market."

"Nein. Ach, nein." Josh should've been there. And, since that hadn't been possible, he should've told her not to go. But that decision wasn't his to make. Not yet.

"She had a birdhouse with her, and Bishop Joe accused her of spending her earnings to buy it, then covering it up with a lie about being robbed. He slammed it down hard enough that it came apart. I brought the pieces home. I hope you can repair it."

Josh didn't know if this could be repaired. The birdhouse, jah. Greta, maybe not. Rage at the bishop mixed with the panic clutching his chest. Greta was out there somewhere, devastated, confused, and alone.

"Where is Bishop Joe?" he demanded. He had some words for him.

"Home. He was the one who called off the search, two hours before we actually agreed to stop looking. And he's declared her shunned until she repents. Preacher Zeke is still in town, searching."

Josh dug his fingernails into his palms as he took a step backward, dislodging Preacher Samuel's hand from his shoulder. He clenched his jaw. When he got to Bishop Joe's....

"Josh, nein. Don't." Preacher Samuel grabbed Josh's upper arm with an iron grip. "Wait. Just wait. David and I have been discussing what to do. Look for Greta, jah. A given. We're leaving as soon as we get Martha home. But we need wisdom from der Herr in dealing with Bishop Joe, and I don't have clear direction yet. Losing our tempers is not the answer, though."

Something needed to be said. Something needed to be done. This had gone on long enough. The man was out of line, even if he was a bishop "ordained by der Herr." He'd changed so much in the past year, and not for the better.

"Let's go." Josh had to find her. She could stay with his family if she didn't want to go home.

"We're not doing anything without praying." David grasped Josh's other shoulder.

"Out loud." Preacher Samuel bowed his head. "Heavenly Father...."

Greta huddled on a bench in the city park, the rain soaking through her dress and running down her face. What did it matter? She was an outcast from her community. From her own family. Maybe not shunned yet, but run off by the bishop. Condemned by Mamm.

What was the next step? She couldn't go home. But what other option did she have? She had nein money. Probably didn't have a daed anymore. She hadn't stuck around long enough to find out what had happened, but when she'd returned to his hospital room to apologize for upsetting him, the bed was empty. Freshly made. Nein sign that Daed had even been there.

She'd been afraid to ask the nurses. What if he'd died? Would his blood be on her hands?

Tears blurred her eyes again. She buried her face in her hands and started sobbing afresh. *Ach, Daed....* He would never hug her again. Never hold her kinner.

"Sweetie? Are you okay?"

The bench creaked as a woman sat on the other end. Englisch. The one who'd given her a ride from the farmers' market.

"Is your mom still at the hospital?"

Greta shook her head.

The woman slid a tiny bit closer. "Do you need a ride home?"

She shook her head again. She would never go home. *Never.* Even if it was her only option, she couldn't do it. If Josh had managed to leave three years ago, with no plans in place, then so could she. She would find a place to sleep to-nacht, someplace out of the rain....

Rain reminded her of the waterfall. She was glad she'd snuck outside to spend time with Josh last nacht. Her final moments with him. She caught her breath as a fresh wave of tears arrived. She was barely conscious of the woman wrapping her arms around her. Pressing another cold bottle of water into her hands. Did she carry an endless supply?

The first one, Greta had drained and left in the hospital room, tucked inside the crate with the few remaining jars of jam and her ruined birdhouse.

She choked on her tears.

"Shhhh. It'll be okay."

Nein. It'd never be okay. Not until Gott stopped throwing curveballs her way.

"Honey, my husband and I run a halfway house for Amish runaways. If you need a place to stay, we have an extra bed. There are other Amish kids there. Boys and girls who are going through some of the same stuff as you. We'll keep you safe, off the streets, and offer guidance on adjusting to our way of life."

Had Josh found a place like that? A halfway haus?

Greta sniffed. "I can't go home," she confessed.

"Then come with us, honey. It's raining. At least come for the night, have a warm meal or two. You can decide in the morning what you want to do next."

Somehow, the woman maneuvered Greta off the bench and into the backseat of her SUV. The man in the front wordlessly started the engine and drove off.

Preacher Samuel directed the driver to the Petersheims' haus. "We need the prayers of Reuben and Viktor," he said to Josh.

Once they pulled into the driveway, Josh tugged his hat low over his face, for added protection from the rain, then got out, followed by David and Preacher Samuel. The three of them crowded onto the tiny porch. As Josh reached out to knock on the door, it opened.

"Kum on in," Esther greeted them. "We're having pie and koffee. Sit down and join us." Then she peered past them to the van. "Ach, nein. What's wrong?"

Viktor and Reuben rose to their feet as the men shuffled into the kitchen. Anna sat in her wheelchair, holding the sleeping boppli.

"It's Greta." Josh's voice broke.

Preacher Samuel put his hand on Josh's shoulder again as he recounted the story.

Viktor grabbed his hat and slapped it on. "Grossdaedi, you stay here with Grossmammi. I'll take them to town. Esther, get the extra room ready for Greta. Once we find her, she can stay here." He reached for his shoes. "This settles what side of the Amish fence I land on, for sure." He speared Preacher Samuel with a harsh look. "I won't have my sohn grow up like this. He needs to learn the gospel of grace."

Josh swallowed the lump in his throat. "Will there be enough room in your pickup?"

"Recently traded it in for one with an extended cab." Viktor shoved his feet into his shoes. "I'll send the driver home—she must be tired, anyway—and get the truck from behind the barn. Wait here." He opened the door and went outside.

Preacher Samuel turned to Reuben. "He must've made his mind up prior to this, if he bought a new truck already."

The older man shrugged. "He said he hadn't, but I think we always knew which way he would go. Even though he tried to conform for Esther. For us." He sighed. "That pickup is a huge thing. Not sure how we'll ever get Anna into it. Esther has to use a step stool."

"Do you think the bishop needs to go to the doctor again?" Anna asked softly. "His reaction to Greta was rather extreme, ain't so? Blaming her for her daed's bad back and his heart attack? Especially since he's been having medical problems of his own. His frau asked Esther and me to pray about it the other day."

Preacher Samuel snapped to attention. "I hadn't heard. What's going on?"

"You'd have to talk to him. That's all I was told. Just that he has bad headaches, so they are getting tests done. We need to pray for him."

As Viktor's big black truck rumbled to a stop in front of the porch, Esther pressed a quilt into Josh's hands. "Take this. She'll be wet and cold. Bring her straight here. We'll deal with her family situation in the morgen."

Josh nodded his thanks, for the quilt and for her confidence. Esther seemed certain that they would find Greta. But, given how many hours she'd been gone, she could be anywhere.

Assuming....

His stomach hurt.

Nein. He wouldn't assume the worst.

Chapter 19

The storms continued through the nacht, with strong winds and hail that pounded the tiny window in the basement where Greta's hosts had set her up. Even though the bed was soft, warm, and dry, she tossed and turned, unable to sleep. The wail of the tornado sirens was much louder here than at home, on the outskirts of Jamesport.

Her hosts—she couldn't recall their names right now—had told her they'd talk to her in the morgen.

When that time arrived, she forced herself out of bed and peeked outside, hoping for some clue as to her location. She couldn't see beyond the wood slat fence lining the property. Tree branches and leaves littered the yard, likely due to the damaging winds.

Hopefully, Josh and his family had harvested all the blueberries in time.

Josh.... Did he know she'd run off? And why?

Because of her shameful behavior. Her guilt over causing Daed's death. Tears welled up in her eyes. For the first time, she empathized with Josh's departure from the Amish. The urgent need to get away. Though she doubted his sweet mamm would ever kum down on him as hard as Mamm had on her.

But her reasons for fleeing were valid, considering the bishop's accusations. He placed the blame for all her family's woes squarely on her shoulders and had warned of further repercussions unless she made a kneeling confession in front of the church.

The weight of it all threatened to break her. *Shunned.* It'd already cost her all she held dear. Daed. Her cousins, aenties, and onkels. Josh. The dream of a quiet, peaceful life. Of a cabin by the waterfall in the woods at the edge of the farm.

Never again would Josh hold her and kiss her.

A tear trickled down her cheek. Greta swiped it away and looked for her dress, anxious to get out of the strange-feeling pajama shorts and tank top her hosts had given her to sleep in. It was a gut thing she didn't have a roommate to see her in such an indecent state, though there was an empty twin bed against the opposite wall.

Her dress was gone. In its place was a stiff denim skirt and a T-shirt that read, "Hand over the chocolate, and no one gets hurt."

This was a strange world she'd landed in. She was definitely out of her comfort zone. But there was nein other way around it. She'd have to make the best of the situation.

She picked up the jumper and eyed it dubiously. At least it would cover her better than the shorts and the tank top. She put the outfit on, then surveyed herself in the full-length mirror on the back of the bathroom door. The hem of the jumper stopped at her knees. She tugged it down, but it didn't do any gut.

She couldn't wait to get her own clothes back.

Her kapp was probably ruined, though. The papery material wasn't designed to get soaked. Her hostess had taken it, along with her black bonnet, to be washed—most likely along with her dress. She'd get them back eventually. Or so she hoped. They couldn't expect her to adjust to the Englisch world that quickly.

She touched her hair, remembering the feel of Josh's work-roughened fingers threading their way through it. Recalling his exclamations over its beauty.

Her stomach clenched. What would he think if he saw her now?

Didn't matter. That wouldn't be happening. She couldn't go back.

It seemed Gizelle had won, after all. The pain of betrayal knifed through Greta.

She gathered her hair back in a ponytail, braided it, and secured it with a hair band. Then she summoned courage and held her head high as she left the room. She could do this.

Her hostess and four teens were sitting around the kitchen table—two buwe and two girls. Probably the Amish runaways her hostess had mentioned the previous nacht.

The Englisch woman stood and motioned to her. "Come join us, Greta. Meet Leah, Rhoda, Daniel, and Nehemiah."

"Hallo," all four said.

One of the buwe winked. "Call me Miah." His voice sounded familiar. Maybe their paths had crossed at a frolic or a singing.

Her hostess handed Greta a bowl and a spoon, then motioned toward an array of cold cereal boxes on the counter.

After breakfast, the others dispersed to do various activities. Her host said that all four of them were taking GED classes, as well as driving lessons. A couple of them held part-time jobs.

A foreign world. If Greta were at home, she'd be getting ready for the farmers' market. Well, not in this weather. She'd be working at home. Baking. Cleaning. Daydreaming of doing the same tasks in the home she would share with Josh someday.

The woman allowed Greta to do dishes after she finished breakfast. She stood beside Greta and dried. Quiet. Not pushing.

Not that Greta had anything to say, other than, "Thank you for letting me stay here."

"It would've been a miserable night to be outside." The woman smiled and laid the dish towel on the countertop. "Okay, sweetie. Let's talk. Help yourself to a drink from the fridge, and have a seat at the table." She poured herself a cup of koffee and sat.

Greta opened the refrigerator door and started to reach for the carton of orange juice, but then she saw the cans of Coke. Much more tempting, since it was a rare treat. She picked one up, carried it over to the table, and sat before pulling back the tab to open it. "I'm sorry, but I don't remember your name."

"Deana. My husband ran away from the Amish years ago, so we want to help other Amish kids."

Deana. Greta mentally repeated it several times, so she wouldn't forget.

"Are you okay after being robbed? How is your mom doing? You said she was at the hospital?"

"Yes. To visit my…my dad." Her voice cracked. She cleared her throat. "He had a heart attack. That's why he was there in the first place, but I think he might have…have died. Alarms were going off, and when I went back later, he was gone. They told me it was my fault."

"You think? You're not sure? Who are 'they'?" Deana raised her eyebrows.

"The preachers. And my mom agreed with them." Greta sniffled. "I wish I knew for sure if he was alive or not."

"Well then, let's call the hospital," Deana suggested. "They won't answer that question, due to privacy laws, but if I ask to be transferred to his room, we'll know if he's there. What's his name?"

"Andy Miller."

Deana pulled out a cell phone, fiddled with it a few moments, and then held it to her ear, waiting for what seemed to Greta like hours.

"Yes, thank you," she finally said. "Connect me to Andy Miller's room, please." She waited again. Then put her other hand over the mouthpiece. "They're transferring the call," she told Greta. "That means he's still there—still alive. Do you want to talk to him?"

"Can I?" Greta's heart leaped into her throat. Daed was still alive. She couldn't keep from smiling. She grasped the phone—it was so lightweight, compared to the one in the shanty—and held it to her ear.

"Hallo?" a male voice said.

It didn't sound like Daed. But it sounded familiar.

"Onkel Samuel? It's Greta. Daed's okay, ain't so?" Her voice broke.

~

Josh was wet and frustrated. While Preacher Samuel and David had searched the hospital again, he and Viktor had searched everywhere they could think of where a homeless person or a runaway might sleep. They'd both been runaways, after all, and they knew where the homeless usually camped out. Under bridges and docks. In alleyways and sheltered doorways. On park benches. And although they found some men in some of those places, and even a few females, there wasn't any sign of Greta.

Josh fidgeted in the front seat of Viktor's pickup. They were parked in the business district of town, where they had agreed to meet up with Preacher Samuel and David. He stared out into the rain, the grayness, hoping that his personal ray of sunshine—Greta—would walk toward them. Maybe wearing the green dress that matched her eyes. But she didn't appear.

David Lapp did, though. Alone.

Maybe they'd found Greta, and she was with Preacher Samuel. He hoped so.

David approached the truck, steadied by his cane. He opened the back door and climbed inside. He leaned his cane against the seat beside him, then took off his hat, held it just outside the open door, and shook the water off before closing the door.

"Nein sign of her, then?" Viktor asked. "Preacher Zeke said he'd call the hospital this morgen after checking to see if Greta returned home during the nacht."

David shook his head. "Have you eaten breakfast yet? I'm supposed to pick up something for Preacher Samuel."

Viktor pointed at the golden arches across the street. "What about McDonald's?"

Food? Who cared about food? Josh just wanted an idea of where to search next. He felt a strange urgency to find her, as if she might be in danger.

"Let's go through the drive-thru." Viktor started the truck. "We can take the food to the hospital and eat there." He backed out of the parking lot.

David put his hat back on. "Why don't I go in and order? It just dawned on me that Greta might've gone to a women's shelter, like the ones they have in Lancaster. Not sure if there are any nearby, but it's worth asking."

Viktor's brows shot up, and he glanced at Josh. "Gut idea. You sure you want to go inside? I could just ask at the drive-thru window."

"I'll go in," David said. "Easier to ask in person than to shout through a drive-thru window, ain't so?"

Josh shrugged. He couldn't blame his friends for wanting to eat, but his own stomach was in knots. He didn't think he'd be able to keep any food down. Besides, they should be praying. He should be praying. *Lord Gott—*

"Besides, who's to say Greta isn't in the restaurant?" David asked. "Going in will give me a chance to look around."

That was a gut call. Josh perked up. They hadn't checked any fast-food places or diners.

Viktor drove across the street and found a parking place next to the building.

"I'll go in with you," Josh said. He put on his hat and opened the truck door.

Viktor turned to him. "Order me a koffee, please. Make it a large. I need lots of caffeine after being up all nacht. Ach, and pick out one of their breakfast sandwiches and some hash browns."

Josh led the way inside, followed closely by David. They both took the time to scan the restaurant tables. There was a flash of green, similar to the shade of one of Greta's dresses, but it was a man's raincoat. Josh frowned as he went to stand in line.

He empathized with Viktor's need for caffeine. He ordered himself a Coke. Fatigue was compounding his fear for Greta and his rage at the unfair way the bishop had treated her. Not to mention his frustration that Gott didn't seem to be hearing his prayers.

When the cashier brought out their order, Josh took the bag and lifted the cardboard drink carrier from the counter, then glanced over the crowd one last time.

Tears burned his eyes.

"I can carry the food," David offered as he joined him. "I talked to a few employees, and none of them knows about a local shelter." He frowned. "I'll ask at the hospital. Someone there should know for sure. Or could check online for us."

Discouragement trailed Josh all the way to the truck. He opened the door and handed the drinks to Viktor before climbing in. "I don't know where else to look." He let out a sigh. "Maybe we should just stay at the hospital awhile. As close as Greta is to her daed, she's bound to show up sooner or later if she's still in the area."

Or so he hoped. Of course, he never would've dreamed she would've left in the first place. In fact, he'd been almost positive they would find her sitting on a bench in the park gazebo, crying.

His stomach churned. Gut thing he hadn't ordered breakfast for himself.

Viktor lifted his brown koffee cup from the cardboard carrier. "I don't know what to say, either. If she hasn't gone home, she's holed up pretty gut somewhere." He glanced over his shoulder at David. "And I'm sure Josh will agree when I say that when I left the Amish I didn't stick around the area. I was outta here."

Josh nodded. And kicked at the floor mat. "But she's a girl." *A woman.* Not that it didn't mean she wouldn't leave. But he knew Greta. It didn't seem likely. She loved her daed. Loved her cousins. And loved him, or was starting to again. "She's here, somewhere. Has to be."

David reached over the seat for his koffee cup. "Okay. But where?" He looked around again, as if expecting her to appear.

"I don't know." And that frustrated Josh to nein end.

Ask, and it shall be given you; seek, and ye shall find; knock, and it shall be opened unto you.

Josh frowned as the verse from Luke came to mind. He hadn't exactly been asking. Seeking, jah. But he hadn't asked. That should've been the first step. Instead, he'd panicked and let his friends pray.

He bowed his head. *Lord Gott, please give us a sign to let us know whether Greta is here—or not. Wherever she is, take care of her, and bring her back to us. To me.*

"Greta, praise Gott." Onkel Samuel's voice came through the foreign-feeling device.

Greta pressed the phone tight against her ear. "How is Daed?"

There was nein answer.

"Onkel Samuel? Hallo?"

Still nein answer.

Greta put the phone down on the table, blinked back a fresh round of tears, and glanced around the room, not wanting to look her hostess in the eyes. She didn't want to see her pity.

Deana reached for the phone and slid it into her pocket. "Your uncle was there?"

"I think he…he hung up…on me." She hated the way her voice quavered.

"That's to be expected. You've probably been shunned."

Greta winced, but she was probably right.

"I know it's easier said than done, but try to forget about your family. You're part of mine now." The older woman reached across the table and squeezed Greta's hand. "You know your dad is alive, but we'll consider it best for you to stay here."

Greta was relieved to know Daed was alive, but she wanted to see him. Maybe she would wait until she thought Onkel Samuel had left. If she was indeed shunned, she didn't need the pain of having the people she knew and loved turn their backs on her. Daed wouldn't be able to—not while he was lying in bed. He would still talk to her. They would discuss her thoughts and concerns, then work it out somehow. Reach an understanding, even if she didn't like the punishment.

She would have expected the same from Onkel Samuel. After all, hadn't he said, "Praise Gott"? And asked where she was?

Maybe she wasn't shunned, despite what Deana believed.

Hope flared.

"Can you take me to the hospital to see Daed? Please? You said you would take me this morgen if I wanted to go."

Deana grimaced. "I don't think that's a good idea. My husband told me how shunning works, and I don't want to see you go through it. That aside, they sure won't want to see you dressed like you are." She sighed.

Greta slumped. Even if Onkel Samuel had sounded glad to hear her voice, he had hung up on her.

She was still an outcast.

Maybe it was best she stay here and get acclimated to the Englisch world. Josh would be hurt, and she hated causing him pain; but she had nein choice. She wouldn't be able to bear being shunned by him.

He'd get over her.

Probably much faster than she would get over him.

If she ever managed to.

Chapter 20

Josh hurried into Andy Miller's hospital room. He'd scanned every room and hall he'd passed on his way there. "Nothing. Not a sign of her." His face tightened. His eyes burned.

Preacher Samuel looked up from his seat beside the phone at the head of the bed. "Keep the faith, Josh. Der Herr knows exactly where she is."

"But I don't." Josh handed him a cup of koffee, feeling the sting of conviction over his lack of faith. He had the urge to find a quiet place and do nothing but pray, but he needed to keep hunting for her.

"Morgen, sohn. You'll find my girl, ain't so?" Andy grasped Josh's hand and stared into his eyes, desperation in them.

"Morgen, Andy." Josh handed him the mug of weak-looking tea on his hospital tray. "I'll do my best." He swallowed the stubborn lump in his throat—again—and revised his statement. "I will find her, Gott willing." Something in Andy's eyes reached Josh's heart. He squeezed the man's hand, then pulled back.

Preacher Samuel cleared his throat. "She c—"

"So. Preacher Zeke called? She didn't go home?" David asked, handing Preacher Samuel the food they'd ordered for him.

Josh frowned. If only she had gone home. But she'd been run off by the bishop and rejected by her mamm, and now had been missing for close to twenty hours. Nein, she wouldn't have gone home. More likely sitting in a park. But he and Viktor had gone through them all. Twice.

"He called. She's not home. However...." Preacher Samuel turned to Josh. "Greta called here."

"What? Really?" Josh couldn't believe Preacher Samuel had waited so long to tell him. *Danki, Lord.* "What did she say?"

Preacher Samuel shook his head. "Nothing helpful, I'm afraid. Our call was quickly disconnected, and she didn't phone again. But I think she's somewhere in town. She didn't sound afraid or endangered. I'm sure she'll eventually kum in to visit Andy. She asked about him before I lost her."

Lost her. In more ways than one. If they'd had more time to talk, would she have asked about Josh? He immediately regretted the selfish thought, even as he wished he'd had more time with her to convince her of the feasibility of a future together.

But none of that mattered right now. She wasn't here. She was so close, and yet so far away. Josh resisted the urge to slam his fist into the wall. *Where is she, Lord?* He hated feeling so out of control.

David looked at Andy. "If she comes to visit, you'll tell her to stay, ain't so? Tell her to kum home?"

Viktor looked up from where he crouched against the far wall, his untouched meal beside him on the floor. Had he been praying? "She can live with us until things are resolved with the bishop. And the community and your family."

Andy eyed him steadily. "She's my dochter. She needs to be at home. But they are transferring me to a hospital in Kansas City as soon as I'm stabilized for the bypass surgery." He looked at Josh. "Sohn, I understand you have responsibilities other than Greta, but...."

Josh swallowed. If he understood Andy right, he wanted Josh to find Greta. His other responsibilities grated on him. But Andy was right. Josh needed to work, too, both on his family farm and at the Millers'. He did it out of love for Greta, though. Might be better to devote the time he would have spent helping them to searching for her. He'd reduce his hours at the farmers' market as much as he could afford to, though Mamm had asked him to start selling berries in addition to the other items.

But Mamm would understand. Greta was more important than making money at the farmers' market. She was more important than anything, including his contracted book. Which he hadn't touched for days.

Andy picked at a loose string on the blanket that covered him.

It would hurt Andy's family, losing Greta's income from the farmers' market. Maybe he would ask Mamm and Linda to set up a display for the Miller family in their barn, where they sold berries.

"I'll keep looking, Andy," he assured him. "Do you want us—my family—to sell your baked treats and canned goods until Greta comes home?"

Andy considered that a moment. "Jah, danki. That would be most appreciated. Gizelle isn't the cook Greta is, but I'm sure she would be willing to help her mamm with the baking."

Preacher Samuel stood. "I believe we're all willing to help you, Josh. We know you have to work. You also have that book to write. A book that I'm sure is needed, for a purpose far beyond whatever we can conceive of right now." He put a hand on Josh's shoulder. "For now, though, we've done all we can. We've spent all nacht looking for her, and we need to return to our families and our other responsibilities. She'll show up. And when she does, whoever is visiting Andy will bring her home."

"We'll take shifts," David suggested. "That way someone is looking for her all the time. I can go first."

"I will." Josh stared at his friend. "I'll go first."

"Fine." David nodded. "I'll pray she's found today. But if not, I'll be back to-nacht. We'll meet in the lobby."

"Might be better to have Josh or me take the nacht shift." Viktor tossed his empty koffee cup into the trash. "We're street savvy and—no offense, David—not handicapped."

"Right. Like I can't beat people off with my cane," David quipped.

Josh tossed his empty Coke cup into the trash. The sugary liquid sat heavy on his stomach.

He appreciated his friends' attempts to cheer him up, but he wouldn't smile again.

Not until he found her.

~

The days stretched by endlessly. Greta had lost track of how many had passed since Deana and her husband, Hugh, had taken her in. She stared out the window at the hot sunshine blazing down. At least the haus was air-conditioned.

The home was equipped with a security system that needed to be deactivated by either Deana or Hugh whenever someone left, or an annoyingly loud siren went off, while the security company received a simultaneous alert. This, Greta had learned the hard way, when she opened the door to walk around in the backyard. Video cameras continually surveyed the perimeter of the property. Who needed so much security?

And every time Greta asked her to take her to the hospital to visit Daed, Deana had something else more important to do. Usually, working on her computer while watching a TV show that gave Greta a headache. A "soap opera," Deana called it.

Greta had nothing to do. There were nein baking supplies in the haus, and not even a single book. The washing machine and clothes dryer did all the laundry with little assistance required. Greta couldn't comprehend how the machines could have "eaten" her dress and bonnet—the excuse Deana had offered after the items had been missing for quite some time.

Resentment was beginning to build within Greta. Why had Deana offered to take her home that first morgen, only to renege indefinitely? Why couldn't she sit at the hospital with Daed while Deana ran to the grocery store or went for a dentist appointment?

The woman had offered to cut her hair for her. She wanted to give her a "cute little pixie cut," whatever that was. Greta had refused.

Deana had time to cut her hair, but not enough to take her to visit Daed?

It was like she was a prisoner in this haus. Except that a prisoner wouldn't be allowed to go to GED classes or take driving lessons. Not that she'd actually enrolled in either one yet.

Greta stared at the door off the kitchen. Maybe Deana or Hugh had forgotten to activate the alarm. Not likely, but she walked over and checked the control panel. Sure enough, it was live.

Would Deana object if she wrote a letter? It should have been a silly question. Greta was legally an adult. She should be able to write whomever she pleased. And visit Daed if she pleased. She shot a glower at the woman's back. But she didn't know how to get her way. Sneaking out of a tiny rectangular basement window was different from a normal-sized window on the second floor. And way different from walking out the door.

She swallowed the bile in her throat and went into the other room. "Deana? May I have some paper and an envelope? I'd like to write a letter."

Deana turned around with a slight grimace. "Oh, honey, no. I'm sorry, but it's not a good idea to contact your family. I don't mean to be unkind, but they'll probably just throw the letter away, and—"

"It's for my cousin. She's not Amish." Not yet, anyway.

Deana shut her eyes. Briefly. "Okay. You can write your cousin. I'll have Hugh drop it in the mail the next time he goes out. You can give your cousin our P.O. box, in case she wants to write back to you. I'll jot the address down for you." She opened a drawer and pulled out a sheet of lined notebook paper and an envelope. "Just set it on the table when you're done." She handed Greta the paper and a black pen, then turned back to the computer.

"Thank you." Greta started to walk away, then hesitated. Josh had mentioned wanting her to proofread the notes from his trail journals for a manuscript he was working on. If a publisher had found them, they had to be online, ain't so? If only Greta knew how to access them.

"Would you mind showing me how to use the computer sometime?" The words were out before she could stop them.

Deana turned again, this time with a smile. "Absolutely, honey. I'll show you how, right after you write your letter. We have an old laptop you can use."

Greta was grateful, but still pretty peeved. Deana had plenty of time to teach her how to use a computer, but no time to take her to see Daed?

Of course, Daed might not even be at the hospital anymore. She wondered again how many days she'd been here. Four or five, maybe. She'd asked Deana to call the hospital several times. Presumably, she had, but never in front of Greta. And she always said, "No one answered in his room."

Greta went downstairs to her cellar bedroom, sat at the desk, and began to write.

Dear Esther,

I'm in Cameron; I don't know exactly where, or I'd tell you. An Englisch couple took me in. The frau was at the farmers' market the day I was robbed—

Wait. Greta's blood chilled. *Miah.* That was why his voice sounded familiar.

He was the one who had robbed her.

Josh hadn't slept since Greta's disappearance, and the fatigue was beginning to wear on him. The day after she went missing, Andy's doctor had deemed him stabilized enough to be transferred for bypass surgery.

In the waiting room at the hospital in Cameron, Josh picked up a newspaper someone had discarded and thumbed through it. There were a few personal ads, some of them expressing birthday wishes. If he took out an ad, saying something like, "Greta, kum home. Love, Josh," would she see it?

It was worth a try.

The newspaper office would be closed now, since it was after five. Tomorrow, he'd stop by and try to compose a suitable ad.

Viktor strode in and sat next to Josh. "Any luck?" He handed him a cold can of Coke.

Josh shook his head. "I *finally* found someone who knew where the shelters are located. She gave me the address of the women's shelter, but not the abused women's shelter. She said it was 'secret.' I don't think Greta would be in that kind of shelter, anyway. But the person I talked to at the main shelter said that nobody matching her description had kum in."

Viktor grimaced. "She's not in a shelter, anyway. But she is here, or was, yesterday. She's…she's not safe." He handed Josh an opened envelope, addressed to Esther. Postmarked in Cameron.

Dear Esther,

I'm in Cameron; I don't know exactly where, or I'd tell you. An Englisch couple took me in. The frau was at the farmers' market the day I was robbed.

I can't tell you more. I'm __________. I'd love to know how Daed is. When ____ calls the hospital, she says they put the call through, but he doesn't answer.

Please write me at post office box number ______.

Tell Josh I'm sorry. So sorry. I remember what he said right before he left. "There's a consequence for every choice you make." I made a very bad choice.

Greta

Josh's stomach churned. Someone had censored the letter, blacking out any potentially identifying details.

Leaving nein way of contacting her.

Chapter 21

Greta wiped her sweaty palms on her denim skirt and bit her lip, determined to master the mystery that was the Internet. Since Gott didn't care about her, she needed to find a way to help herself.

The computer was easier to navigate than she'd expected. She caught on quickly when Deana showed her how to use it, then left her alone to "play."

And play she would. Since Esther must not have received her letter last week, judging by her failure to respond, Greta needed to try another way of contacting her family. But how did one get in touch with another party who had nein access to a computer?

Rachel occasionally used a computer at the store, and Josh was the only Amish man she knew who owned a laptop. But she didn't know where to start with either of them. She stared at the blinking cursor in the "to" field within the e-mail account Deana had set up for her. So close, and yet so far away.

Outside Greta's room, the vacuum cleaner hummed to life. Deana hummed along with it. Greta gripped the computer tighter. She needed to make the most of this opportunity. But where to start?

She opened the window Deana had shown her for something called a search engine, then typed in "Appalachian Trail Journals." And whimpered when 256,000 results were listed. Now what? She didn't have any idea where to start.

A search for "Josh Yoder" pulled up nothing related to her Josh. And hadn't he mentioned that the hikers all used trail names, anyway? Either they came with one in place, or the trail named them. Something like that.

She forced herself to breathe slowly, calmly. She didn't want to let Deana know that her reason for using the computer was fear, not boredom.

She rested her chin on her hand and stared at the screen as she tried to remember other details about what he'd told her. What was the subtitle of his book? "My Life as Ex-Amish." Or was it spelled "X-Amish"? A search of the latter yielded a bunch of results. She clicked on one of them, then found herself on a page with a picture of the Josh she knew and loved.

Her heart ached with longing for him. But now was not the time for pining over lost love. It was time to find a way of escape.

She began to read.

My first day on the Appalachian Trail. Dan insisted I stay sober for this experience. I doubt I will. (Sorry, Dan. Depends on whether the memories follow me here or not.)

His drinking habits had pursued him that long after he'd left? And who was Dan?

It was windy and barely above freezing. Didn't realize Georgia got so cold in April. Dan and I walked around the visitors' center, and I signed in as a thru-hiker. Before Dan left, he took a lot of pictures to document my trip, which made me uncomfortable, and pressed a cell phone into my hand. Told me he wanted to see photos posted on my trail journal. He'll be the only one following me, since my family is Amish. Besides, they don't even know I'm doing this. We haven't exactly been in contact since I left.

Greta's heart squeezed in sympathy. So, this is how it felt to be on the other side.

I feel obligated to do what Dan asks, since he outfitted me for this journey and is going to continue his assistance by sending supplies to various post offices along the way for me to pick up. Finally, he said, "Go with God, Josh. Listen for Him." I snorted in disbelief and started on my hike up to Springer.

She agreed with his mind-set, and snorted along with him. Then she glanced at the door to make sure Deana wasn't watching. The vacuum cleaner was so noisy, she couldn't tell what was going on.

The falls alone had 604 steps to the top. Yeah, I counted. It was pretty windy at times. I met a man on the trail who'd hiked up to Springer the night before. He said temperatures had gotten down into the 20s, with 70-mph winds, snow, and sleet.

Greta shivered.

I got to Black Gap Shelter about 5:30 and set up camp. Afterward, I hiked down a hill to get water that came out of the mountain. I built a fire and cooked hot dogs and s'mores. A man who introduced himself as Lion King came in after dark and camped in the shelter. He asked if I wanted a trail partner. He seemed nice enough, but I don't want company.

Greta frowned. He might not have wanted to be around other people, but she sure would love some friendly company. She didn't even have a friend here anymore, since the other two girls who'd been living in the haus had decided to return home, Deana said. Leaving just Greta and the two buwe. It seemed strange since they'd talked the nacht before about their plans for today, and going home hadn't been mentioned by either of them. It also seemed odd that they could leave, while she wasn't allowed to even visit Daed. It also seemed odd for this group to rob her at the farmers' market and then rescue her at the hospital.

A tear escaped.

She brushed it away.

Nothing added up. She shivered. If only Josh were there to wrap his arms around her. To comfort her.

She had to get a message to him. Somehow.

She studied the trail journal page, not knowing what to look for. There were options to "share" and "tweet" the page, but she didn't know what those meant. And she didn't see anything that would allow her to reply. Maybe the next page would have that option. She clicked "next."

> *Day two. I talked to Lion King and someone named Broom-man before we broke camp. Lion King had thru-hiked before and shared that a couple of months into his hike, he had a pretty good beard, and sometimes he'd have food in it and not know it. One night, he woke up, and there was a mouse eating food out of his beard. I can't imagine allowing a beard to grow, since that's how Amish identify themselves as married. And I'm not. Since I left, I doubt that the woman I love—I'll call her G—will ever welcome me back into her life. Though, truthfully, I doubt I'll ever return. I miss her, though. More than she'll ever know. And I'll never stop loving her. If only I could do things over…*

If only.

If only he hadn't made a mistake, felt guilty, and run away. If only she hadn't snuck out of the haus with her hair down and incurred Daed's heart troubles as punishment. She supposed she deserved whatever would become of her for having been so sinful.

She reread the last several lines of Josh's second entry. Tears stung her eyes. Josh loved her. She'd been in love with him, too, back then. Still was.

I hiked up Springer Mountain for a few pictures (happy, Dan?) and signed the register to officially begin my hike. Lion King made a pop can stove for me to use. I never would've thought of such a thing. Very interesting. Two pop cans, some tape that doesn't melt, and a lot of patience. I'll have to remember how to make them. A ridge runner who works for the Appalachian Trail Conservatory joined us and gave me some information on water sources and bear canister requirements. Finally lost Lion King and Broom-man when I took a side trail to Long Falls. I set up camp just short of Hawk Mountain Shelter. I think a bear joined me during the night. I could hear something big sniffing around. And I think that bear is wearing my new sunglasses. I do hope he enjoys them and that, maybe…just maybe…the rascal will send me a photo of how he looks with them on. I really liked those new sunglasses.

Greta found a smile.

"Greta?" The door opened, and Deana stepped in. "What are you doing, honey?"

Greta clicked to return to the main page. "Just reading something I found online."

"We're starting a movie in the living room. I'm making popcorn. Come join us."

It wasn't an option. It was an order. How many movies had she seen now? All of them of scary, sinful, disturbing things. She shuddered. And it would put her in close proximity with Miah. She still hadn't figured out how to confront him about robbing her. He owed her family the money he'd taken. Maybe she should just tell him flat out that he'd stolen money from a family that desperately needed it for medical bills. But the Amish preached that if someone stole something from you, he needed it more, and you ought to surrender it joyfully, as if giving der Herr.

If der Herr cared, then He would've made sure Miah got caught. Or would've stopped him from robbing her in the first place.

The Amish had never met Miah. Perhaps he *wanted* the money more than Daed did.

"We'll expect you upstairs in a few minutes." Deana left the door open.

Greta glared after her as she shut the laptop. Deana had been at the farmers' market before the police arrived. She'd been there before Miah robbed her.

Was she involved in the robbery? Was it all part of a kidnapping scheme?

None of it made any sense. Deana had taken Greta to the hospital and left her there. She'd kum back later, during the rainstorm, and "rescued" her. How could she have known that Greta would flee the hospital? She couldn't have.

Trying to figure it out gave Greta a headache.

And Miah, with a gun.... Did Deana know he carried a weapon? If not, would she be concerned if she found out? Or would she just smile her fake smile?

There were so many things she didn't understand about this haus. About her situation. About why she was being forced to stay here.

Increasingly against her will.

Greta went upstairs. Deana was making popcorn in the microwave, from little bags labeled "Extra Butter." Daniel was taking soda cans out of the refrigerator. Nein sign of Miah. Gut.

Deana looked up and smiled. "Good news, Greta. We found a job for you. Since Leah left, her boss has graciously offered you her job. You start tomorrow."

Daniel froze. He looked over his shoulder at Greta, then quickly returned his attention to the fridge.

Greta's stomach knotted. Jah, Leah left. And she *couldn't*. She took a deep breath to calm herself. "What about the GED classes and driving lessons?" She tried to keep her hands from shaking as she tore open a bag of popcorn and dumped the hot kernels into a bowl.

Deana laughed, but it wasn't a happy sound. "You won't need them, honey. Either Miah or Daniel will take you there."

"But…." Not that Greta had really wanted the classes. Deana was right—she'd never need them. Especially if she could figure out how to defeat the haus alarm system and leave. Go home, to her family—and to Josh. But every attempt so far had failed. Did other Englisch homes have this much security? Nobody went in or out without typing in a code.

Maybe working a job would be a gut thing. Leah had worked in a restaurant as a server. She'd worn horribly indecent clothes—her "uniform"—but the restaurant doors wouldn't be guarded. Greta might be able to slip out and disappear. Or she could send word via a letter that would actually get mailed. Or maybe a helpful person would call the phone shanty for her and get word to her family.

"I'll help carry the popcorn into the other room." Greta tried to appear helpful and compliant. Grateful.

"Thank you, honey." Deana put another bag in of popcorn in the microwave. "I'll pick out a movie." She left the room.

Greta ripped a bag open with more force than necessary and dumped the contents into a bowl. Her hands trembled uncontrollably.

Daniel put two more soda cans on a tray. "You still want a Coke?"

She nodded.

He stepped closer. "Tell me about your family."

Greta looked up in surprise. Nobody here had ever asked. "My dad hurt himself during harvest last fall. He needed back surgery, but we couldn't afford it. Mamm took care of him, while my younger brother went to school and tended to the farm, and I started work at a local grocery store to bring in some money to help with bills. But it wasn't enough. Then my dad had a heart attack...." Tears welled in her eyes, but she blinked them back. "My sister took over my job at the store, and I started selling things at the farmers' market. It was the only money we had coming in. And then I was robbed." Her voice broke. "And was brought here. I don't know how they're surviving without my income. Or how Daed is doing. Or if Gizelle has her claws firmly in my Josh. Or if they even miss me."

Wow. She'd really dumped on him.

Daniel studied her. Glanced over his shoulder. "She may be my aunt, but...."

Her stomach flipped. "She said you were a runaway Amish."

He rolled his eyes. "She says a lot of things. Most of them are lies. The two other girls were from Iowa, I think. She 'lost' their clothes, just like she 'lost' yours."

Greta glanced down at the stiff denim skirt that barely skimmed her knees. She hated these clothes.

Daniel pulled another can out of the refrigerator. "I don't approve of what she's doing, but it's not like I have a choice. She's paying my way through college if I 'cooperate.' She's also helping my dad out with his medical expenses. He has diabetes, and the drugs are expensive. Aunt Deana swears she'll cut his payments and make my life hell if I don't. But stealing money from a family that needs it is just wrong. You won't see anything of the money you earn here, either. She'll tell you she needs it handed over for room and board. And then you'll be sent to Kansas City." He didn't make eye contact with her.

"What's in Kansas City? Why will I be sent there?" She couldn't go further away from home.

"A bigger, better job. Or so she'll say." Daniel looked over his shoulder again and lowered his voice to a whisper. "Look, I like you. I hate to see this happen to you. Give me your address. I'll make sure the stolen money is sent to your parents. Along with a note from you, if you write one. But you can't mention it to anyone. Not like you'll ever escape. Not even from the restaurant. Someone will be watching you the whole time. I can't do anything about that." He sounded regretful.

Escape. So, she was a prisoner. Her stomach churned. And the microwave timer must've been set on too long, because this latest bag of popcorn stunk. "What're they going to do with me? If I'm a prisoner, why find me a job?" She clenched her fists.

Daniel blew out a breath. "Sex trafficking. You're gonna be sold as a prostitute and probably end up hooked on drugs."

Greta forgot how to breathe as she stood there and stared at him.

He looked down, his face reddening. "Sorry. And you have to pretend like you don't know, because your drug addiction will get an early start if you resist. The owner of the restaurant is involved in sex trafficking and drugs, like Deana. He likes to check out all the girls first. I think he keeps some for himself. He owns a club in Kansas City, too. It's to your advantage if he likes you."

Gott, if You're real—and I know You are—if You care at all about what happens to me, then deliver me from this.

She didn't feel anything. Her prayers probably still hadn't passed the ceiling. Either that, or they'd been diverted to an answering machine Gott never checked.

Now she knew her lot in life.

"Terrifying" didn't begin to describe it.

She picked up the bowls of popcorn and staggered into the other room.

She would spend the next hour or two thinking of a way to escape—while the future awaiting her if she didn't was depicted on the big screen mounted to the wall.

The next morgen, Greta went into the bathroom and splashed cold water on her face, hoping to wash away the tear streaks and insomnia-induced dark circles. She heard a noise in the bedroom and peeked out. Deana set a stack of clothes on the bed. "Here's your uniform for at the restaurant. You get to start work today. Isn't that exciting, honey? A real job. And if you do well enough, you'll earn tips. Wear your tennis shoes, because you'll be on your feet a lot."

Tennis shoes. The one thing that remained from the day she'd been kidnapped.

"Have you ever worked as a server?"

"No." Maybe admitting her lack of professional experience would prompt Deana to reconsider. Of course, she'd done plenty of serving at Amish weddings, funerals, work frolics...every family meal could probably be considered a serving experience.

"Well, it's not that hard. All the other girls caught on fast." She smiled. "Go ahead and get dressed now, honey. Come out as soon as you're ready, and we'll take you to work and introduce you to your boss." Smile. Smile. Smile.

Greta swallowed the bile that rose in her throat. When Deana had gone, she took the clothes and pulled the pants on—her first time wearing men's clothes. They didn't feel tight, but they hugged every curve. The shirt did, too, and its neckline was cut low, showing a lot of cleavage. She looked around the room, trying to find something to wear under it that would make it more modest, but she couldn't find anything.

She stared at herself in the mirror, then averted her eyes in shame. Why did she have to dress like this? It was worse than when she'd slipped outside in her nacht-gown and robe. Far worse.

She was beyond hope now. Did Gott understand that she had nein choice?

"Honey? Are you ready? It's time to go." Deana's voice was just outside the door. "Miah is getting the car."

Greta opened the door. "I'm not your honey. Don't call me that."

Deana didn't respond. Maybe she hadn't heard. Or maybe, considering the end she planned for Greta, her term of false endearment should be the least of her concerns, and Greta should just learn to tolerate it.

Somehow, some way, she would escape this.

If only she could rely on Gott. *You've got this, ain't so?* The prayer was sarcastic, at best.

Even so, a strange sense of peace filled her. She cringed, regretting her sarcasm.

Trust Me.

Josh hung out at the Cameron post office as often as he could. It was a quiet place to sit on a bench with his laptop and type paragraphs he hoped made sense. Greta never came in, not that he expected her to. He offered a physical description of her to all the employees, but nobody reported having seen her.

Seemed the post office was a bust, but he was running out of options. Ideas. Time. Greta had been missing for over a month now. How long until her body was found in a shallow grave somewhere? *Gott, where are You? Where is she?*

David was supposed to meet him at a local restaurant today. They'd been visiting different ones, hoping to find someone who'd seen Greta. Just before the agreed-upon time, Josh tucked his laptop under his arm and headed for the restaurant on foot. His head pounded, probably from a combination of sleep deprivation and worry.

A chime sounded when Josh opened the door, and a hostess with short blond hair greeted him. She gave him a once-over, staring at his clothes. He snatched his hat off as he averted his eyes from her too-tight black pants and pink shirt that showed too much cleavage. "Table for two, please."

She picked up a couple menus without a word and started walking away.

Rude. Should he wait there or go after her? After a moment's hesitation, he followed her to a small table.

She laid both menus down on the table. "What do you want to drink?"

"Water, please."

"Your server will be with you shortly to take your order." She turned on her heel.

Right. He set his laptop on the table, placed his hat on top of it, then sat down and opened the menu. The prices were expensive. Maybe he'd order just a side salad. It wouldn't stay with him long, but it seemed to be the cheapest thing.

Out of the corner of his eye, he saw another set of legs in the same tight black pants. The server set a glass of ice water in front of him. "Have you decided what—Josh?"

Joy flooded him as he looked up. His heart nearly stopped at the sight of Greta in that pink shirt, cut immodestly low. Her strawberry blonde hair was pulled back in a long braid.

Danki, Lord. "I—I've looked all over for you." He could hardly speak. What was she doing here? He jumped up from his chair, aching to pull her close. To kiss her. To hold her.

She backed away, glancing over her shoulder. "Shh. You don't know me, okay? Someone is watching." There was a frantic tone in her voice. "If you're ready to order...?"

Josh's blood ran cold, and he dropped back into the chair. Resisting the urge to glance around, he opened the menu again and pointed to something. He had nein idea what. Nor did he care. "What do you mean, someone is watching?"

"Since when did you start ordering off the senior citizens' menu?"

Josh's face heated. "A hamburger. Medium well. Who's watching, Greta? And why?"

"Do you want fries or a baked potato with it?" She moved closer, angled her body slightly, and lowered her voice to say, "How's Daed?"

"Baked potato. He's home. Recovering from a successful heart bypass surgery."

She nodded.

He forged ahead, feeling encouraged. "They miss you. *I* miss you. And you need to know, Bishop Joe finally asked for financial help for your daed…and for himself, since he was diagnosed with a brain tumor. Please, kum home."

Tears glimmered in her eyes. She glanced over her shoulder again. "I…I can't. I'll be right back with your order, sir." She took the menu from him and hurried off.

Josh watched her disappear through a swinging door. Then he looked in the direction she'd glanced before leaving his table. A man sat at a booth, staring at Josh. His eyes were dark. Hard. Dangerous.

Nein wonder she seemed terrified. Had she been with that man all this time? What had he forced her to do? Josh's gut twisted.

He unrolled the napkin and laid out his eating utensils. Unwrapped the straw and stuck it into the glass. Squeezed the slice of lemon on the edge, then dropped it in the water. Gave it a stir with his straw. And glanced at the man again.

He still stared back, scowling.

Greta came back through the door with a large tray loaded with food. She carried it to a table of diners nearby and delivered their meals. Never looking his way. Pretending she didn't know him.

He'd pretend, as well. *Gott, please give me wisdom.* He glanced at the front door of the restaurant, looking for David. He needed to be warned. And they needed to figure out what was going on.

Five minutes later, Greta stopped at his table, carrying a plastic basket. "Here's your complimentary bread and honey butter, sir. Let me know if you need anything else." She avoided his gaze.

"Are you in danger?"

She didn't need to answer. He *knew* she was.

Her steps faltered, but she walked away without comment.

Greta's stomach churned. It was such a relief to see Josh. She wanted nothing more than for him to whisk her away, to safety. But Miah was watching her every move, and he carried a concealed weapon. She wouldn't put Josh in danger. And with Daniel's warnings about the likelihood of Deana drugging her if she didn't cooperate fully....

On the other hand, if Daniel had been there instead of Miah, maybe she would've attempted escape. He wasn't in agreement with his aunt's dark designs. But then again, that didn't change the situation with the restaurant owner.

At least Daniel had warned her, even if he'd done nothing to help her escape.

Her eyes burned.

Would Josh be in danger if Miah found out that she knew him? Would her family?

Bile rose in her throat.

Best to make Josh think she wanted to stay.

The furthest thing from the truth.

When Josh's order was ready, she grabbed the plate and headed to the dining room.

David Lapp sat across from Josh. *Fantastic.* Another person she had to pretend she didn't know. Hopefully, Josh had told David to pretend the same.

As she approached the table, the two were leaned over it, talking. Neither one looked at her. She put the plate down. "Enjoy your meal, and let me know if there's anything else you need." She turned to David. "Did you want to order anything, sir?"

David kept his eyes on the menu. "They announced my upcoming marriage to Rachel. Thursday. She wants you to stand up with her." He turned the page. "Viktor's here. His truck's parked just outside the door."

Viktor? If he knew she was in here, he'd…well, he wouldn't be calm, like Josh and David. Though she sensed that their show of composure was hanging by a thread. Could it be that Gott cared a smidgen for her, and had sent these three men to help her? The peace she'd experienced that morgen so long ago morgen had since vanished.

Trust Me. The words replayed. But how could she? She glanced at Miah again. His eyes warned her not to try anything.

"I *can't* leave. Would you like some koffee? Or something to eat?" *Accept my answer and just go. Please.*

David shook his head. Closed the menu. "I ate at home."

"Where can I find you?" Josh asked, his eyes on David.

"Let me get your bill." She walked to the cash register and printed his check. At the bottom of the paper, she scribbled, *He has a gun. Just leave. Please.*

Greta picked up a carryout container and carried it back to the table with the check. "You can pay on your way out. Enjoy your lunch." Then she went back to the kitchen again, wishing she could go somewhere private to cry. Or, even better, walk out the door and get in Viktor's truck.

But Daniel had warned her that someone would be watching her at all times, especially when she went anywhere near the service door. Sure enough, every time it was within view, so was a man with his eyes on her.

The next time she came out of the kitchen, Josh and David were gone.

Chapter 22

Pain wrenched Josh's heart as he carried the plastic container holding his untouched food out to Viktor's truck. He would rather be carrying Greta. But if the man watching her really carried a gun, doing that would endanger Greta, as well as the rest of the restaurant staff and patrons.

He opened the driver's side door. "We need to kum up with a plan."

Viktor's brown eyes darted from Josh to David and then back. "You found her." He didn't smile.

"She's in there, working as a waitress. She says someone with a gun is watching her, and she asked us to leave. She's scared, understandably. She's in danger."

"We could wait outside and rescue her when she comes out." David opened the back door and put his cane on the seat. "But I don't think that will work. If she's guarded, someone will probably accompany her. Maybe we could follow them and see where they take her, then call the authorities. I know the Amish frown on getting the police involved, but—"

"What can they do? She left home of her own accord. We have nein proof she's being forced to stay there, or that someone with a gun is guarding her. Nothing. Except that she's scared." Josh raised his hands in frustration.

"Get in." Viktor reached for the door handle. "I'm going to back in to a parking space, near the employee parking. We'll follow them. Esther will be so excited when we bring Greta home to-nacht.

Worrying has turned her into a basket case. And Grossmammi hasn't closed her Bible for weeks. Not that it's a bad thing."

David climbed into the backseat. "I know. Rachel's been the same way. She actually suggested going to town and trying to retrace Greta's steps, imagining where she might have gone. Preacher Samuel and I told her nein. We don't know what happened to Greta on the day she disappeared. I'm so glad we stood our ground. Whatever Greta stumbled into, we don't want Rachel to get caught up in, as well."

Josh's stomach hurt. He walked around in front of the truck and got in the passenger seat. *Lord Gott, please let this work. You know I love Greta. I know You do, too. Please help us rescue her.*

My thoughts are not your thoughts, neither are your ways my ways....

What did der Herr mean, planting that particular verse in his spirit? Josh's head pounded. Did it mean Gott wasn't going to rescue Greta? That her being in captivity was part of His will? How could that be? Nothing gut could kum from this. Absolutely nothing. *Lord....*

Viktor shifted into drive, drove to the back of the lot, and parked.

After an eternity, a new shift of waitresses started to arrive, all of them clad in the same immodest outfit. Finally, Greta emerged, led by the dark-haired man who'd stared at Josh. He kept a tight grip on her arm.

Viktor made a growling sound.

It grated at Josh, too, but he ducked down in the seat when the man appeared to be scanning the parking lot. He didn't want to get Greta into trouble.

Josh heard a vehicle door slam, then an engine roar to life.

"She's in a green minivan," Viktor said. "They're pulling out."

After a moment, Josh straightened as Viktor started his pickup.

He waited for an opportunity to merge into the traffic. Josh watched the green minivan turn onto a side street. Viktor made the same turn moments later, but the minivan had vanished.

Viktor muttered something under his breath.

Josh nearly choked on the tears that were forming.

Ask...seek....

A failed attempt, Lord. I asked...I searched. What more do You want from me?

Knock.

Josh stilled. His brain whirled as he tried to decipher the message. Was he supposed to physically knock on doors? Or pound figuratively on the doors of heaven through prayer?

Cast all your cares upon Me....

"We need to pray," Josh blurted out.

Viktor glanced at him. "We've been praying."

"I mean, down-on-our-knees, intercessory-type prayer. All of us."

"I was thinking the same thing," David said. "Storm the doors of heaven. Viktor, let's head home and get Preacher Samuel. We're going to pray until...until...Acts twelve. I need a Bible."

"What's in Acts twelve?" Viktor turned onto another side street, then turned around in the cul-de-sac.

"I don't know. It just came to mind. Let's go home, get Preacher Samuel and his Bible, and pray."

Miah gripped Greta's arm so hard, she'd probably bruise as he yanked her through the garage doorway into the kitchen. Deana was pressing buttons on the microwave as Miah shoved Greta into the room. "She's not going to work. Too close. People know her."

Greta cringed. Would this be enough for them to try to drug her?

Deana turned around with a scowl. "Who?"

"Two Amish men. They seemed relieved to see her. I think they tried to follow us, but I lost them."

Despair washed over Greta. Too bad Viktor hadn't managed to tail them. Then again, she didn't want him or Josh or David getting hurt.

"Are you sure?"

"Positive."

Deana looked at her. "Who were those men, honey?"

Like she would tell the truth. "Just some guys from my community."

"And what did you say to them?"

"Nothing. Just…'Enjoy your lunch.' Stuff like that."

Deana's face contorted with rage. She advanced on Greta, wielding a paring knife. "Want to tell me the truth?"

"That *is* the truth!" Greta couldn't keep from shouting. For once, all the boldness she'd schooled herself to tamp down during scoldings from Mamm was unleashed. "Why would I tell them that I was kidnapped? Why would I tell them you were planning on selling me as a prostitute, when I knew Miah was there, watching me? I know he has a gun. He's the one who robbed me at the farmers' market, and—"

The force of Deana's slap knocked Greta's head sideways. "Missing money is the least of your concerns. You won't be staying here much longer. We'll ship you off soon enough. In the meantime, lock her in her room. I'll contact the restaurant. Perhaps they'll know the names of the men, especially if they used a credit card."

They wouldn't have. Greta doubted Josh even owned one. And David hadn't ordered anything. But she didn't say any of that. Instead, she winced as Miah gripped her arm and dragged her down the basement stairs. He shoved her into her room, hard enough that she fell to her knees in front of the bed.

He yanked her up and spun her around to face him, jerking her arms behind her and holding them tight. "You're gonna be a hooker, and you know I'd love to sample the goods." His finger inched out, sliding down her cheek.

She jerked back, repulsed by his actions, by his words.

He pulled her nearer, his finger moving further south, down her neck, then lower, to the skin revealed by the deep *V* of her neckline. She trembled with fear. With rage. "But you're more valuable, untouched." He shoved her backward, and she missed the bed, falling on her bottom, her head hitting the mattress. "She might bring your supper down, or she might not." He slammed the door behind him. She heard the lock click.

"I'm going to call him," Deana said from just outside the door. "I want to ship her out this evening. Before she brings trouble to us."

Tears flowed down Greta's cheeks. Why had Gott allowed her to see Josh today? Was it some cruel trick to make life worse? She'd never escape from this room, from this house—so far removed from her quiet, peaceful Amish world.

Shipping her out that evening.

It seemed hopeless to pray.

She got up off the floor and started pacing the room. She had to think of a way to escape.

When Deana brought her supper down—*if* she brought supper down—maybe she could shoulder past her. She might make it to the main floor, but she wouldn't escape the haus. And it'd probably land her in deeper trouble. Like, drugged and unconscious during the transport.

She dropped to the bed. Then she noticed the laptop on the bedside table. She reached for it. Reading Josh's trail journals would comfort her. She might never see him again in person, but at least she could "visit" him through his writing—for now.

Instead of trying to find the spot where she'd left off reading the last time, she started on the page that had popped up on the screen.

I think I am soaked clear to the bone. It has rained so much in the past several days, even my waterproof backpack is saturated. My tent, my clothes, my shoes may never dry out. I may never dry out.

My head is pounding and my mouth is dry. I need a drink. Maybe, if I reached my hoped-for miles, I'll find someone there with beer, whiskey, or something else to share. Or I'll find trail magic.

Dan, I'm sorry. I've wandered the Appalachian Trail for weeks, over a month. And God is nowhere to be found. Is this all there is to live for? What is my life? I lost all hope of reconciliation with my family, with G. God has rejected me. Forgotten me. And I am struggling with my very life. There is no meaning. No purpose. Nothing worth living for.

Tears ran down Greta's cheeks as she whispered the words that echoed the despair of her own heart. What had changed in Josh's life to put happiness back into his eyes?

The next entry, a few days later…

Some excitement today. Somewhere in the distance, I heard a shout of "Look out!" I ran through the woods as fast as I could. A wall/avalanche/river of mud was washing a hiker away. I watched in horrified fascination, realizing I would never reach him in time. He was going to die. And there was nothing I could do.

And then I realized that the river of mud had shifted and was coming straight toward me. I scrambled up on a boulder, threw my backpack behind me, and braced myself. Then, as the man drew near enough, I reached for him and somehow pulled him out of the mud and helped him stand on the rock. He struggled to get footing, his mud-coated shoes slipping this way and that. Finally, he seemed to be able to stand on his own. He looked at me, and a glimmer of recognition lit his eyes. In his current state, he could have been anyone. I hadn't exactly allowed myself to make friends out here.

I'd remained alone. Angry. Sullen. Silent.

He stood there, shaking, gasping for breath, while I held him up and yanked his backpack off, and tossed it behind me, near mine. Then I released him.

He fell to his knees.

I swore, half afraid he'd fall back into the mud, to his death. But he shook his head. Instead, he started giving God credit for saving him, saying He'd rescued him from the miry clay and stood him on a solid rock.

He was delusional, thinking I was God.

And then I realized that wasn't it. He didn't mean me at all. He gave full credit to the almighty God.

The God who'd abandoned me had rescued him. How fair was that?

Greta gasped, her hand moving to grasp the low neckline of the pink shirt. She clutched it close to her heart.

I internally cursed the very God he praised. But then, his words started reaching into my conscience as he said things I'd never heard before. Things like God's grace, and how it wasn't about works. How he wasn't good enough, and didn't deserve to live, but God had saved him, anyway. How he owed Him his life, his heart, his soul, his all.

Something stirred inside me. And I realized...I did, too.

God has a purpose for me. Me. Joshua Yoder. X-Amish. Me, even though I don't deserve a second chance.

I fell to my knees beside this mud-covered man as he begged for forgiveness, and that's when I recognized his voice. We'd met before. Broom-man.

He prayed out loud. Praised. Had a God-experience like nothing I'd ever seen or heard of. I wanted the same experience. I held on to his spiritual coattails, listening, getting caught up, feeling that great need, until it became mine. And as he cried and begged and worshipped, I cried and begged and worshipped along with him. And inside, something changed. I completely surrendered myself to God. I was His. And He was mine.

Greta's heart raced. If only she could be free of the burden of guilt. If only she could know that Gott cared about her as confidently as Josh knew Gott cared about him.

I need to hike with the man I rescued. I need to find out more about the grace that he talked about. I believe it, and I recognize it as truth, but I need to learn more so I can go back and share it with my people.

As soon as I've learned enough, I'll answer God's call to go back home. To the Amish. To my family. To G. To serve Him somehow, as a missionary, or evangelist, or preacher. As a witness.

Lord, help me to be capable of this task You're calling me to. If it is Your will, let me be welcomed.

I won't ask for G *to forgive me for leaving her. I won't ask her to love me. But I hope someday she'll understand that I had to leave, to find God.*

And that, maybe, if He wills it....

The tears started again. If only Gott would find her.

If only she could find a way of escape. Maybe, if she could find Josh's Appalachian Trail journals, she could find a police department and somehow leave a message on their site.

She typed in "Cameron, Missouri, police department." But when she clicked on the first search result, the words "Access Denied" flashed across the screen.

What else could she try?

Footsteps sounded on the basement stairs. Seconds later, the door opened.

"I'll take that." Deana's voice was icy-cold as she snapped the laptop shut and picked it up. "Here's some tea. It'll calm you. Help you sleep." She set a steaming cup on the bedside table. "And change out of the uniform. They need it returned."

Gladly.

The door latched shut behind Deana. The lock clicked.

Greta's heart trembled. Her last connection with Josh was gone, just as she was beginning to understand....

She sniffed, the tears starting afresh. Gott truly had abandoned her. Abandoned her family. All because of her sins, according to the bishop. Her transgressions. She would never be gut enough to make things right.

Greta looked for the denim jumper and shirt Deana had given her, but she couldn't find them. None of the articles of clothes she'd had hanging in the closet that morgen was in the room. Maybe they were in the laundry. With nothing else to wear, she changed into the tank top and shorts Deana had left her to sleep in.

Greta threw the hated black pants and pink shirt as hard as she could against the door. They landed in a heap on the floor. Then she paced the room as she ranted at Gott and told Him exactly what she thought of Him. Of His indifference. Of His neglect.

Wait. Josh had thought Gott abandoned him, too—just before he became convinced of the opposite. Gott hadn't abandoned him. He'd been there all along. Was it possible that Gott knew where she was? That He cared what happened to her? To her family? She remembered the anonymous donations of food and a cow, the deer that had been delivered. All of them seeming to point to Someone who loved her family and was looking out for them.

Could it be that He loved her, too?

Trust Me.

The memory of those two words washed through her, bringing both comfort and conviction. In her unbelief, she'd ignored the Gott who loved her. She'd pushed Him away, claiming He didn't care.

Gott, please forgive me. Please…please help me.

Maybe He would kum through in the eleventh hour.

She needed to give this more thought. Spend more time in prayer.

She went back to the bed.

Shipping out that evening….

Ach, Gott.

Greta picked up the tea and raised it to her mouth….

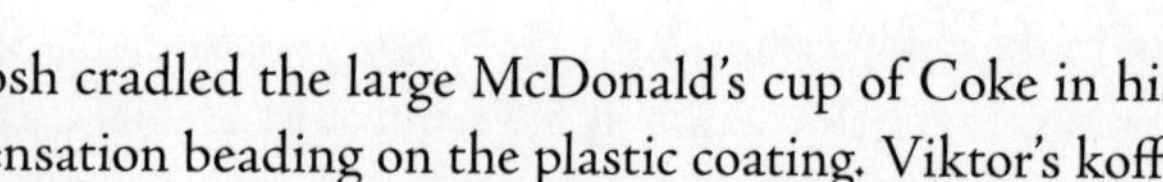

Josh cradled the large McDonald's cup of Coke in his hands, condensation beading on the plastic coating. Viktor's koffee sat in a cupholder in the console. In the backseat, David was silent. Josh turned around. His friend stared out the window, seeming lost in thought. Probably still trying to remember the wording of that verse from Acts 12.

They were on the outskirts of Jamesport, passing the greenhaus, then the Amish supermarket where Greta used to work. *Ach, Greta.* Then going through town to the other side and down the dirt roads.

Soon they pulled into Preacher Samuel's driveway. He came out of the barn, joined by his sohn Sam. Viktor cut the engine but didn't get out. Instead, he pushed a button to lower the window beside Josh.

When the two men approached the window, Josh cleared his throat. "I— We— She—" He stammered to a stop. Swallowed. *Calm down.* "We found her. She's working as a waitress at a restaurant. But she said she was being watched. By someone with a gun. And couldn't leave." He wiped his eyes. "We waited until her shift ended and tried to follow after, to see where she was taken, but we lost them."

Preacher Samuel's gaze turned serious. "Recently, I've heard of Amish girls disappearing from other districts, many of them mere kinner in their rumschpringe."

"Sex trafficking," Sam muttered.

Josh's blood ran cold. He stared at Preacher Samuel's sohn. Nein. They couldn't do that to his Greta.

Preacher Samuel stroked his beard, his forehead furrowing. "I never considered that, Sam, but I'm afraid you might be right." He turned back to Josh. "So, you found her but lost her."

"Jah. Both David and I feel that we need to pray. Storm the doors of heaven. Now."

"I need a Bible," David said from the backseat.

"I'll get mine." Preacher Samuel stepped backward. "There's a hunting cabin in the woods, not too far from here. It's owned by Englischers, but they said we could use it for our Bible studies. I'll get the key." He turned and strode toward the haus.

Sam opened the back door of the truck and climbed in next to David. "If you think you're going to pray Greta home, I'm going to have to see this."

David slid his cane off the seat to make more room. "Nobody ever said we're going to pray her home, though that's not a bad idea."

"If you pray her home, then I'll know He is who you say He is."

Another thing to pray about. Sam had been asking questions—lots of questions—ever since David had risked his own life to save him. When they were still enemies.

Sam scooted over to make room for Josh, who yielded the front seat to Preacher Samuel and joined the other two buwe in back.

Josh closed his eyes. *Gott…ach, Gott….* He knew what he wanted to pray, but the words wouldn't kum. Instead, a refrain began—*Ach, Gott…ach, Gott*—and repeated over and over in his head. Maybe the Spirit knew he needed to pray something different.

Preacher Samuel came out of the haus, climbed into the truck, and handed the Bible back to David. "Here you go, sohn." He turned to Viktor. "Take this road to the Y, then take the right. I'll point out the right dirt road when we reach it."

Five minutes later, the truck bounced down a narrow rutted road in the woods. A small log cabin came into sight. Stones and logs circled a fire pit in the front yard. Preacher Samuel got out and approached the door. He knocked, waited a moment, then unlocked it.

Josh jumped out of the cab and hurried inside. The sooner they started storming heaven, the better.

A flashlight lantern sat on the rough-hewn table. Josh flipped it on as David pulled out a chair and sat, his finger already marking a spot in the Bible. "You're going to love this." He waited until everyone else found a seat, then started reading. "Acts twelve. '*Now about that time Herod the king stretched forth his hands to vex certain of the church. And he killed James the brother of John with the sword. And because he saw it pleased the Jews, he proceeded further to take Peter also….*' I'll skip ahead to verse five: '*Peter therefore was kept in prison: but prayer was made without ceasing of the church unto God for him.*'"

Chapter 23

Greta didn't know how long she prayed—for rescue, for forgiveness, for salvation. Finally, a new sensation of peace flooded her being. And she liked it.

Despite her newfound confidence that things would somehow work out, the situation still seemed hopeless. Her eyes burned with unshed tears. She got up off her sore, stiff knees and climbed into bed. Her legs had fallen asleep, and they tingled as the blood returned to them. Hopefully, Gott would still listen if she prayed in a more comfortable position.

Outside her door, she heard noises. Bumps. Muffled voices. A stifled scream. A door slamming, followed by a female crying. Had Deana kidnapped another Amish girl? Greta sat back against the wall and drew her knees to her chest. She shivered uncontrollably, but not because she was cold.

She must've fallen asleep at some point, because the next thing she knew, she jerked awake, her eyes opening to darkness and a subtle scent she couldn't identify. It didn't smell like Deana's preferred perfume but sweeter, richer.

She glanced at the glowing red numbers of the digital clock beside her bed. Two a.m. Not even the moon lit her room. She lay there, as still as she could, not daring to breathe. What had awakened her? Was it Deana? Or Miah, coming to "ship her off"? *Ach, Gott, not Miah.* Bile rose in her throat. She fought to keep still. They would expect to find her drugged unconscious by whatever Deana had added to the tea Greta had dumped in the sink.

Fear not.

The message, spoken not audibly but in her spirit, seemed to crowd out the terror. The strange sense of peace from earlier started to return.

Suddenly, a faint glow appeared beside her bed. It outlined a dark form…a person. But he didn't seem familiar. Nor did his presence cause her to panic, oddly enough.

Kum quickly. Nein time to tarry.

His words seemed to kum from nowhere and everywhere. She swung her legs over the edge of the bed, not questioning the command. The dreamlike quality of his presence made her trust him. He moved toward her bedroom door—which was closed and locked—and opened it. Greta hurried into the dimly lit hall, and he shut the door behind her without a sound.

The door to the other basement bedroom, usually open, was shut. But Greta heard silence—nein more crying. She hesitated.

The man shook his head. ***Hurry.***

She followed him upstairs, into the dark kitchen, through the living room, and to the front door. It also opened at his touch.

Greta held her breath, bracing for the blare of the alarm. But it didn't go off, even though the flashing green light showed that the system was activated.

Follow Me.

Was this a dream? She looked around. A squirrel scampered up a tree, and a night bird sang from its perch in the branches. *Freedom.* Something she'd taken for granted before she was abducted. She took a deep breath, this time catching the scent of roses.

The man moved down the abandoned street to a dark car.

Get in.

She opened the car door and slid in. Her rescuer—somehow, she knew that's what he was, and not a man sent to deliver her to Kansas City—walked around and got in behind the wheel. In the brief time that the interior lights illuminated his features, she glanced his way. He had a beard and wore Mennonite clothing. But she didn't know who he was. She didn't know how he'd been able to get in and out of locked doors without a key, or to get out of the haus without setting off the alarm.

She still couldn't believe they'd made it this far without being caught. Feeling a ping of panic, she looked back at the haus with a shiver, half expecting to see someone coming after them. How was this happening? Where was he taking her?

I'm taking you home.

After answering her unspoken question, the man started the car and drove off, waiting to turn on the headlights until they'd left the neighborhood.

Her heart leapt as she thought about home. Tears burned her eyes. Gott had actually rescued her.

Maybe.

Watching out the window, she began to recognize various landmarks. The local greenhaus. The store where she used to work. The business district of Jamesport. Then the back roads near her family's haus. Past Onkel Samuel's haus and the schoolhaus. But instead of taking the left in the road, he went right at the Y. "Wait—"

Trust me. I know.

But he didn't take her home. Instead, he pulled to a stop in the middle of the woods, of all places.

This is where you get out.

Confused, Greta shifted, unfastened the seat belt that she didn't remember buckling, and slid out. She turned to look at the man.

This is the way. He pointed down a trail she hadn't noticed. ***Walk about a quarter mile, and you'll reach a cabin.***

Right. She glanced over her shoulder at the rough path leading through the dark woods, lit dimly by the light of the moon when it wasn't obscured by clouds.

"Are you sure?" She turned back to the car. "Where am—"

She was alone.

The car was gone.

Gone!

Her heart raced.

This had to be a dream. Cars didn't just disappear down dirt roads without a sound. People didn't vanish. Slumping with disappointment, she closed her eyes, afraid to open them again and cause this wunderbaar dream to vanish. A shiver of cool nacht air rippled across her skin, and she hugged herself.

An owl screeched somewhere in the canopy of trees above, startling her eyelids open.

She was still in the middle of a road in the woods. This had to be real.

Had Gott sent an angel to rescue her? Did He still do that?

Her heart filled to overflowing with gratitude. *Danki, Lord Gott. Danki.*

She wouldn't question it anymore. Not now. Not when, whatever the cause, she was still free.

Biting her lip, she backed up a few steps and started down the trail. She jumped at another screech from the owl, then started running. Sharp stones cut into her bare feet. She winced and stumbled but didn't slow her pace, instead moving to the grassy strip between the wheel ruts.

She rounded a curve in the path, and there stood a tiny cabin, soft light shining through its windows. She stopped under a tree and stared, suddenly having second thoughts. How did she know this was a safe place? She could be walking into another trap, similar to the one she'd just escaped.

Even so, she felt compelled to approach. Her feet insisted on it. She climbed the rough steps, then stood outside the door as another bout of insecurity overtook her.

Gott, I can't.

Knock, and the door shall be opened unto you.

Maybe so, but what would she find on the other side?

After a moment, she raised her hand and tapped on the door. A woodpecker would've made more noise. She backed away, ready to run if she needed to.

Rustling sounds came from within. Footsteps. A second later, the door opened.

A bearded man stood silhouetted in the doorway. *Onkel Samuel.* Her breath caught, and tears clouded her vision.

His eyes widened, his lips parted, and he stared for what seemed like a minute. Maybe two.

Greta's face heated as she remembered she wore nothing except the indecent tank top and shorts. Her long braid was uncovered. She crossed her arms over her chest, wishing for something to cover the rest of her.

"Josh." Onkel Samuel's voice broke with a strange sob, and he stepped aside.

Josh took in the appearance of the girl in the doorway for a long moment before the truth registered. *Greta.*

He caught his breath. The men around him gasped as he shot to his feet. "Ach, liebling." He rushed over and gathered her to his chest, then swept her up in his arms. The chilled skin of her arms as they wrapped around his neck did nothing to calm him. She was returned to him, at last. She pressed her face into his neck and began to tremble. He moved her to the low futon across the room, where he sat and held her in his lap, indifferent to the others' gazes, to the impropriety of his actions.

Greta burst into tears. "You're real." She burrowed into him. "It's *not* a dream."

"Nein, liebling, nein dream. I'm here, and you're safe."

Viktor dropped a blanket over them, probably just as much to cover her body as to warm her.

Josh shouldn't be seeing her in her current state, but he didn't care.

"Danki, Gott. Danki."

Around them, praises and prayers of thanksgiving burst forth. Josh watched as Greta's eyes widened at the unusual outbursts. It wasn't the Amish way. But their way needed to be shaken up. Gott needed the honor and praise.

Josh would explain that later. For now, he just nuzzled her neck. She smelled…different. A musky floral scent. Not like the mixture of vanilla and cinnamon he was used to. It didn't matter. It was her hair, her eyes, her lips. It was her. His Greta.

She still trembled in his arms.

"Shhh. I have you, liebling. You're safe." He rocked a little and rained tiny kisses from her ear to the corner of her lips.

"I was scared. So scared. They wouldn't let me leave. They locked me in a basement room, and they were going to ship me off to-nacht. They were selling me as a…." She lifted her face to his. "A prostitute." These words she whimpered.

Prostitute. Josh's stomach roiled. He held her even tighter, trying to shield her from even the memory of her experience. It was just as Sam had suspected. *Ach, dear Lord…just in the nick of time. Danki, danki, danki.*

"How did you escape?" David asked her.

Greta shook her head. "I don't know. Some man—he looked Mennonite—he appeared in my room and told me to follow him. He opened locked doors without a key, and got us outside without setting off the home security system alarm. He drove me in a car as far as the end of the trail leading here, and then he vanished when I got out. Really. Just…gone." She used the corner of the blanket to wipe a tear from her cheek.

"An angel." Sam sounded stupefied. "Just like in the Bible. Like Peter."

Josh tugged Greta against his chest again, with one hand splayed against the side of her hip. Warmth was finally returning to her skin, and yet, for the first time, the contact didn't send flames of passion searing through his veins. Deep gratitude was all he felt. *An angel. Ach, Lord.* Fresh tears filled his eyes.

"I thought He'd rejected me. I turned my back on Him…and yet He loved me enough to rescue me." Greta's voice held awe.

"God is infinitely more committed to you than you ever will be to Him," Preacher Samuel said quietly.

Danki, Lord. It became a continual refrain.

He pulled her closer still.

An angel.

The tears escaped. Poured down his cheeks. Dripped off his chin.

"Ach, Lord. Your mercy endures forever and ever."

Chapter 24

Josh wiped his hand over his wet face and tried to wrestle his emotions under control. He rubbed his eyes and glanced around the room. Not that he cared what others thought of him, crying like a boppli. It wasn't every day that Gott moved in such a way.

Sam looked at David. "Gott has proven Himself beyond what I thought He was capable of doing."

Smiling, David reached for his cane, glanced up at the loft, then propped the cane against the wall and stood without its assistance. "Kum with me, Sam. We need to talk." He picked up the Bible and shuffled toward the ladder.

Preacher Samuel caught Josh's gaze for a brief moment before he turned to Viktor, tears glittering in his eyes. Sam grabbed the lantern and followed David, leaving the room in pitch darkness.

"Gott has moved in miraculous ways," Preacher Samuel said quietly. "Seems revival is starting to sweep across Amish country."

"Seems so. And badly needed, for sure," Viktor agreed.

"Can't see a thing down here," the preacher said. "I'm going to try to sit. Hopefully, not on Greta's lap."

Greta hiccupped.

Preacher Samuel touched the top of Josh's head, then lowered himself beside him on the futon. "We need to keep praying, buwe. Gott has begun something here."

Greta moved off Josh's lap. Now that she'd finally begun to feel safe, she was uncomfortable with that level of familiarity around her extended family—and more aware of Josh's hand resting on her hip, his fingertips touching her thigh. A slow, growing burn made its way through her veins.

Josh seemed reluctant to let her go. Nein sooner than she scooted off than he drew her tight against his side, his arm settling around her bare shoulders. She adjusted the blanket to better cover herself. Not that anyone could see her in the darkness. But she knew…and Gott knew.

Gott, I'm so sorry for doubting You. She dipped her head. *Help me to learn to trust You more. To know that, nein matter what, You will be there for me. I don't know what's going to happen with my family yet. I don't know how I can go home and face Mamm and Gizelle, especially after all the lies….*

The thin strap of the tank top slid down her arm. Despite the blanket covering her, she yanked it back up.

And especially dressed like this. If they thought my morals were bad before…

And Bishop Joe. If she reappeared with Josh, wearing indecent clothing…. She sniffled. And the bishop had been scandalized by her messy hair when she'd ridden in a convertible.

Though, the "punishment" of being forced to marry Josh no longer held even a thimbleful of revulsion. She'd gladly see it enforced.

Nein, the bishop would kum up with something far worse.

Like forcing her to kneel and publicly confess all the things she'd been falsely accused of doing.

But after facing the prospect of a life of prostitution, kneeling and confessing—even to wrongs she hadn't committed—seemed easy.

Greta straightened, jerking out of Josh's arms. "Onkel Samuel? Am I shunned?"

"Ach, liebling. Don't worry. Everything's going to be okay." Josh reached for her, drawing her back to his side. He didn't want to let her out of reach. Terrified she'd vanish again.

"Don't worry?" Greta pulled away again. Her voice was tight. Josh had nein choice but to let her go. "But that means...."

Preacher Samuel grunted.

Greta slumped. "Then I really am shunned? She said I was." She leaned against Josh once more, as if needing the contact as much as he did. "Why aren't you shunning me?"

"Who's 'she'?" Josh asked instead. He wanted a name. He ran his hand down Greta's arm and back up, then tucked her closer against him.

Across the room, a chair creaked as Viktor shifted.

Dawn colored the sky outside the windows, filling the cabin with dim light.

Preacher Samuel exhaled a heavy sigh and leaned forward, resting his elbows on his knees. "Bishop Joe isn't in his right mind, Greta. He has a brain tumor. It's affecting him mentally, making him unreasonable at times. We don't know yet if it is cancerous or not. But the bishop reacted to your appearance without taking into consideration that he might be operating under a misconception. In this case, as far as I'm—we're—concerned, the shunning isn't valid. Besides, Bishop Joe didn't tell anyone in the community, so the word hasn't gotten out."

"Bishop Joe has a tumor? Ach, Josh did say something about that. I forgot. Will he be all right?" Greta pulled the blanket tighter around herself.

"It's in the Lord's hands."

"But does my family know why he reacted that way? Will I be allowed to return home?" She choked on the words.

"Doesn't matter," Viktor stated. "Esther and I have decided. You'll kum stay with us. Neither Esther or I have joined, so it won't bother anyone."

Josh tucked the blanket under Greta's chin. "Or you could kum home with me. Mamm would love to take care of you." *And you'd be near me, so I could keep you safe.*

Preacher Samuel coughed. As if he wasn't in complete agreement with that plan.

"We'll face Greta's family in the morgen," he said quietly.

Greta slumped. "Maybe it'd be best if I looked for another place with some Englisch friends in Jamesport. Away from here. I don't want to cause problems for anyone."

"Nein!" Josh hadn't meant to yell, but he must have, judging by the way Greta jumped. He reached for her hand, intertwining her fingers with his. "You're not leaving again. You can't. How can you even consider it, after...?" He pressed his lips together and shook his head.

"It's not as if I want to, but...." She looked up.

He followed her gaze.

Sam appeared at the edge of the loft, holding the lantern. David started down the ladder, clutching the Bible.

Preacher Samuel stood. He tugged at his beard, then dropped his hands to his side. Then he lifted them across his chest. And released them again.

David handed him the Bible and gave a single nod.

Preacher Samuel laid it on the table. When Sam stepped off the bottom rung of the ladder, the preacher reached for his sohn and pulled him into his arms. "Praise Gott. Praise Gott." Tears flowed unhampered down his cheeks.

Viktor came to his feet, a grin appearing on his face. "Two miracles in one nacht."

"Three." Greta looked up. "I found Gott, too." Her voice broke. She glanced at Josh, then down at the floor. "She let me use an old laptop. I found your trail journals."

Josh cringed, remembering some of his entries. But then he grinned as his conversion came to mind. She'd found der Herr as a result. He pulled her closer and leaned into her, intending to steal a kiss. But then, centimeters away from making contact, he remembered their audience and angled his head to give her a chaste kiss on her cheek. "Who's 'she'?" he asked again, but that last comment seemed to answer his question. "Your kidnapper?"

"Jah. Deana. I first met her at the farmers' market. I think she targeted me and was even behind the robbery. She set me up so I would go with her willingly. She seemed nice. At first."

Josh scowled. At least he had a name.

"We need to get home," Preacher Samuel said. "Our families will wonder what happened to us." He released Sam. "I'll kum by Viktor's about an hour before noon to get Greta and take her home. We'll see what happens from there. I know Andy will be glad to see her. I think Martha will be, too." He lifted a shoulder.

Viktor yawned and stretched. "Jah. I'm in need of a gut nap or a strong cup of koffee. Maybe both."

Josh helped Greta up and lifted her long, silky braid out from under the blanket. He rested his hand on her back as they walked outside, then lifted her into the backseat. She scooted over, and Sam got in the vehicle from the other side and slid over next to her.

Josh climbed in and shut the door, then patted his lap. "Sit here, liebling."

Color crept into Greta's cheeks.

"There's room on the seat," Sam pointed out. "David's in already. We're only a little squished. You just want an excuse to hold her."

Josh couldn't deny that. He wrapped his arm around her shoulders again. "Preacher Samuel, I want to go with you when you take Greta home."

Preacher Samuel tugged at his beard again. "I know you want to be with her, sohn. But this time…I think, nein. Not a gut idea. I'll make sure we kum by afterward to tell you how it went."

We. As in, Preacher Samuel and Greta?

His heart hurt.

Beside him, Greta winced.

Evidently Preacher Samuel didn't expect it to go well.

Chapter 25

Greta's stomach ached. She wanted to curl up in a ball and cry out all the tension. And she never wanted to leave the safety of her home again. But that wouldn't be an option.

Not that her home was safe. Nein, she might have escaped one nightmare, but another still remained. Gizelle seemed to be behind some of her problems. Greta wondered how her sister would react to her return after feeding Bishop Joe half-truths on the heels of half-truths she'd told Mamm. Maybe she could hope for a smile from Daed.

Viktor drove his truck behind the Petersheims' barn and parked. Greta shifted away from Josh's side, but Viktor looked back at them with a slight grin. "You two have until Esther hears Greta is in the truck. Five minutes, give or take. Keep it decent." He winked at Josh, lowered the windows, then got out.

Greta's face flamed. Just like Viktor to take them behind the barn and leave them there. Unchaperoned.

Not that she minded. But she would have preferred being by the waterfall again, or walking down the dark road, hand in hand. Somewhere secret. Not orchestrated by someone else.

The door slammed shut, and Greta watched as Viktor stalked around the corner of the barn. Josh grazed her hand with trembling fingers. "I was going crazy worrying about you." He reached up and smoothed her braid. "I missed you."

"I missed you, too. Terribly." She shivered. "I never intended to go away for long, but when I went to the park after Daed's heart attack, I was sure I was shunned. Then Deana showed up, and she seemed so nice. So understanding. I didn't know what else to do."

"So you went with her willingly?"

Greta nodded. "It wasn't so bad, at first. Deana told me that she and her husband ran a halfway haus for runaway Amish kids. And there were two other Amish girls there who seemed really nice. Deana promised she'd help me get my GED and my driver's license, and she said she'd take me home if I wanted to go, but it was all lies. She wouldn't let me go to the hospital to see Daed or anything. And then I realized Miah was the one who robbed me. Her nephew Daniel told me what they actually did with the girls. And then I got scared.

"I think they kidnapped another girl. I didn't see her, but last nacht, before Gott rescued me, I heard crying."

Josh turned to face her. "There are real halfway houses out there. I think there's one in Cameron."

Greta shrugged. "You probably heard about Deana's. I have no idea if they actually help Amish buwe or not. But the girls...." Greta shook her head. "I thought she was an angel of mercy, taking me in out of the rain, and hugging me. But then it was just scary. I'm worried about the girl who was crying in the other bedroom."

"You know who is involved. You mentioned three names. You know where the haus is. And we know which restaurant they forced you to work at. We'll go to the phone shanty later and report it to the police."

"Jah, I guess that's a gut idea." Greta glanced out the window. "Ach, Esther." She scooted across the seat and out the door, then fell into her cousin's arms.

"I couldn't believe it when Viktor said you were out here." Esther hugged her tight.

Greta clung to her. "I'm so glad to be back."

Josh shut the truck door and rested his hand on her lower back for a moment, then moved away. "I'm going inside."

Probably to suggest to Viktor that they call the police.

Greta shivered. She would be scared to leave the house if Deana wasn't apprehended. Afraid to go to town. Panicky to be alone. And what about the others she might have endangered by escaping? She'd written Esther's address on the letter Deana's husband was supposed to mail for her. What if they'd kept it to use in tracking her down? The thought of Deana out there somewhere, knowing where Greta worked, where she lived, brought a deep sense of dread. The woman could take her again, and there wouldn't be an angel to save her the second time. Greta would never be able to leave home without looking over her shoulder.

"Let's go inside," Esther said. "I have an extra dress you can wear until you get your own clothes at home."

If she were even allowed to darken the doorway at home. Greta's stomach churned with anxiety.

Would her life end up ruled by fear? If only she could feel that elusive peace again. Or breathe in that heavenly scent.

While Josh and Viktor reported everything they knew about the situation to Viktor's grossdaedi, Esther hurried the blanket-wrapped Greta upstairs for a bath, presumably, since Josh could hear water running.

It'd be nice to have his Greta returned to normal. Modest clothes, the prayer kapp, scented like vanilla and cinnamon....

He couldn't wait to resume courting her.

Josh didn't want to leave the Petersheims', but it didn't seem right to linger when his host kept smothering his yawns behind his hand. Besides, Josh needed to get home and let his family know Greta had been found, not to mention start catching up on the work he'd let go while she was missing.

Mamm would be so relieved at the news. Despite the unofficial shunning, she would probably invite Greta for dinner and prepare all her favorite foods.

It'd been too long since she'd had dinner at his home. Too long since they'd played a game of Scrabble after the dishes were done. Talking, laughing, enjoying each other's company. The last time had been before his departure.

Josh pulled in a deep breath and glanced around the kitchen table at Viktor and his großeltern. "I'll see you later, jah? Danki for all your help, Vik, and for your prayers, Reuben. Anna."

"I'll keep praying for the whole situation," Reuben said. "Especially for her healing. She'll have a lot to work through, for sure."

Josh nodded. He'd never considered the emotional trauma Greta had suffered. He would have to be sensitive of that. "Tell Greta I'll see her later."

Viktor nodded. "Will do."

Josh pushed the screen door open and stepped outside. Even though it was early, the sun beat down with a force, and the humidity made it hard to breathe. Hopefully, rain was in the forecast.

He walked until he reached Preacher Samuel's haus, then climbed the porch steps and opened the kitchen door. "Hallo?"

Rachel poked her head out from the sewing room. "Ach, Josh." She came into the kitchen, carrying a garment made of blue material. Probably her wedding dress. "Daed just told us the news. I'm so glad Greta's safe. I'll go see her later. Daed went to get Preacher Zeke. He wants him along when they take her home." She fingered the blue material.

Josh glanced away. "I offered to go with him, but he said nein."

Rachel raised one shoulder in a shrug. "He said something about stopping in to visit the bishop, too. I'm so excited she's back. She'll be able to by my side-sitter at my wedding. Well, if Bishop

Joe pardons her. I asked Bethany Weiss to be a side-sitter, too, as Esther can't, since she's married."

Josh pinched the bridge of his nose as he studied Rachel, wondering if there were any questions in that speech that he needed to answer. "Um, jah," he finally said. "Might be gut to visit Bishop Joe." He had some words of his own that he wanted to say to the man, but Preacher Samuel had already cautioned him against doing so.

"Daed said they were planning on selling her into prostitution." Rachel's eyes were wide. "Isn't that scary? Hard to believe there are people like that nearby. And that some of the other Amish girls who we'd assumed had run away might actually have—"

The screen door breezed open and then slammed shut as Sam strode into the kitchen. He stopped and stared at Josh for a second, then grinned. "Hiya. Didn't you just leave?"

"Jah, but I have something else to tell your daed. Greta mentioned some names when we were talking. And I want to call the police. I know it's not our way, but we need to protect other girls from falling victim to the same scheme. Given the current situation, I didn't think he'd have a problem with it; but thought I'd let him know, since the police might want to talk to Greta. To me. To David. And maybe even to your daed."

"Names, huh?" Sam got out a glass and filled it with water, then took a long swallow as Rachel returned to her sewing room.

"Jah. Deana, Miah, and Daniel."

Sam's brow furrowed. "You know, there's a guy in my one college class named Dan. He's mentioned an Aunt Deana a time or two. Maybe when I go to class later today, I'll talk to him. If Daed thinks it's okay."

"Maybe not, in case you tip them off and they flee." Josh lowered his chin. "I guess I need to head home. When you see your daed, would you tell him I stopped by? He was going to give me an update, anyway, but I need to talk to him before long."

"You got it." Sam nodded. "And, hey—if you don't mind, pray for me? I've got some decisions ahead of me."

"I will."

As Josh left the Millers', a heaviness descended over him. Maybe it was just the sudden calm after the raging storm of adrenaline. Or maybe it was from a lack of sleep. Either way, his spirit seemed to deflate. His eyes burned with unshed tears.

Josh stopped at the shanty nearby and picked up the phone. He didn't care what the preachers would say. Something needed to be done. If he got in trouble for his actions, then so be it. Other Amish girls might be in danger. Relief fluttered in his stomach at the thought of Greta being home safe, where she belonged.

Once assured that nein ambulance was needed, the emergency dispatcher promised to send an officer out to talk with Josh right away.

As he started the mile walk home, he couldn't help but worry about Greta.

Would she be welcomed by her family? Would Bishop Joe change his mind?

Or would the shunning become official and stand?

~

At the sound of hoofbeats and buggy wheels in Esther's driveway, Greta pressed a hand to her stomach, willing the contents to stay put. She got up from the bed in the spare room, where she'd been attempting to nap, and glanced out the window.

As she'd feared, it was Preacher Samuel and Preacher Zeke.

Time to go home and see her family.

She shouldn't be afraid, but terror filled her. Would she be able to hold her tongue around Gizelle, after all the false accusations she'd made that had propelled her into the horrific mess she'd just escaped? Could she ever forgive her sister?

She quickly redid her hair into the approved style, secured Esther's spare kapp over it, and checked the borrowed dress to make sure it was smooth and securely pinned. It was gut to be attired in the familiar way, instead of in the strange-feeling, immodest clothes she'd been forced to wear for weeks.

Footsteps sounded in the hallway. Then someone tapped on the door.

"Greta?" Esther whispered. "Are you awake yet?"

If only she'd been able to sleep.

Greta opened the door. "I'm just about ready. Do you have an extra pair of flip-flops to lend me? And will you pray for me?"

"For sure. But the preachers want to talk to you first. They want the whole story from the beginning, including the accusations Gizelle made about you."

Bile rose in Greta's throat. She didn't want to talk about all that. She wanted to forget Gizelle's lies. Forget Deana. Forget the awful experience, most of all the threat of being sold into prostitution. But she supposed Preacher Zeke would insist on hearing everything, in order to decide whether the Amish community at large ought to shun her. Preacher Samuel had said that he would disregard any shunning that was enforced, but he couldn't speak for everyone.

Esther frowned with concern. "You're looking rather sick. If you don't want to do it, I can tell them you're ill."

Greta shrugged. "I'll have to face them sooner or later." She swallowed, trying to control her nausea.

"I just made some mint tea. I'll pour you a cup. That will help to calm you."

"Nein, but danki." Greta wrung the fabric of her dress. "Nothing will help."

"Prayer will help, Greta. And those who love you will support you, nein matter what." Esther gave her a hug.

Greta could hardly believe she'd needed the reminder. *Lord, forgive my unbelief.* She moved toward the stairs. "Danki, Esther."

Moments later, she stepped into the kitchen. The two preachers stood before her, looming large. Preacher Zeke's expression was stern. Where were Anna and Reuben? They'd probably been asked to leave, so the preachers could talk to Greta alone. With nein witnesses.

The nausea returned, and there was nein controlling it. She spun around, almost colliding with Esther, and dashed into the bathroom.

Chapter 26

Josh strode up the long driveway to his parents' home, hoping he wouldn't find a squad car already parked between the haus and the barn. Mamm and Daed, not to mention his older brother and his brother's frau, would be alarmed if a police officer showed up looking for him.

He'd overstepped boundaries, calling 9-1-1 without an official okay from Preacher Samuel.

When Josh rounded the bend and saw nein police car out front, he blew out the breath he hadn't realized he was holding, then yawned. Staying out all nacht, mixed with all the stress of the previous days, had wiped him out. But his stomach grumbled in complaint of its lack of breakfast.

Josh glanced at the sky, noting the position of the sun. Probably about eight. He'd missed breakfast but might be able to talk Mamm into making him a fried egg sandwich to eat on the way out to work.

Daed came out of the barn, leading two draft horses. "Ach, gut. You're home. We need your help in the west field."

Sometimes, he thought it might be nice if his parents were to ask him where he'd been. Especially after he'd been gone all nacht and had important news to share. So much had happened.

"Daed." Josh's voice cracked. "We found Greta." He blinked back the fresh tears that stung his eyes, but one managed to escape. He wiped it away. He'd cried enough already.

Daed's gaze searched his. Compassion lit his eyes. "I'm sorry, sohn. I hoped you'd have better news."

"What do you mean, better news? It's the best. She's back now. I'll explain what happened."

Daed glanced at the horses, then looked toward the field. "I'd like to hear it. But you go on in and clean up, and I'll meet you in the kitchen. I'm sure your mamm would like to know, too."

Josh ran his hand over his chin, feeling the stubble. If he looked disheveled enough that Daed had noticed, it must be bad. He backed up a step. Hesitated. "The police are coming."

Daed turned abruptly to face him again, the skin around his mouth etched with lines of concern. "You'd better hurry, then."

Apparently, the same restraint that kept Daed from asking about his whereabouts during the nacht stopped him from inquiring why the police were on their way. But maybe it was simply that Daed trusted him. If so, that was a new thing since his return. He'd grown into a man—no longer a bu.

Josh turned and jogged to the haus. Mamm wasn't in the kitchen. Probably in the basement, since he heard noises coming from down there. He hurried upstairs to the spare bathroom for a quick shower, then changed his clothes.

When he came back downstairs, the kitchen was still empty, but a laundry basket full of wet clothes sat at one end of the table, waiting to be taken outside and hung to dry. And at the other end of the table sat a metal mixing bowl of rising dough, next to the faded old fabric Mamm used for rolling out dough. Jars of cinnamon and sugar sat nearby.

Josh's stomach growled yet again at the thought of cinnamon rolls. It was almost empty, save for a few nibbles of the burger he'd taken to go from the restaurant where they'd found Greta.

A low murmur of voices came from just outside the open screen door. Josh peeked out the window. Mamm, Daed, and two police officers stood on the front porch. Mamm wore a pinched look, clearly not thrilled to have had her daily schedule interrupted by strangers—and the law, no less. Daed probably felt the same way, but his expression was more schooled. All four glanced at Josh when he opened the door and stepped outside to join them.

At least he wouldn't have to tell the story more than once. Though he did fear missing out on the cinnamon rolls if the police officers asked him to go with them.

"Joshua Yoder?" One of the officers peered at him. "We had a call to come to this address."

"Jah—yes." Josh had given some information to the dispatcher taking the call, but he didn't know how much of it, if any, had been communicated to these officers. Their faces gave nothing away.

Josh swiped his hand over his freshly shaven jaw.

"Why don't you tell us why you called." The officer who spoke, the one wearing a pair of black sunglasses, scowled at Josh as if he'd interrupted an overdue koffee break.

Were police always so stern? Josh's stomach twisted as he recalled the destructive fireworks at Viktor's haus that had prompted his first encounter with the law. Those officers had been scary, too. Especially to an already terrified adolescent.

"Jah—yes, sir. Have a seat, and I'll tell you the whole story."

But only Josh's parents sat. Then Josh leaned against the porch railing and began his story.

"It all started when my girl, Greta, went missing."

Esther came into the bathroom and set a glass of murky-looking water on the counter next to Greta. "Rinse your mouth with this. It's baking soda." She rubbed Greta's upper back. "You don't have anything to fear, Greta. Onkel Samuel is on your side, and Preacher Zeke just wants to hear the story from you before he makes any judgment call. You know he's a reasonable man."

Preacher Zeke did have a reputation for being kind, as well as for getting to the heart of a matter before he made any decision. Onkel Samuel would go with her to face her parents and also to talk to the bishop, if they decided Bishop Joe was in the wrong. Even so, Greta wasn't ready to deal with the fallout from this past month. She might never be ready.

Taking a deep breath and pressing a trembling hand over her stomach, she forced herself to straighten and reached for the glass as Esther left, closing the door behind her. Greta rinsed her mouth several times, then scrubbed her face to eradicate any traces of her tears. Then she reached for the doorknob. *Lord Gott, I need You.*

She received nein audible answer, but a sense of peace flowed through her. If Gott could send an angel with a car to rescue her, then surely He could help her talk to her onkel. She sucked in a breath and opened the door.

In the kitchen, Esther was serving the preachers mugs of koffee and a platter of sweet bread. When she moved for the door, Greta found her voice. "Stay. Please. I need you."

Esther hesitated. She glanced at the preachers, then nodded before taking a seat.

"Sit down, Greta," Preacher Zeke said, his voice kind.

Greta pulled out a chair and lowered herself into it.

"Why don't we start at the beginning? Have you and Gizelle had discord among you?"

Of course, he would want to broach that issue first. Greta thought she would rather talk about her month of captivity, or her miraculous escape, than to tattle on her sister.

She took a deep breath. "I didn't think so. We've always gotten along just fine…at least, until she took my old job at the Amish Country Store, and Josh started coming around. Then she started lying. For example, she said she was out with Josh the nacht of Daed's heart attack…things like that. I'm not sure if she wanted to make me jealous, or what."

Preacher Zeke nodded, as if her response explained everything. "And did you go outside in your nacht-gown when Josh visited? With your hair down?"

"Jah, but I wore a robe over it, tied shut. And my hair was in a braid." At least that particular time. "And another time, I wore a dress, but my hair was loose." The preciousness of the memories battled with a powerful sense of shame, but she realized she would do it over again if she had the chance.

Across the table, Onkel Samuel leaned close to Preacher Zeke and whispered something. The minister nodded, then turned his attention back to Greta. "Tell me about the robbery at the farmers' market and your subsequent abduction."

Greta didn't know if she would have called it an "abduction." She'd gone willingly, after all. But maybe it counted as an abduction since she hadn't been allowed to leave of her own accord.

She took another deep breath and then told them the whole story.

When she concluded, Preacher Zeke took a final swig of his koffee, then stood. "I've heard enough. We'll go see Bishop Joe now. I want you to kum with us, Greta."

She felt a surge of panic, but it quieted when Onkel Samuel gave her an encouraging smile.

Esther went over to the door and picked up her ruby flip-flops. "Do you want me to kum with you?"

Onkel Samuel shook his head. "She'll be fine. You stay here and take care of your own. I'll either bring her back later or stop by to tell you what happened."

"Danki, Esther." Greta gave her a hug before putting on the flip-flops. "Keep praying."

Esther nodded. "None of what's to kum will even begin to compare with what you've already been through. You can do this."

Jah, she could. She still didn't want to face the bishop—or her family. But with the help of der Herr, she would.

All too soon, Onkel Samuel guided the horse into Bishop Joe's driveway.

Preacher Zeke glanced back at Greta. "Your onkel and I will handle this. You keep quiet unless you're spoken to."

Greta nodded. *Gladly*.

They found the bishop seated in the quiet kitchen, holding a dish towel to his head as he rocked slightly in the chair.

Reminded of his brain tumor, Greta found her anger toward him abating. Her eyes welled with tears of sympathy.

Bishop Joe opened his eyes and glared at the group, as if they had nein right to bother him. Neither preacher acknowledged the look. Instead, Onkel Samuel pulled out a chair for Greta, then sat next to her.

The bishop lowered the towel from his head. He grimaced, his eyes clouded with pain. "So, you returned. Are you willing to kneel and confess?"

Sharp words burned on the tip of Greta's tongue. Somehow, she kept them from coming out. Instead, she merely nodded.

"Now, hold on a minute." Onkel Samuel took the lead. "Zeke and I just had a long conversation with Greta, and we feel the girl has done nothing wrong."

Greta brightened. The preachers would support her? *Danki, Gott*.

"Jah, she went outside her haus in her nacht-clothes and with her hair loose," her onkel conceded, "but she didn't do it deliberately to cause sin in the heart of man. And you know our own fraus and dochters do the same at our homes."

"But she's been rebellious and disobedient. And she stole her family's money." Bishop Joe waved his hand at her.

She bit her tongue and glanced at her onkel.

"I don't want to talk about this," the bishop went on. "You handle it. Shunned for six weeks after confession." He added a decisive nod, then winced.

Preacher Zeke raised an eyebrow, then cleared his throat. "Do you think you should be bothered with church decisions at this time? Maybe you should step back and let Samuel and me handle your duties until you've finished treatments."

Bishop Joe unwrapped the dish towel, adjusted the ice pack inside, and bundled it up again. He frowned. Hesitated.

Greta held her breath.

The bishop nodded. "Jah. My frau and I have discussed this. I'm not stepping down. But I authorize you both to act on my behalf." He pressed the towel to his head again. "Handle Greta as der Herr wills. And since Preacher Eli passed on to glory, we need to ask der Herr to call another man to step in as preacher. You work out the details of both. I'm done." He pushed to his feet and groaned. "I'm going to take a nap."

Onkel Samuel's smile flickered. He glanced at Greta as a door shut. "We'll go talk to your parents." He stood.

"And tell them…what? That I'm shunned for six weeks after I kneel and confess?"

Preacher Zeke raised his eyebrows at her admittedly impudent question. "I don't think you've done anything for which you need to kneel and confess to the community at large." He pushed his chair back. "You're not shunned."

"Danki." The whispered one-word response was all she could manage. She rose on shaky legs, feeling suddenly hungry and wishing she'd eaten some of the sweet bread at Esther's. For now, she feasted on joy.

The community would gossip. People would look at her as if she'd done the things she was accused of. They would wonder how she'd gotten away with her sins.

But it didn't matter what the community thought of her.

Gott alone had the power to forgive sins. And He had forgiven hers. She smiled, remembering the sensation that had washed through her as she'd prayed and confessed. The feeling of newness that had claimed her innermost being. The wonderment at the mercies of Gott.

A verse she'd memorized from Psalm 51 came to mind. *"Purge me with hyssop, and I shall be clean: wash me, and I shall be whiter than snow."*

~

As Josh described the man guarding Greta in the restaurant—the one she'd claimed carried a gun—one of the officers worked on a corresponding sketch.

When he finished, Josh nodded, suppressing a shudder. Even on paper, the man radiated evil. "Looks like him."

The other officer raised an eyebrow. "If this is the man I think he is, your girlfriend stumbled into a drug organization. The FBI made a drug bust late last night."

"Drugs?"

"That, among other things, is bad enough to get the FBI involved." The officer stood. "Where will I find Greta?"

Josh's stomach churned. She wouldn't have any idea the police were coming to talk to her. And he had nein way of warning her. "Viktor Petersheim's farm." He gave directions. "But she may not be there. Preacher Samuel said something about taking her home." He told them how to get to her haus.

The police officers both nodded, then turned to leave. Josh followed suit, going back into the haus. Mamm had gone inside long ago, once she'd been assured that the officers weren't taking Josh away for committing some crime. Daed had gone toward the field once he'd heard the story. Josh would be expected to follow. Immediately. But he really wanted to go to Greta. Reassure himself that she truly was safe.

But he couldn't.

Besides, Preacher Samuel had said he'd bring Greta out and update him.

He had nothing to do but wait. Hope. Think. Pray.

Mamm met him in the kitchen, her fists resting on her hips. "Joshua Kenan Yoder. When exactly were you planning on telling me Greta was home?" She nodded toward the open window.

He opened his mouth, but she rushed on, "You're going to go get that poor girl and bring her here so I can show her some loving care."

Josh grinned. "For sure. But right now, she's with the preachers. We'll have to wait our turn."

"I expect your daed told you his big news."

Josh shook his head. "Nein. But I'm supposed to help him in the west field. What's going on?"

Mamm smiled. Shrugged. "Maybe he'll mention it."

Chapter 27

Greta's heart thumped as the buggy neared home. She pressed her hand to her stomach, afraid she'd be sick again. At the same time, she wanted to weep for joy.

Home.

Tears burned her eyes, but she willed them to stay put. Better to be stoic and not show her emotions—especially not knowing what would happen. Would Mamm reject her? Would she be allowed to see Daed and William? Would Gizelle be home and start filling the preachers' ears with more lies? Greta rubbed her clammy hands over her borrowed dress. At least she could stay with Esther.

How could she even begin to forgive her sister?

"Forgive us our debts, as we forgive our debtors." The verse flashed through her mind, and she cringed. Gott *expected* her to forgive Gizelle for her lies, and Mamm, too, for taking other people's word for everything and rejecting Greta without giving her a chance to explain. It hadn't been their fault Greta had run away. She'd made the decision all by herself.

Help me, Gott. I can't do it on my own.

I am with you always.

Greta blew out a breath as the buggy rattled over the gravel and came to a stop.

William stepped out of the barn and approached the buggy. As he reached for the reins, he glanced up and met her gaze. "Greta! You're back." He dropped the reins and ran around the buggy to the entrance, clambered into the backseat, and pulled her into his arms. "Ach, we missed you. Please don't run away again."

She wasn't sure how to respond. She hadn't exactly run away, but William didn't know the details of her absence. "I missed you, too." Her voice broke as she returned his embrace.

She doubted she would receive a similar greeting from Mamm and Daed. The normal way of welcoming a runaway teen was more...unwelcoming. It was ignored. More of an "Ach, you're back." Wasn't that how Josh had been treated when he'd returned? She'd overheard him telling a friend that while he'd been permitted to kum home, his parents had acted as if his absence were nein big deal. Sad. Only his true friends had welcomed him. And Greta couldn't count herself among them. Instead, she'd shunned Josh for breaking her heart.

She'd changed so much since then.

Onkel Samuel glanced back and smiled before getting out of the buggy after Preacher Zeke. "Kum on." But before heading toward the haus, Onkel Samuel paused and bowed his head in prayer.

Was he nervous, too? Greta's stomach flip-flopped like a fish out of water. She wiped her sweaty palms on her dress once more, then slowly followed William out of the buggy.

William took off at a run. "Greta's home. Greta's home!"

She stood on wobbly legs, staring at the haus.

The *quiet* haus. She didn't notice any movement inside the windows.

She swallowed the bile rising in her throat.

I can't do this.

My grace is sufficient.

She took a tentative, trembling step forward. Then another. She looked over her shoulder. Preacher Zeke held the reins. Onkel Samuel still stood by the buggy, his head bowed.

Danki, Gott, that he's praying for me.

The squeaking of the door hinges grabbed Greta's attention.

And Mamm flew out. Down the porch stairs. Across the drive. Arms outstretched.

Greta's heart started beating again. *Danki, Gott, for acceptance. For welkum.*

Daed followed at a much slower pace, but he had a huge grin spread across his face.

She took a few faltering steps toward them as she watched their approach, and all the torment and indecision washed away in a flood of relief. The tears she'd been holding back now overflowed, and she let them come.

Greta collapsed in Mamm's arms, crying. Daed came up behind her and wrapped his strong arms around them both.

Home, sweet home.

Josh lifted another watermelon into the wagon. As he straightened, he noticed a buggy pulling into the drive. Preacher Samuel? Jah. And Preacher Zeke. He didn't see Greta, though.

Daed carried another watermelon over and loaded it. He glanced toward the haus and frowned. "Why are the preachers here?"

Coming on the tails of the police, the preachers' presence probably did seem suspicious. He should've thought to warn Daed of this planned visit. He'd been too consumed with thoughts of Greta. Of Mamm's comments. Of the police officer's sketch and his mention of drugs. Of the ongoing mystery of whatever it was Daed wanted to talk about, which hadn't kum up in the last hour they'd worked together in the west field.

"Preacher Samuel promised to stop after he and Preacher Zeke talked to Greta's parents."

Daed's chest rose and fell. "Well then, guess you need to go see what's up. Ain't so?"

Josh nodded, even though Daed had already turned back to the watermelon patch, and hurried to the haus. The preachers met him outside the barn as Mamm and his sister-in-law came outside. Both women stopped on the porch, wiping their hands on towels. He stopped in front of the men and bit his tongue to keep from demanding, "Well?"

Mamm and Linda said something to each other, then turned and went back inside the big haus.

"She's home," Preacher Zeke said. "The parable of the prodigal sohn, revisited."

Preacher Samuel nodded. "Welcomed with open arms. Gizelle is at work, so we'll need to make a return visit to talk with her." His expression grew stern. "And the police arrived to talk with Greta. Took matters into your own hands, ain't so?"

Josh cringed. "I stopped by to ask permission. But you were gone. I didn't want what happened to Greta to happen to another Amish girl. I talked with Sam, and the phone shanty was right there, and...." He shrugged.

"I would've given permission. This situation demanded police intervention." Preacher Samuel tugged at his beard. "A couple things more, Josh. Preacher Zeke and I are both serving in Bishop Joe's stead until he recovers." He gave him a serious look. "We are going to have a drawing on Sunday for a new preacher. We need you to pray that the right man is called."

David. Ach, Lord, let it be so. "I will, for sure." He grinned. The last time they'd seriously prayed, Gott had answered in a dramatic way.

"You might want to consider paying a visit to Greta after supper to-nacht, so she's out of the haus when we talk to Gizelle."

Josh's smile grew. He'd planned on it, anyway. "I'll do that."

"We're going back to our families, and we'll see you later." Preacher Zeke gave him a reassuring smile as he adjusted the brim of his hat.

Josh thanked them for stopping by, then returned to the melon patch.

Daed looked up as he approached. His eyebrows rose.

Josh filled him in, adding that the preachers wanted him to go to Greta's that nacht.

"Not like you weren't already planning on it." Daed's lips twitched with a smile. "You given any thought to where you and Greta might live if marriage is in the future?"

"Not really." As the youngest sohn, Josh was set to inherit the family's property. But he'd waived that right when he'd left. The farm would go to his brother and Linda. "I suppose I should start thinking on it."

Daed pointed toward the land to the west. "Eli Schwartz is thinking of selling his farm. He came over and spoke to me about it, in case you might be interested."

Josh glanced in that direction, thinking of the barn and big farm-haus, close together, according to Amish tradition. The horses and cows in the pasture. It was so near, it almost qualified as being at home. *Danki, Gott, for a second chance.*

"We could expand for more crops…even merge the two farms into one," Daed went on. "With all three of us working together, shouldn't be too much. Of course, with Andy's back and heart problems, you might have it in mind to live with him and his Martha."

While Josh was still willing to help out at the Millers', he didn't want to move in with Greta's family, mainly because of Gizelle. "I might consider Eli Schwartz' place. Did he say how much he wanted for it?"

Daed shook his head. "Just getting the word out. Let's deliver these melons to the sale barn, and then we'll go talk with him."

It warmed Josh's heart to be moving forward with plans for his future with Greta. But Reuben's comment about praying for her to heal emotionally came back to haunt him. How much time would she need?

Lord Gott, help me to be sensitive to her needs.

Greta was so glad to be home, in spite of Gizelle's dismissive "Ach, you're back" and snippy attitude. Even the most mundane of tasks, like washing the supper dishes and putting them away in their proper places, was wunderbaar.

Gizelle swept the crumbs out the door while Mamm scrubbed the table and chairs in preparation for the preachers' visit. As far as Greta knew, Gizelle was unaware of their impending arrival. She wondered how it would go. Would Gizelle feed them more lies? Or claim that Greta had spoken falsehoods about her time in captivity?

Too bad she had proof....

Would Josh kum by? Probably so, since she'd stayed home rather than going out with Onkel Samuel.

She couldn't wait to see him, but she was hesitant to leave the safety of the haus, for fear that Miah might be waiting in the shadows with his gun. A shiver ran down her spine at the memory of the sketch the police officers had shown her. Josh had done a gut job describing him. After they'd questioned her, the officers had murmured something about an ongoing investigation, leaving her with more questions and fears than answers.

She wiped the last dish dry and put it away as a buggy pulled up the drive and came to a stop. She peeked out at the preachers and swallowed the lump that had suddenly formed in her throat.

Daed pushed to his feet, his movements slow. He was still in need of back surgery, but he would have to wait until he'd completely healed from his heart bypass. He met her gaze and gave her a tentative smile.

And even though she wasn't the one they were coming to talk to this time, Greta's stomach churned.

The preachers made their way slowly up the porch steps, as if they carried the weight of the world on their shoulders. Daed opened the door, and they entered as Mamm set a plate of cookies on the table.

"James Bontrager's dochter, Lizzy, has disappeared." Preacher Zeke dropped into a chair. "Last nacht. She'd gone into town with friends. They said a woman called her over to her car, asking for help finding something. She got into the car, and the woman never brought her back. We're afraid...our girls are not safe. These people have to be stopped."

Lizzy Bontrager was one of Gizelle's best friends. Greta watched as her sister gasped, covering her mouth with one hand.

Was Lizzy the girl Greta had heard crying in the basement bedroom? Her legs began to tremble with fear for her.

"The police said they'd investigate." Daed glanced out the window, then went to open the door again. "Josh. Gut to see you, sohn."

Greta's heart pounded into overdrive. A few seconds later, Josh entered the kitchen, carrying a birdhouse. Her birdhouse. Her stomach fluttered.

Josh nodded. "It's been a while."

"Danki for all you did to find my girl."

"Of course." Josh's gaze settled on Greta. "Do you want to go for a walk?"

Greta shook her head. "Nein, I can't." Fear twisted her gut.

With a smile, Josh held out the birdhouse. "I repaired it, liebling. With all the original promises still intact."

She took it from him and held it against her heart. "Danki." Her smile wobbled.

"Sure you don't want to go for a walk?"

She glanced at Onkel Samuel. "I'm not sure I can leave."

Her onkel gave her a sympathetic look. "Just stay within sight. You're going to have to leave the haus sometime."

"Or maybe just to the barn," Josh suggested. "William is out there."

"We'll watch from the window." Daed moved to stand in front of it.

Greta took a deep breath, set the birdhouse down on the counter, and put on her shoes. She moved to the doorway.

Josh caught her hand in his. "Stay close, liebling." His voice was strong. Confident.

As they walked across the yard, she leaned into his strength. Tried to absorb it.

When they entered the barn, William poked his head out of a stall. He grinned at Greta, then ducked back inside.

Josh tugged her toward the stall where he'd slept the nacht of Daed's heart attack. He shut the door behind them, then reached for Greta's hands and stood there for a long, silent moment, gazing into her eyes. "I'm so glad you're back, liebling." He tugged her closer, into his arms. She could feel them trembling.

She pressed against him. "Ach, Josh."

"Eli Schwartz is selling his farm. Daed and I went to talk to him. Daed's thinking about expanding, and Mamm thought you might be willing to work in the sale barn. She mentioned the idea of putting up surveillance cameras. They wouldn't be hooked up or anything, but they might help deter theft. We've never had a robbery at the farm, but we'd want you to be comfortable."

That was thoughtful. "Are you going to move out of the dawdihaus, then, and into the Schwartz' haus?"

Josh ran his hand down her back, then up again. The way he'd done the nacht of Daed's heart attack. "Depends on whether a certain girl might want to share it with me someday."

Greta pulled back a little. "Are you asking me to...." She swallowed the rest of her question.

Josh hesitated, his gaze searching hers. Then he shook his head. "Nein, liebling. But I'm talking about the possibility of it, someday."

"Then I suppose I might agree to the possibility of living there someday." Greta flashed him a grin.

Chuckling, he started to draw her toward himself again, but he stopped when they heard the shuffling of footsteps outside the stall.

Greta froze, her smile fading.

Chapter 28

Josh eased away from Greta and peered over the edge of the stall door. He met William's stare.

"Sorry. Just checking," William said. "I've missed her, too." He looked away.

Josh rubbed his hand over his chin, then reached to open the door. "You can join us, if you want."

William hesitated, a look of longing in his eyes. Then he sighed and backed up a step. "I'll catch up with her later. I have chores to finish first."

Oops. Josh hadn't exactly been helping William as much as he should have. But Greta had taken top priority. "I'll help," he assured him. "Kum on, Greta. You can keep me company."

William held up his hand. "Nein, nein. You're courting. I'm sorry for interrupting. Maybe before you leave, if there's anything still left to do...." He turned and walked off.

Glad to be left alone with Greta, Josh pulled the stall door shut again. He sat on a bale of hay and patted the spot next to him.

Greta snuggled up against his side with a soft sigh. "I hate to ask, because I know you wasted a lot of time looking for me, but how's your book coming?"

"It wasn't a waste of time, liebling. I staked out the Cameron post office, asking everyone who came in if they had seen you, and I did a decent amount of writing while I sat there. I pretty much got all the backstory established. The completed manuscript is due to the publisher in six months, and they told me they'd assign me a ghostwriter, if I wanted one. Considering that I've never written a book before, I'm going to take them up on it." It would mean less earnings for him, but it was more important to him to submit a quality story. Besides, he needed more time for farm work. And for Greta.

"What's a ghostwriter?"

"A professional writer who puts the pieces together but doesn't get any credit." He winked. "Using a ghostwriter will give me time to do what I need to do. I know how to type, but I'm painfully slow at it, and I don't have the vaguest idea how to assemble all my experiences into a book. Besides, the reason I wanted you to read my trail journals is because I wanted to share that part of my life with you, so maybe you'd understand why I had to leave. I wanted you to know how Gott had found me on the Appalachian Trail. Seems Gott worked that out for me."

"Jah. I was trying to figure out how to contact you." Greta trembled.

Josh repressed a shudder of his own. He couldn't imagine the horror of what she'd been through. Worse, he didn't know what sort of issues she'd need to work out. Fear of being abducted again, for sure. But had she been violated? He didn't want to ask, so he searched for safer ground. "May I take you to Rachel and David's wedding on Thursday?"

Greta nodded. "I feel I missed so much. Why are they marrying in August? That's early for a wedding. I haven't seen Rachel since that day I filled in for her at Esther's."

"Preacher Samuel chose the date. I think he wanted them married before the lots were drawn for the new preacher, since only married men are eligible. Kind of threw Rachel and her mamm into a panic, but David says they're getting it done. They've had several work frolics over there, for the wedding and for Elsie's quilts." He drew her nearer to him, then gently turned her face toward his. "Greta, I hate to ask, but I need to know. Did they... did they hurt you in any way?"

Tears filled Greta's eyes. "Other than not letting me visit Daed, nein, but I was afraid that *he* would do some terrible things. He... he handled me in some ways he shouldn't have but stopped short of anything serious. Said I was more valuable if I was untouched."

Josh shut his eyes. *Danki, Lord.* At least she didn't have *that* to work through.

He lifted his hands around the back of her head to her neck. His gaze lowered to her mouth. "Do you mind if I kiss you?"

She shook her head with a smile as she leaned toward him.

Josh brushed his mouth over hers, his lips aching with need. With want. She wrapped her arms around his back and snuggled closer as his lips claimed hers.

He struggled to hold himself back, to keep it light; but as she sighed and moved into his kiss, his self-restraint shattered. His arms shook as he kissed her with all the want and the longing he'd felt over the past month.

He slid one hand down to the small of her back and gently lowered her onto the hay bale. "Greta. Ach, Greta." His words came out as a moan.

A shiver worked through Greta's spine as Josh's kisses changed, becoming harder. Deeper. More passionate, as if he wanted to devour her. She reveled in his desire. His hat fell off his head, landing behind her on the hay bale, and she worked her fingers through the silkiness of his hair.

A groan came from deep in his throat, and Josh shifted, more of his weight bearing down on her. Another tremor coursed along her spine. She slid her hands lower on his back.

"Ach, liebling."

His hand slid out from behind her. Rested on her waist. Trembled.

Something banged outside the stall door. Then someone coughed and cleared his throat.

Josh's mouth left hers. A second later, he wrenched himself out of her arms and sat up, breathing heavily.

Greta lay there a moment more, the earth tilting and whirling, and then movement caught her attention. When Onkel Samuel and Preacher Zeke entered her line of vision, she lurched to her feet. Her cheeks burned as she brushed away the straw clinging to her dress. Preacher Zeke crossed his arms over his chest. Her stomach flipped. This was bad. Very, very bad.

Onkel Samuel aimed his gaze toward the ceiling a moment, then lowered it to Josh with a slight smirk. "I see we might be having a talk sometime in the *near* future."

Josh stood, red staining his cheeks. "I...jah. Now, if you want." He sounded out of breath. He swiped his hand over his jaw, then reached behind him for his hat. "Jah, we need to talk. Now." His voice was firm. Determined.

Onkel Samuel's gaze moved to Greta. "We had a discussion with your sister. Everything is cleared up. Wait here, if you would, while Josh and I have a little chat."

Little chat. For some reason, that sounded more ominous than "talk" or even "discussion." Greta's knees shook as the burning desire faded, leaving her drained. Josh followed Onkel Samuel from the stall. Preacher Zeke lingered a moment more, studying her, his lips thin and tight, his eyebrows drawn together, before he went after them.

How embarrassing, being caught in a compromising position by the preachers, after everything that had happened. What must they think of her? Greta dropped back down on the hay bale and buried her face in her hands.

Josh followed Preacher Samuel to the far side of the barn, conscious of Preacher Zeke stalking along behind him. He wiped his damp palms on his pant legs. He could only imagine the embarrassment Greta must feel, if his own were any indication.

He stared at his feet as Preacher Samuel slowed to a stop in front of him. Then Preacher Zeke's boots came into view.

Josh swallowed. Hard. He wasn't quite sure what to say. Where to start.

The silence stretched before him, heavy. Condemning. Or maybe that was his guilt.

Gut thing Bishop Joe wasn't there, too. Otherwise, Josh and Greta would've already been tried and judged with the verdict handed down.

Josh pressed his hands against his pants again and took off his hat. "I…uh, Daed and I talked with Eli Schwartz about buying his farm. I want to marry Greta. This wedding season, if possible."

More silence.

Josh crushed his hat in his hands, shuffled his feet, then dared to look up. The two men before him had some kind of nonverbal communication going on, with hand motions that Josh couldn't decipher. Preacher Zeke raised his eyebrows at Preacher Samuel, but then he nodded.

"I think we might be agreeable to that." Preacher Samuel's voice was dry.

A wave of relief washed over Josh.

Preacher Zeke studied him. "Is Greta aware of your plans?"

Not specifically, but the implication was there. "I haven't exactly hid them. So, jah."

Preacher Zeke turned and walked off. Josh shifted slightly to watch him go. Back to where Greta waited, probably wallowing in mortification. Josh owed her an apology for allowing things to get out of control.

He sighed and looked back at Preacher Samuel. "I'm sorry."

"We understand what it's like to be in love, sohn. The stress and fear both you and Greta have been under recently would be enough to push most people over the edge. But maybe you should keep your courtship public. To eliminate temptation."

Josh swallowed again. Nodded.

"I'm glad you were able to win back Greta's friendship. Her love. I know how badly you wanted to. How badly she hurt you with her shunning when you returned. I prayed. Daily. Love hurts when only one's in love."

It *had* hurt, seeing her efforts to avoid him. He hadn't realized that anyone else had noticed and understood. "Danki."

He heard muffled conversation coming from the stall where they'd left Greta, but he couldn't make out what was said.

A few minutes later, Preacher Zeke returned. "She's agreeable to being approached."

Josh's spirit jumped. He looked down to hide his grin. "Danki. Am I…free to go?"

"Nein." Preacher Samuel shook his head. "You're getting married Thursday, if you're willing. Double wedding with Rachel and David."

Josh blinked. "What? Why? I didn't dishonor her. I—"

Preacher Samuel shook his head, and Josh caught the warning in his eyes.

Preacher Zeke folded his arms across his chest once more. "She might take it better, coming from you."

It would be less like a punishment that way. But still, being forced to marry early grated at him. As if they had done something wrong.

"We won't make you," Preacher Zeke said next, as if he'd read his mind. "Your choice. And hers. But she might be safer as a married woman under your protection, ain't so?"

There was that. Josh nodded. He rubbed his jaw, his heart rate increasing. Marrying Greta—soon. For her protection. His smile fought its way back to his face. "Jah." His voice cracked saying the simple word.

"Not to mention, we're drawing lots for the new preacher on Sunday," Preacher Samuel muttered.

Josh hesitated. That was probably a bigger reason behind the timing they'd chosen. If he and David both got married before the drawing, one of them might be selected. And although the drawing wouldn't be rigged, Preacher Samuel certainly hoped that one of the two of them would be chosen for the position.

But did Josh want the position? He knew David did. He'd long felt the call.

Josh felt called, too, yet his was more toward evangelism than preaching.

He bowed his head. *As You will, Lord. Align my will with Yours.*

"You can go now," Preacher Zeke told him. "We'll see Greta to the haus. William said you would help him with a few chores. After you finish, maybe you can play a game of checkers with Greta. At the kitchen table."

Josh nodded. "May I talk with her first?"

He prayed she would be agreeable to a quick wedding.

Chapter 29

Greta looked up as footsteps scuffed outside the stall door. Her thoughts still whirled, and her cheeks still burned, but her heart fluttered with joy. Josh had approached the preachers for permission to marry her! When Preacher Zeke had asked if she was willing to consider marrying him, she'd barely restrained a squeal. Somehow she'd remained seated on the hay bale, hands folded demurely on her lap, and kept the joy, the excitement, inside.

Jah, she was willing.

But when would be a gut time? If only she could have Esther or Rachel sit with her—her friends, her cousins. But Rachel would marry on Thursday. And Esther had already wed.

The stall door opened.

Josh stepped inside, one hand clutching his hat with a white-knuckled grip. He pulled the door shut, then fell to his knees in front of her.

And bowed his head.

He was praying? What had they said to him?

Greta raised her hands, but she didn't know what to do with them. Whether to touch him or not. After a moment of hesitation, she lowered them, clasped them together, then released them and smoothed her fingers through his hair.

Josh raised his head and caught her hands in his. "Liebling, I…I…." He exhaled and kept hold of her hands while he bowed his head again, for two seconds. Three. Then raised it. "Ich liebe dich."

"Ach, Josh." She grinned. "Ich liebe dich, too."

"I'm so sorry I left you three years ago. If I could do it all over, I would have handled my troubles differently. Please forgive me."

Her breath caught at the pain she saw in his eyes. She would do anything to make it go away. "I forgave you a long time ago, Josh."

He smiled. "Would you give me the honor of becoming my frau? Would you be willing to spend your life with me?"

Greta pulled her hands free from his, then scooted forward and wrapped her arms around him. "Of course, I'll marry you."

He buried his face in her neck with a sigh of relief. "I don't want to be apart any longer than necessary." A quick inhalation. "How would you feel about marrying sooner rather than later?"

Greta ran her hands down his back, reliving the memory of their passionate kisses. Wishing they hadn't had to stop. "Jah. Sooner is gut." Her face warmed.

Josh exhaled again, his breath hot against her skin. "Preacher Samuel suggested a double wedding with Rachel and David on Thursday." Now his tone was hesitant. Reluctant.

Greta stiffened. "They're forcing us to marry, ain't so? But you aren't a member of the church. They can't force you." The shame they would incur.... But then, it would be nothing compared to the plans those Englischers had had for her.

"Nein, liebling." Josh looked up. "Not forced. You have the right to choose. But Preacher Zeke suggested you might be safer as a married woman. And I joined the church while you were... away."

"You did?" She didn't know whether to be glad that he had joined or upset that he hadn't spent every waking moment searching for her. That she'd missed seeing him kneel for believer's baptism. The warring emotions flooded through her, fighting for dominance.

"Jah. I didn't want to do it without your being there to witness, but Preacher Samuel encouraged it. He said you would want me to, since…well, since, if I didn't, we'd have to wait another year to marry. I don't want to wait another year." He fell silent.

Greta hugged him to her as her mind whirled. *Marry on Thursday? Safer as a married woman?* That might be true, because then she wouldn't be valuable…at least not to *them*. She shuddered.

But marry in mere days?

She'd wanted Rachel to sit down with her.

She pulled in a breath. *Lord, what should I do? Marry so soon? Mamm will have all kinds of conniptions.*

Trust Me.

The impression in her spirit was not as specific as she might have liked, but a sense of peace flooded her. She did want to marry Josh. The sooner, the better.

"Jah. I'll marry you on Thursday." She would deal with the stress of that decision later. Mamm would likely vent for a while. But Gott would work it out.

Somehow.

Josh rose up on his knees and brought his lips to hers. "Ich liebe dich."

She sighed and wrapped her arms around his neck as he pulled her against him.

One kiss morphed into two, three, four….

When Preacher Zeke cleared his throat, Josh reluctantly pulled away from Greta, his mind still reeling. His beautiful Greta would be his frau, and much sooner than he'd ever dared to dream.

With the world tilted off its axis, Josh somehow rose to his feet and relinquished Greta to the custody of the preachers before he went to help William with the chores. Not that there were many to do.

Preacher Samuel returned after a few minutes and filled the water trough in the cow barn as Josh was spreading fresh hay around. "I spoke with Andy, privately, after I saw Greta safely to the haus. When we finish the chores, we'll call for Greta and present the marriage proposal to her, the way it should be done." He gave Josh another stern glance. "She knows we'll ask. She's not to say a word until we do."

Josh nodded, barely able to contain his excitement.

Excitement...and fear. He didn't have the vaguest idea where they'd live until he purchased the Schwartzes' farm. But Gott would work that out.

As long as they had someplace to be alone, it would be enough.

Greta's nerves turned somersaults as she went into the haus. She paused to slip off the flip-flops she'd borrowed from Esther, meanwhile telling herself to calm down. She needed to pretend nothing significant had happened in the barn. She turned around slowly to face her family.

Gizelle gazed back, her face wet with tears.

Greta winced. While she was out in the barn kissing Josh, her sister was inside, being confronted by the preachers about her lies. Would she apologize?

Gizelle turned away and went upstairs. Nothing was said. No apologies. Nothing.

Greta needed to forgive her sister, whether she asked her to or not.

Something she was incapable of doing in her own strength. She'd have to trust Gott for help.

But right now, Josh consumed her every thought. Her every ounce of energy.

Greta tried to concentrate as she prepared the dough for cookies so that Josh could enjoy a fresh-baked treat when he came inside to play checkers. *Checkers.* As if she cared about a silly game.

She wanted to check Mamm's fabric stash to see if they had enough to make a dress for her to wear on Thursday. But she didn't feel she ought to, after the preachers told her to keep her pending marriage silent. When Onkel Samuel had a whispered conversation with Daed in the other room, she understood the way of it. The preachers and Daed would present Josh's proposal to her.

She couldn't concentrate on the cookies. She checked and double-checked the measurements of every ingredient so as not to make a foolish mistake. Instead of doubling or tripling the recipe, she followed it to a tee. Three dozen shortbread cookies.

Greta had just removed the last baking sheet from the oven when the door opened and Preacher Zeke peeked in. Daed pushed back his kitchen chair and stepped outside.

Greta stilled, her face flaming. Mamm raised her head and arched her eyebrows.

A low murmur of voices floated in through the open window.

Greta wrung her apron in her hands, her heart pounding out of control. Was this the way she would feel as she knelt in front of the church, promising her life to Josh?

William came inside. "Greta? Daed wants you to step outside a moment."

Mamm's eyes narrowed.

Greta swallowed. Then forced her feet to move. What was she so afraid of? Josh, Daed, Onkel Samuel, and Preacher Zeke were all out there. All men she trusted. And marrying Josh wasn't a bad thing.

Just…life-changing.

She straightened her spine and walked outside. Shut the door. Then faced the four men.

Josh smiled, instantly reassuring her.

Daed beamed, his hand on Josh's shoulder. "Greta, this young man wants to marry you…."

So sweet that it was done this way. Preacher Zeke had asked if she was agreeable; Josh had knelt before her and asked. His was the more meaningful question.

She bowed her head. Nodded. "Jah."

The men exchanged some words, but Greta didn't hear a thing. Her gaze locked with Josh's. Soon she would be his frau.

Several minutes later, the preachers headed for their buggies.

Greta struggled to speak. "Want to kum inside?" she asked Josh. "I just baked some cookies, and we could play checkers...."

He gave her a regretful frown. "I should go, liebling. I need to talk to Daed and Mamm about our plans. They'll be excited, but we need to work out a few details. I'll try to see you sometime before the wedding." Then he winked at her before turning and heading for his buggy.

"Wedding?" Mamm demanded through the screen door.

Daed turned to her, all smiles. "Thursday."

"What?" Mamm reached for one of the freshly scrubbed kitchen chairs and collapsed into it.

Chapter 30

Thursday morgen—the day of his wedding—Josh scanned the weekly newspaper as he ate his breakfast. He couldn't wait to reassure Greta that her captors had been found and taken into custody for alleged participation in a sex trafficking ring. He shoved the newspaper aside and concentrated on finishing his baked oatmeal with bananas.

Not that he was hungry. It wasn't every day a man got married. The only reason he was eating was to prevent his stomach from rumbling in the middle of the silent prayers during the ceremony.

Preacher Samuel's farm shined for the double wedding. The women had spent hours baking, cooking, and cleaning the haus from top to bottom. The men had set up benches, tents, chairs, and tables for the meal following. The Ausbund had been delivered for the evening singing. It would be a long day of sermons, followed by a nacht of fun and celebration. Josh was ready for it all to be over and everyone gone home.

He couldn't wait to marry the girl he'd loved for as long as he could remember.

They would stay in his upstairs bedroom in the dawdi-haus until they were able to move into the farmhaus next door. He wished they could spend their first night alone together in their own home; but, with such short notice, his room would suit just fine.

"Need to get a move on." Daed came into the kitchen, dressed in his black pants, white shirt, and vest. "Don't want to keep your lovely bride waiting."

Josh didn't try to hide the grin that split his face. Nein, he wanted to be there in plenty of time. But he gestured at the newspaper. "Did you read that, Daed?"

"Considering I usually read it the same evening it's delivered, jah. Gut news, to be sure." He lifted his black hat from its hook on the wall. "Heard Lizzy Bontrager was returned, too. Safe and sound. I would've told you last nacht, but you went to visit your girl." He winked and then stepped outside as Mamm bustled into the room.

She stopped mid-stride and stared at Josh. "Why are you still sitting there?"

Josh pushed to his feet. "Just finishing breakfast." He carried his bowl to the sink. "Daed went to get the buggy."

"I'll do dishes after we kum home. That, and freshen up your room. It'll be ready when you return from the singing. Now, you get."

Josh's face heated. His room, soon to be his and Greta's. *Theirs.* "Danki, Mamm." He hugged her.

A marriage—his marriage—to Greta.

A dream kum true.

Greta and Josh spent what seemed like hours in a back bedroom at Onkel Samuel's haus, being lectured by Preacher Zeke about the sanctity of marriage. Then they were presented before the church: her and Josh, Rachel and David. Her stomach quaked, not with butterflies but with birds. Bluebirds of happiness.

At one point during the service, she smoothed the blue dress she had made with Gizelle's help. She still didn't understand exactly why Gizelle had lied—she'd said something about jealousy—but the apology she'd finally made had seemed sincere; and, as Gizelle sat with her head bowed in silent prayer, Greta fully forgave her sister.

Finally, the wedding sermon ended, and the rest of the day passed in a rush.

Before she knew it, she and Josh were at his parents' haus. Her face flamed as she muttered gut-nacht to his parents, and then, hand in hand, she and Josh headed upstairs to his room.

He shut the door behind them, then looked at her for one long, charged moment. A slow smile formed on his lips. "Greta. Ach, liebling. Ich liebe dich. I've waited forever for this day."

"Josh." It was nein more than a whisper. He had experience; all she'd had were some sizzling kisses. Would the rest of it be as wunderbaar? What if she was lousy at it? Would he be disappointed?

She glanced around the room. William had helped bring her belongings over the day before. On the corner of the dresser sat the beautiful birdhouse Josh had given her. It had been struck into splinters and brought back to him for repair. Now it was whole again, unbroken, and stronger than before. Just as her childish love for Josh had been shattered when he left but, through their brokenness and by the healing hand of der Herr, now beat again in her heart, stronger than ever.

All coherent thoughts disintegrated when Josh gripped her shoulders in a warm embrace. The heat of his body radiated through her skin as he ran his hand up her neck until his fingers tangled in her hair. He tugged her to him until her mouth almost touched his. The intensity of his gaze weakened her. Steel blue phased into a stormy gray as his mouth brushed over hers, gently at first, then deepening. Everything inside of her sighed and eased. This was Josh. Her ehemann.

She was finally home.

To stay.

The Budget

Jamesport, Missouri. With the recent homegoing of Preacher Eli King, David Lapp has drawn the lot to minister to the people....

RECIPE

Homemade Soft Pretzels

Ingredients

1 ½ cups warm water (about 110 degrees)
1 tablespoon sugar
2 teaspoons sea salt
1 package active dry yeast
4 ½ cups all-purpose flour
2 tablespoons unsalted butter, melted
Vegetable oil, for the pan
Melted butter, for brushing pretzels
Sea salt

Combine the water, sugar, and sea salt in a bowl and sprinkle the yeast on top. Allow to sit until the mixture begins to foam, approximately five minutes. Add the flour and butter and mix with a wooden spoon until well combined. Knead until the dough is smooth and pulls away from the sides of the bowl. Remove the dough from the bowl, then clean the bowl and grease it well with vegetable oil. Return the dough to the bowl, cover with plastic wrap, and let sit in a warm place until the dough has doubled in size, approximately half an hour.

RECIPE

Preheat the oven to 450 degrees. Line two baking sheets with parchment paper lightly brushed with vegetable oil. Set aside.

Turn the dough out onto a lightly oiled work surface and divide into eight equal pieces. Roll out each piece of dough into a 24-inch rope. Make a *U* shape with the rope, then hold both ends of the rope and cross them over each other, pressing the bottom of the *U* in order to form the shape of a pretzel. Place onto the parchment-lined baking sheets. Brush with melted butter and sprinkle with sea salt.

Bake pretzels until golden brown in color, approximately 12 to 14 minutes. Transfer to a cooling rack for at least 5 minutes before serving.

About the Author

A member of the American Christian Fiction Writers, Laura V. Hilton is a professional book reviewer for the Christian market, with more than a thousand reviews published on the Web.

Her first series with Whitaker House, The Amish of Seymour, comprises *Patchwork Dreams, A Harvest of Hearts,* and *Promised to Another.* In 2012, *A Harvest of Hearts* received a Laurel Award, placing first in the Amish Genre Clash. Her second series, The Amish of Webster County, comprises *Healing Love, Surrendered Love,* and *Awakened Love.* A stand-alone title, *A White Christmas in Webster County,* was released in September 2014. *The Birdhouse* concludes Laura's latest series, The Amish of Jamesport, which also comprises *The Snow Globe* and *The Postcard.*

Previously, Laura published two novels with Treble Heart Books, *Hot Chocolate* and *Shadows of the Past,* as well as several devotionals. Laura and her husband, Steve, have five children, whom Laura homeschools. The family makes their home in Arkansas. To learn more about Laura, read her reviews, and find out about her upcoming releases, readers may visit her blog at http://lighthouse-academy.blogspot.com/.

Welcome to Our House!

We Have a Special Gift for You ...

It is our privilege and pleasure to share in your love of Christian fiction by publishing books that enrich your life and encourage your faith.

To show our appreciation, we invite you to sign up to receive a specially selected **Reader Appreciation Gift**, with our compliments. Just go to the Web address at the bottom of this page.

God bless you as you seek a deeper walk with Him!

WE HAVE A GIFT FOR YOU. VISIT:

whpub.me/fictionthx